TRAIL OF FEARS

SARA R. TURNQUIST

If you would like to stay up-to-date on this and other series from Sara and receive a free ebook, sign up for her newsletter:

https://saraturnquist.com/list

To all whose journey has been difficult.

INDIAN REMOVAL ACT

Thomas Greyson splashed water on his face. Had he only been here two weeks? Certainly, they had been the most trying of his life. Adjusting to this new place and new way of living had proved difficult.

He remained crouched over the bowl, the water beading on his forehead. Taking in slow, deep breaths, he watched the droplets fall into the small pool. Rippling in response, the liquid hypnotized him.

After several moments, he grabbed for the towel and swiped it across his face. If only he could wipe away the stress and frustration as easily as he did those lingering drops of moisture.

"Come, Greyson. No time for pretty-pretty face."

Thomas jumped; his gaze searched out the source of the intrusion. Glancing toward the now open door of his small cabin, he saw his new friend. Atohi's long dark hair framed his rigid features. The man had no sense of privacy. Perhaps it was not so important in this culture. Nevertheless, Thomas doubted he would have made it this far without his guide.

Atohi let the door shut, disappearing as the wooden barrier slammed into place. Would he not wait for an answer?

Thomas released his grip on the towel and moved to follow.

Stepping out of the cabin and into the bright sun proved brutal. Thomas raised a hand to cover his eyes.

Where was Atohi?

The solid figure of his retreating friend was already several paces away. It would be best not to linger, not even to let his eyes adjust.

"Wait." He reached back to secure the door.

Atohi turned. "I go, you go. No wait."

So, the man also had no sense of patience.

Jogging, Thomas closed the distance. It would do no good to arrive so far behind his guide. No, that would not bode well.

Thomas picked at the corner of his vest. When a thread came loose, he caught his nervous habit and forced his hands to his side.

But why shouldn't he be nervous? This meeting could change everything—how the people received him, whether he would be allowed to continue teaching the children, and if he could proselytize. That was of utmost importance.

"What should I expect?" Thomas matched his step to Atohi's.

"Expect men. Men in a circle." Atohi spoke simply, as if to a child. He did not pause his step or his speech.

Thomas stifled a laugh despite the tension building within. "I meant, what will they think of me?"

"I not know what they think. Maybe they think good. Maybe not. I not know."

As if the tribal council wasn't intimidating enough! This would be the first time they had convened since Thomas had come to live among the Cherokee.

"What I mean to say is, how should I conduct myself?" Thomas rubbed the back of his neck. It did not soothe the hairs standing on end.

Atohi grunted. "Should not ask so many silly questions."

Thomas halted. *Silly questions? Is that what Atohi thinks?*

Atohi continued walking, neither pausing nor looking back.

Thomas shook his head and raced to catch his guide once again.

The remainder of their walk was silent. What was he to say? And though he might describe it as uncomfortable, Atohi seemed rather at home in the stillness.

Tendrils of smoke curled and reached for the clouds just above the tree line. As well, the smell of burnt wood and ash reached Thomas's nostrils. Were they close? The faint sound of drums beating caused his heart to thump louder.

Swallowing hard against a suddenly dry mouth, he worked to make his breaths even. Was he so put off? So worried? He took a moment to turn his heart and mind heavenward.

Lord, You are in control. May Your will be done.

As he refocused on his surroundings, the trees opened to a clearing. There, among the teeming of natural life, sat the distinguished men of the tribe.

Ten men in their prime sat in a semi-circle around a small fire, conversing in a language he'd yet to master. Did they talk about the state of affairs of the tribe? Perhaps they discussed particular members of the tribe—how they fared this season. Maybe they shared who would need assistance and who prospered.

Atohi did not stop until he was an arm's length outside the circle.

Were they to stand so close? Would they not be intruding on the private matters of the council?

Unmoved by Thomas's reluctance, Atohi stood his ground, watching, waiting.

Thomas fought the urge to drop to his knees in supplication but remained upright and stepped to Atohi's side. He would have to trust his guide.

At this distance, he could make out the lines of the stern faces, illuminated by the flames. His breath caught, and his pulse quickened. These were a proud people. He stood as straight as possible, chin up, mimicking a confidence he didn't feel.

The tribe's councilmen continued their discussion as if nothing had happened. No one acknowledged or seemed to realize that Thomas and Atohi stood just beyond their intimate gathering.

Time passed, but some moments later, a quiet came over the circle. A break in their discourse?

Should he introduce himself? Was that what they waited for? That was why he came.

He stepped forward.

Atohi's hand shot out.

When Thomas's eyes caught Atohi's, there was no mistaking the rebuke, though his eyes never moved from the council members' circle.

Why was Thomas to wait?

Atohi still would not look in his direction.

Thomas let out a long breath. This would be one more thing he needed to accustom himself to. He wanted to show respect and meet their expectations. So, he remained silent while the council picked up their interchange once more.

Time passed as he stood quietly, waiting to be addressed. Sweat beaded on his forehead from the strain of standing still. How long would this continue?

Ow!

Atohi jabbed his arm.

Jerking his head toward his guide, Thomas wiped at his forehead and rubbed his injured arm.

Atohi tilted his head at the group of men.

Thomas shifted his gaze in that direction.

Ten sets of eyes were upon him.

His heart skipped a beat.

Gathering his wits and sending up another quick prayer for wisdom, he forced his feet to carry him into the open space created by the semi-circle.

"Great men, I bring greetings from the American Board of Commissioners for Foreign Missions." His voice broke. He clasped his hands behind his back as they, too, were shaking.

Atohi, still standing just beyond the circle, translated.

Thomas continued, "I am honored you have decided to allow me to live among your people. It is my hope that my presence will be to our mutual benefit and will lead to a greater understanding between our peoples."

The men of the council exploded with speech, shooting words and phrases back and forth, some even thrown in Thomas's direction. Arms and hands flung toward him.

Thomas fought the urge to shrink back. He furrowed his brows and bit at his lip. *What are they saying? Why are they so enraged?*

Finally, the older man at the top of the semi-circle spoke. His voice was strong and sure, a deep baritone that demanded attention. Was he the chief of this tribe?

All discussion halted. Had he called for silence? Some of the men hung their heads.

The chief spoke again.

Atohi, translating for Thomas, seemed to be the only man who dared open his mouth.

"We have come to understand that there are many opinions on this matter. But we agreed to welcome this man into our village. He is under our protection and will enjoy our good will. This is what I say."

Some of the men nodded, their faces drawn and serious. Others turned away.

The chief's eyes leveled on Thomas. And the words that he spoke, though indistinguishable to Thomas, were deciphered by Atohi. "Welcome to our home, missionary. We ask that you respect our customs and beliefs and keep your heart open to hear what we say. I hope you may see there is much to learn, not only to teach."

Thomas held the man's gaze, pushing his earlier trepidations to the side. He squared his shoulders and firmed his posture.

The chief's dark eyes shone with life. Thomas saw in the lines on the chief's face the story of a man who had lived many years for his people, who concerned himself with the needs of his people. How many tough decisions had this man made in his lifetime?

Thomas respected what he saw. Bowing his head, he measured his words. "I am eager to learn."

Though he kept his eyes on the chief, he saw in his periphery the untrusting gazes of some of the men. They peered with menacing glares.

He ignored them. With determination.

Today, he would focus on the faces in the group that gave him hope. Those whose eyes were bright with expectation.

And trust that God was at work.

Adsila carried a bucket of fresh water into the house. It was a delicate balance, trying not to slosh too much onto the floor. But she was rather skilled at this chore. If only the handle wouldn't dig into her hand so. She made her way to the stove and relinquished her burden. Rubbing her hands together, she attempted to ease the soreness in her palm.

"Thank you," Mother said, moving her hands over the heated surface, busying herself with preparations for the evening meal.

Looking about the room, Adsila noted Father's empty chair. Why had he not returned? What could have kept him? She fought to ease the tightness forming in her chest. There was nothing to worry about. He would be home soon.

Brushing hair from her face, she took a deep breath. The council meeting must have ended by now. Perhaps he was on his way this very moment.

What manner of strange mood would he be in? These meetings always put him off balance. Did they remind him of things past? Times forgotten? It was no secret, even to her, that he mourned the things that would never be for his children.

Glancing at Tsiyi studying at the dinner table, her heart weighed heavy. Her younger brother would never know what it was to live in a tent as their people had for centuries. In truth, her own memory of that time had faded. Many moons had passed since they built this house of wood.

Running a hand down her skirt, she remembered the feel of deer-skin against her flesh. Not anymore. Now she wore a gingham dress. The adjustment to the cotton clothing had not been easy. It was course on her skin and gathered tightly to her figure in places. She tugged at the waistband. How old had she been when her people stopped wearing animal pelts? Trading their ways for more 'civilized' clothing. Too young. Still, she could remember…

The door creaked.

Her gaze turned.

Father's tall form appeared in the doorway, and she moved to greet him.

"Good day, Father." She nodded as he entered.

He smiled and reached forward, placing a hand on her shoulder. "Good day, my daughter."

His skin, tanned and worn by days spent in the sun, appeared to have deeper lines than usual. His hand lay heavy this evening. As heavy as the burden he carried for his people?

Blinking at her, he squeezed her shoulder before letting his arm fall.

He continued into the house, pausing by Tsiyi. Placing the same hand on her brother's head, he rubbed at the dark hair. Moving farther into the house, he stepped to Mother.

Adsila averted her gaze. The happenings between her mother and father were theirs alone. She stepped to the cupboard, and as she pulled out the cool sturdy tin dishes, she heard the whisperings of her parents. Was that a giggle she heard from Mother?

As she set the bowls on the wooden table, Father came and eased into his chair.

She placed a dish in front of him. "How was the council meeting?"

A clank sounded from the kitchen.

Adsila turned.

Mother's stirring spoon had hit the side of the pot. Had she dropped it?

Adsila frowned. Her boldness never settled well with Mother.

Father leaned back and met her gaze. Unlike Mother, he never seemed disturbed by Adsila's questions. "There was much to discuss. It has been too long since we met."

Adsila nodded.

Worries over the council members' farms and livelihood took increasingly more of their time. They hadn't the opportunity to meet as often. Gone were the days of hunting for short spurts, leaving ample daylight for matters of tribe and home. The strains of farm life were difficult. All the more so for men who had enjoyed a much different life. But that was before.

Mother brought the large pot of stew to the table. Touching Tsiyi's shoulder, she directed him to put away his schoolwork.

Adsila slipped into her seat. Her thoughts were awhirl with questions, but they would have to wait. Such conversation would not be allowed in Tsiyi's presence.

After Mother sat, the meal could begin.

They ate in silence. Did Mother and Tsiyi also feel the weight of the meeting upon Father? Who would break the stillness? Disturb the moment?

"What have you learned in school?" Father took a bite and leaned forward, eyeing Tsiyi.

"We learned about water today." Tsiyi shrugged. Had he no thought in his head?

"Water? What do you need to know about water that you do not already?" Father's eyes darkened, and his brows came together.

Adsila held her spoon to her mouth, glancing from Father to Tsiyi.

Tsiyi didn't seem to notice the change in Father's temperament. He slurped his soup and continued. "It has three states: water the liquid, like we drink, water the solid, like when the pond freezes in the winter, and water as steam, like when Mother boils a pot on the stove." Was he so mindless? Did he not understand Father's concern?

She rolled her eyes.

"Hmmm." Father turned his attention to his food. Clearly, he did not see the point in spending time on such nonsense.

She took another bite, but the intensity of Father's eyes turned her stomach. Turning the vegetables in her stew with her spoon, she waited.

"Mr. Greyson said it was like God." Tsiyi's eyes widened as he chewed from one side of his mouth.

Her back straightened as she tried to catch Tsiyi's eyes. That would get a rise out of Father for certain. How could she warn her brother?

"Like the Great Spirit?" Father refused to use the Christian name 'God.' "How?"

Try as she might, Tsiyi would not look in her direction. It was hopeless.

"He said God exists in three forms: God the Father, God the Son, Jesus, and God the Holy Spirit." Tsiyi's eyes lit up.

"Hmmm." Father was quiet for a moment. Then he spoke, "But the Great Spirit is one."

"He said that, too. Mr. Greyson told us that God is three, but He is still just one God. Just like all forms of water are still water." Tsiyi continued to shove food into his mouth as if not bothered by Father's reaction.

Father remained silent. Did he not have a response to this? After a few moments, his tone deepened. "What do we know of the Great Spirit?" His face was a blank canvas.

"The Great Spirit created all things and presides over all things," Tsiyi recited, chin high.

"Yes. Unetlanvhi is all places, at all times, and knows all things. And lives above to watch over. There is none greater." Father's mouth was set, drawn in place.

"But, Father..." Tsiyi leaned over his plate. "What if—"

"There is none greater." Father's firm voice filled the small cabin.

Tsiyi's shoulder's drooped. "Yes, Father."

Adsila scooted her bowl forward, long since finished. Something wasn't right. What happened at that meeting? She looked at Mother.

The older woman's gaze met hers, eyes serious. She knew it, too.

"I think," Mother said, standing and reaching for the empty dishes, "It is time you two got fresh air."

Tsiyi's mouth spread across his face. "May I run to Mohe's house and ask if he can come to the creek?"

Mother nodded.

Tsiyi was out the door before Adsila could stand.

She stepped in that direction as well, but as she reached for the latch, she halted.

Turning back to her parents, she took a deep breath and gathered her wits. "Mother, Father, I want to stay."

Both sets of eyes were on her.

Mother's were wide, but Father simply blinked.

"Adsila," Mother began, her voice harsh and scolding, "You—"

Father held up his hand. He tilted his head then nodded for Adsila to continue.

She stepped forward, sucking in another breath through her teeth. "I am old enough, and I want to know about the affairs of our tribe. I'm a member of this tribe, and it affects me, too."

Father continued to watch her but said nothing.

"I'm not a child anymore. I'll be married someday... soon." She choked on the last words but kept her features firm as her argument poured out like rushing water. "And I want to be treated fairly... as an adult."

Father's features betrayed no sign of what he might be thinking.

She kept her chin high.

After a long moment, Father waved an open palm toward her vacant chair.

A rush of blood pumped through her body. She pushed a breath out and stilled her limbs to contain her excitement. Then she settled into the chair.

Father eyes did not leave her face. Was he gauging her reaction? A slight smile broke through his exterior.

Mother took her seat as well. Her features were passive, but her posture was tight. And she would not look in Adsila's direction. Did she not agree with Father's decision?

That stung. So, Mother did not think Adsila was old enough. It was no matter. Father's word was final. She shifted her attention to Father and refused to so much as glance at Mother.

Father's eyes became clear and serious. "There was much discussed. But one matter is of great importance." His gaze caught Mother's.

Something passed between them that Adsila could not identify.

Her nails scraped across the back of her hands. Was she playing with her fingers? She pressed them into her lap.

"What is it?" She cringed at the lingering silence.

Father sighed. "The United States Congress passed the Indian Removal Act."

A strangled cry escaped Mother's lips, and her hand flew to her mouth. Did this mean something to her?

Adsila looked between them.

Their faces were downcast.

Mother's eyes glossed over, and Father reached for her hand.

Adsila's palms stung. She had dug her nails into them. It took effort to unclamp her hands.

An uncomfortable quiet fell over the room.

"What? What does this mean?" The words burst from her before she could stop them.

Father's gaze jerked toward her. His dark orbs, too, were glassy.

Clearing his throat, he blinked away any hint of tears. So proud. "It means we are to be moved from our lands, the lands our ancestors have inhabited for generations, to lands west of the Mississippi River."

Her stomach lurched. A knot formed in her middle and it weighed a hundred pounds.

"B-B-But," she stammered. Where were her words? "They can't do that! It's not right! It can't be. Not even by their laws."

Father gave her a long look. His eyes were deeper in that moment. The lines in his face seemed so, too. He was worn. Worn by the decisions he and the council made over the years and worn by the decisions that were out of their hands.

"You are still young, my daughter. You do not yet know the true nature of the white man. He will find a way to get what he wants."

She couldn't speak. Her head swam, and her skin became clammy. Even breathing was a struggle.

What were they going to do?

Lillian Greyson closed her Bible and laid it in her lap, the aged leather binding was warm.

The Psalms brought no joy, Proverbs no wisdom, and the Gospels no hope.

Not today.

Not when her thoughts were so clouded.

She couldn't see past the fog of worry to find the peace that passes understanding, which God promised she would find in Him and His Word.

Not lately. And not today.

How could she see past herself to focus on God when her youngest son, her Tommy, was in the midst of great tribulation?

How her heart ached for him. Why couldn't he be more like his brother and sister? If only he could have found a 'regular' vocation, marry, settle close to home, and start a family. Here.

Why did he have to become a missionary?

Why couldn't God call him to be a preacher in Charlotte?

She did want her children to follow God's path for their lives, but if she were honest with herself, her idea of God's plan maybe had a narrow scope. And God was big. Had she not taught her children that very thing?

Newspaper crinkling drew her attention.

Her husband glanced at her, his paper now drawn down past his face.

"Finished your reading already?" Arthur pulled his pipe from his mouth.

"It's no use." She set her Bible on the side table.

He cocked his head to one side.

She could not disguise the demons that plagued her. Not from her husband. He knew her too well.

"Thomas is a grown man, Lillian. We have to let him live his own life." He brought his paper down to his lap.

"But the Indian Removal Act..."

"Has nothing to do with him." His voice was firm, face drawn. "He is a protected citizen of the United States."

"That's what they said about the Indians." Her own voice sounded meek. Did her concern have to be so ridiculous?

"Absurd," he confirmed, putting his paper to the side, a harsh motion. "They're not like us." His chest puffed, and his free hand clenched into a fist.

She nodded, lowering her head and looking at her lap, fidgeting with the fabric of her skirt. He spoke the truth.

"Besides," he continued, "I think we can rest assured that our government will take care of the Indian removal as delicately as possible. No one wants trouble." He spoke with gentleness, but his voice did not invite discussion.

She sighed. Her husband was wiser about these things. Splaying her hands, she studied her fingernails.

His tone softened. "If it will make you feel better, why don't you write the boy a letter?"

"What a marvelous idea!" She clapped her hands.

Without further prompting, she moved to her correspondence desk and pulled out paper and pen. It took only a handful of seconds to gather her thoughts before she began.

Dearest Thomas, I hope this letter finds you well...

Thomas let out a deep sigh. Having finished his lessons for the day and dismissed his students, he took a moment to gaze over his humble classroom. Was he reaching them? His students performed well in their subjects, but had he made any lasting impact? He sighed again as he rubbed chalk dust from his hands. Perhaps only time would tell.

He gathered his things and made short work of closing the small schoolhouse. As he stepped out of the makeshift building, a breeze flowed over him. His eyes slid shut. If only it could take his worries and cares with it. The burst of air washed over him and refreshed his senses. And he allowed it. For several blissful moments.

His shoulders tightened, and his brow furrowed. What interrupted his peace? The children. Their eyes stared into him even now. Wanting, hurting, asking for something deeper than grammar and equations. It was important they get good instruction in these basic subjects; but it was vital they learn about God, about Jesus, about the Gospel.

Opening his eyes, Thomas gazed across the landscape. There were a few cabins visible from this vantage point. The Cherokee, his mission field, had proved more resistant than he had anticipated. His studies had taught him how much they'd given up to become 'civilized.' Much of who they were now lay in the past. Curious.

He began the walk toward his own cabin.

Did the Cherokee believe he now asked them to give up the last bit of their culture? Their religion? Was that the reason for the difficulty he had acquainting himself with his neighbors?

He had been invited to sup with Atohi and his family once a week, and he had the school. Beyond that, no one would open their doors, or their hearts. Or listen to the message he brought. No matter what the chief said, he was an outsider.

He spotted his cabin on the horizon. The structure's modest proportions were nothing compared to his parents' large home in Charlotte. But it belonged to him.

What would his mother think of him living in such a tight space? Unthinkable! Inhumane! And all other such craziness. But the little house had been more than adequate.

Ducking, he stepped through the door and set his school supplies down. He crossed his arms as his gaze wandered about the small space. It needed a good cleaning. There were dirty plates and a pile of clothes in the corner—it made him long for one day of the housekeeper's time.

But as much as this humble abode belonged to him, the chores did as well.

Not today.

He needed respite for his soul. Having no one to talk to or share his concerns with, he often found himself in need of time alone with God. Grabbing for his knapsack, he walked back into the sunlight.

Today he needed space. From this village. From these worries.

Working his way up the creek, he left any semblance of the known behind as he sought a quiet spot in which to commune with God. He lengthened his stride, and the worries of the past days faded as the cabins diminished in his view.

He pulled at the strap of his knapsack, reassured by its weight. It was but a slight burden, bearing only his Bible, a block of wood, and his whittling knife.

From his youth, his father worked with him to whittle, using first soap and a dull blade. Soon after, he graduated to wood and a real blade.

His mother encouraged him to pursue art and sculpting as he grew, but his true passions lay with God's direction—the mission field. Still, there was nothing like using his hands to create statuettes of birds, squirrels, and many other things in God's natural world. But it could never be more than a hobby.

Glancing back, the village had long since disappeared. Perhaps now he should look for a place to nest down. Then he might read and study to his heart's content.

And pray.

Perhaps even work the knife over the block and bring something new into being.

A tree nearby stood tall and proud. The grass around it appeared a lush seat. Nature's chair, already prepared for him.

He stepped toward the aged oak, placing a hand on the trunk and shrugging the knapsack from his shoulder. Gazing up the height of the tree, he wondered at the storms it had weathered. Would he, too, prove sturdy enough to stand such tests?

Water splashed. Where did that come from? It seemed close. Should he concern himself with it? Maybe it was nothing more than a wild animal further upstream.

Or was it?

He wouldn't have to go but a few feet.

But would it be dangerous to sneak up on an animal with no rifle?

The splashing continued.

Didn't sound too large, he wagered.

He pulled the bag over his head, the strap resting across his chest, and stepped in the direction of the sound. The creek made a sharp turn a few yards upstream.

Following the bend, he kept his footfalls as soundless as possible and slowed his steps as he drew ever nearer.

The sounds were so clear now. For certain, he was only a few yards from the animal. He came to a stop and, holding his breath, lifted a shaking hand. This was nonsense. There was nothing to fear. Steeling himself, he pushed the tree limb to the side.

A young Cherokee woman stood in the creek, water to her knees. More striking—she wore a traditional deerskin dress.

He had never seen such, except in pictures.

Belted at the waist with fringe on the hem and on the sleeves, it was rather... becoming. And because of the depth of the water, she had hiked the skirt until the hem only covered her to mid-thigh. Long, black hair hung loose, flowing about her shoulders.

His face warmed. He wanted to turn away, to back up, to slip from this scene. In truth, he should. But he couldn't.

She was captivating. The young woman hummed a tune that could have been as old as her people. And she moved back and forth in the water to a rhythm all her own. Was she from a nearby village? Perhaps she sought the same thing he did—solace.

Yes, he should go. Should have gone before now.

Moving one foot back, he put his weight on it.

Still, he could not tear his eyes away.

As he pressed back on that foot, the ground moved underneath him.

And he slipped.

When he stopped sliding down the small embankment, he was in the creek.

Jarred. And well deservedly so. But as he moved, nothing seemed broken, thank the Lord.

He opened his eyes and shifted forward, squatting on his toes. And the blunt end of a rather large branch greeted him. Mere inches from his chest.

Two angry deep brown eyes glared at him from the other side of the scary-looking limb.

His hands shot in the air.

"What are you doing here? Spying on me? White man!" Her voice was strong, harsh. Not at all like the gentle cadence he'd just heard.

"No." He backed up as he rose, almost tripping on the smooth stones in the creek.

She kept step with him, not allowing for one inch of distance to come between him and the branch.

"I was… I was walking along and came upon you… by accident" He tried to find his words.

"By accident? You expect me to believe that?" Her eyes flashed. One side of her dress kept slipping down, exposing a perfectly browned shoulder.

He lowered his eyes. "I promise you. I am the village missionary. My village is three miles… that way." Raising a hand a hair higher, he pointed behind himself.

"Missionary? So, *you* are the one teaching our children lies." Her voice gave no hint of softening. She raised the branch higher so it was in his face.

"Yes. I mean, no! I mean…" He touched the branch with one finger to ease it back down.

Clearing his throat, he attempted to speak more firmly. "I am the missionary sent to teach. But I speak only the truth."

Her lips curled into a snarl. "I suppose that is what *you* believe." She lowered the branch… slowly.

"Please." He stuck his hand over the lowering branch. "My name is Thomas."

She stared at his hand, eyes dark and hard. "You should make your way back to the village before it gets dark, Missionary." Taking a step back, she left no room for argument.

He let his hand fall to his side. Still, he could not just let it be.

"And you are?" he called after her.

"Someone who doesn't trust you," she said as she backed away from him, her gaze continuing to follow his every movement.

Pursing his lips, he lowered his eyes. What more was there to say? He swallowed against the tightness in his throat.

One more person who didn't trust him.

His hands balled into fists. Was there nothing he could do to change his plight? Moving toward the embankment, he stepped out of the creek.

But before he began his climb, he paused. Nothing would excuse him not being a gentleman. He ground his teeth. "Shall I escort you back to the village?"

No answer. Not even a sharp rebuke.

He turned.

But she had vanished.

Walter Buckner made his way to the capitol building, his steps slower than usual. Two things were true: one, the senator would already be in his office and two, the senator would not be in a pleasant mood.

With his head down, Walter tried not to think on what the day would bring. Which only made those thoughts run rampant. Would the senator be angry? Would he take it out on the staff?

Mph!

Walter collided with something solid.

"Watch where you're going," a voice said in a coarse tone.

He looked up. One of his colleagues smoothed his jacket as he regained his composure.

"Sorry, Harry. I… my mind was somewhere else."

"No worries. We're all a little uneasy these days." Harry flashed him a winning grin. The same one that had probably gotten him into politics and would keep him there.

"Walk with me?" Harry waved toward the building looming in front of them.

Walter nodded, taking up step next to Harry, trying not to rush.

Silence fell between them, but Harry broke it soon enough. "What do you think of Senator Frelinghuysen's six-hour filibuster?" A sly smile pulled at Harry's lips. "And all for nothing. I tell you, your boss..."

"What?" Walter's tone was more abrasive than he'd intended.

"I was only..."

"I know." He softened his voice. "But you have to respect the man, standing for his beliefs... especially when they aren't popular."

Harry quirked a brow but didn't speak further.

"He has to have nerve to do that." Why did he feel the need to defend the senator?

Harry nodded. "That's true. But don't you think he should keep his evangelical Christianity out of his politics?" His voice was plain, matter-of-fact even. "I daresay he won't go far if he doesn't."

Walter wanted to remind Harry that the position of United States Senator is quite a distinguished honor. Especially for someone who 'won't go far.' But he bit his lip. No good would come of it.

They entered the building in silence and soon approached the hallway that divided their paths.

Harry nodded as they separated. "See you later, Walter." Then, with a quirky smile and a wink, he added, "Keep your head on straight."

"I will." He plastered a smile on his features. "Sorry again about bumping into you."

"No worries," he called without turning his head.

Walter continued the several feet remaining to the offices of New Jersey Senator Theodore Frelinghuysen. Lanterns were on, but there was no movement within. So, the senator had arrived, but no one else.

Opening the door with as little noise as possible, he set his things down on his shared desk and sighed. Must he intrude on the senator's privacy? But it was his duty to check on the man and ensure there wasn't anything he needed.

Making quick strides through the large space, he made his way to the inner office's door. The barrier to the senator's inner sanctuary was cracked. Still, Walter knocked with soft raps. Even the slight movement caused the door to open a hair's width more. Were the hinges so well-oiled?

"Senator Frelinghuysen? It's Walter… uh… Mr. Buckner." He could not get used to the way in which the senator addressed his staff so formally.

"Yes?" came the gruff response.

Was that an invitation? With nothing further forthcoming, he assumed it to be so. As he opened the door enough to slide halfway into the room, he noted that there were no lights illuminating this room.

The senator sat in his large chair, its back to the door so that the senator could face the grand window. Which was, as of yet, the only source of light.

A Bible sat opened on his desk.

"Sir, can I get you anything? Coffee, perhaps…?" Walter's voice sounded strangled, even to him.

"No, Mr. Buckner. I'm quite all right."

Was he as deep in thought as he appeared? "Very well, sir." Walter pivoted, preparing to extricate himself from the inner office.

"Mr. Buckner?"

He heard the senator shift.

"Y-yes, sir?" Walter almost tripped over his own feet spinning back toward his boss.

"What do you think about this business with the Indians?" The senator inclined his face toward Walter, his features offering no clues as to what Walter should answer. Did he want Walter's honest opinion?

He almost crumpled under the weight of such a question from his superior, the man who, in many ways, held the reins on his future. This man's opinion mattered to so many. Walter's opinion hadn't mattered much to anyone… ever. But this great man asked for it. Dare he give it? It may be his only opportunity.

"I think," he started, clearing his throat. He must not draw out his answer, but his mind became a blank. What could he say now? There was nothing!

He looked to the senator. The man had not moved. Just sat. Waiting.

Drawing in a deep breath, the clouds around his thoughts parted. "That is, I believe they were told to assimilate and they would be fine. They did, and now everything is not fine."

"Hmmm," Frelinghuysen murmured. He made no further sounds.

Was this space for Walter to continue?

He swallowed hard. Could the senator hear it? Fighting the urge to wring his hands, he continued, "I do hope the Act is carried out in the way it was written… for everyone's sake."

At that, Frelinghuysen turned his chair to face Walter. The senator's eyes seemed to pierce Walter's; face drawn and serious. "I will tell you this, Mr. Buckner. President Jackson has never been much on the letter of the law."

Adsila laid her mother's deerskin dress in the heirloom trunk. She smoothed her hands over the fine hair. Would it be for the last time?

Mother and Father did not know about her jaunts in the wilderness. What would they think if they did? Would they be proud of her for keeping the spirit of their people alive? Or would they scold her for her inability to let go? Would they be afraid? For what would have happened if a white soldier found her instead of that missionary?

Still, she could not help but smile when she remembered the way the angles of his face played as he looked at her. He couldn't hide his thoughts. Were all white men so obvious?

Her smile fell. It was him, after all, and his people who were responsible for the wrong wrought upon hers. No, he didn't deserve any more consideration. Not one more thought.

Pulling her hair into a braid, she stood and moved out of her parents' partitioned off room.

Clanging pots sounded from the direction of the kitchen.

Mother was already hard at work.

Adsila had best help prepare dinner.

She finished with her hair and smoothed over the folds of her cotton dress before stepping into the main living area.

Her breath caught.

There he was.

The missionary.

At her family's dining table.

How?

"Adsila," Mother said, interrupting her thoughts.

Her gaze met Mother's, who smiled a bit too broadly.

What was going on? Was something amiss?

"This is Tsiyi's teacher, Mr. Greyson. Tsiyi found him by creek and invite him to dinner." In Iroquois, she said, "That brother of yours, I don't know what to do with him!"

"How nice." Adsila felt the edges of her mouth creeping up.

Thomas had risen when Adsila entered the room. As she met his gaze, his eyebrows shot up.

"Nice dress."

Was that all he could manage?

Mother gave them both a strange look—brows furrowed, mouth drawn.

"I mean, nice to meet you… Adsila." Thomas's cheeks turned as red as poppies.

"Where is Tsiyi?" She sidestepped Thomas.

"He out to field to get Father." Mother stirred dinner, still smiling at Thomas. And in Iroquois, said, "Although what your father is going to say… I'll tell you what your father's going to say. He say, he's going to straighten out one young Cherokee brave, that's what your father say."

Thomas smiled at Mother but he shifted. Was he uncomfortable with a language foreign to him flying around?

"Mother's English is not so good," she explained. Then grimaced. Why should she care what he thought? Or how uncomfortable he was?

"Ah," he muttered as he relaxed back into the chair.

The door opened, and her head jerked that way.

Father and Tsiyi entered the house.

Thomas stood once again.

"Hello, sir." He extended his hand.

Again with that hand.

"Thomas. Thomas Greyson. I am honored that you would have me into your home to sup with your family." His voice sounded sturdy. Much more so than she expected.

She watched Father as he met Thomas's eyes. Would he throw the man out? He would not let the white man stay after all the… the inhumanity brought about by his people!

Father raised his hand to grasp Thomas's.

She let out a breath she didn't realize she held. What was that? Had she been worried for the missionary? For what reason?

"I am called Gawonii. Wife is Inola. Please," Father said in a pleasant voice. "Sit. Wife is good cook."

Thomas smiled, taking his seat again. "I don't get the pleasure very often."

Father nodded and sat across from Thomas. "Wife cooking great pleasure."

Mother blushed as she placed the venison stew in the middle of the table. In Iroquois, she told Tsiyi to wash for dinner.

Adsila grabbed bowls and spoons from the cabinet, setting them around the table before sliding into her seat. Not long after, all were seated and eating.

A few moments of awkward silence followed. Were her parents expecting her to play host to this man, relying on her English? She couldn't. She wouldn't.

Why wouldn't Father say something? She kept her eyes on her dinner, not chancing an unspoken command from her parents.

At last, Father's deep voice filled the emptiness. "It is good you teach young ones about water." Father's eyes met Thomas's. "Not so good you teach about God."

She almost choked on her bite of vegetables, swallowing hard. Such a heavy comment so early in the meal.

To his credit, Thomas seemed unmoved. "It is my calling to teach about God. He told me to preach the good news."

"Remember what chief said. You respect. Keep heart open. Learn." Father's voice remained pleasant though his eyes were serious.

She hoped the missionary would take note of the precipice he walked.

Thomas nodded. "Then tell me." He leaned forward. "What would you have me know?"

"I would tell of Great Spirit." Father's eyes were bright.

Now, here we go. She took a deep breath and resisted the urge to roll her eyes.

"The children have mentioned the Great Spirit." Thomas smiled at Tsiyi. "But I'm not sure I understand."

Father looked to Adsila. She squared her shoulders under his scrutiny.

Of course, his English would not suffice. So, he spoke in Iroquois.

She translated, meeting Thomas's gaze.

"Unetlanvhi is the Great Spirit. The Great Spirit lives above and presides over all things. The Great Spirit is all knowing, He is everywhere, and is all powerful. And He is Creator."

"That sounds like the God of the Bible." Thomas nodded.

Father continued, as did she. "Signs, visions, dreams, and powers are gifts of the spirit. Our world is intertwined with the spirit world.

"Hmmm..." Thomas mumbled. There was more silence as he stared at the surface of the table.

What was he doing? Thinking on what he had heard?

At last, he looked up. He jerked a little. Was he taken aback that they all stared at him? If so, he recovered well.

"Thank you," he said to Father. Then he looked to her. "And thank you. You have both given me much to think about."

The dinner bowls were quite empty now, and Mother stood to gather the dishes.

"It was a wonderful meal." Thomas nodded to Mother.

She smiled.

"I tell you, Greyson," Father said. "Wife cooking…" He made a motion with his hand over his tummy.

They all laughed. It was easy to get caught up in the warmth of the moment, but Adsila did not forget for one second who Thomas was—a white man. And the white man meant greed and untrustworthiness.

Lillian sat on a sofa in the parlor, her most beloved book raised to just below her face. Her brows came together. How many times had she read this same passage? Did Emma truly disappoint Mr. Knightly again? Not her favorite part. Then why had she reread it no less than five times in the last half hour?

Enough!

Grunting, she turned the page. A bit harsher than necessary.

She looked to the binding. If she weren't more careful, she might tear the page.

"Darling?" a voice broke through the silence.

She startled, eyes cutting toward the intrusion as she dropped the book into her lap, a hand flying to her chest.

All was well. Only her husband.

"Arthur!" Sucking in a breath, she let it out over several seconds. "You surprised me."

"As it would seem." His mouth was drawn, but his eyes danced. Was he concerned? Or amused?

Still heaving, Lillian leaned forward and retrieved her book from where it had slid onto the floor. Once it was settled once more on her lap, she met his eyes.

His lips curled into a smile. "I have something for you."

"Oh?" Should she hang on to her anger? But as she looked at his smile, she could not help but press her own lips into a smile as well. Perhaps it was only for his sake. Still, it was a smile.

He reached into his jacket pocket and produced an envelope. "This came today."

A letter! She had watched and waited for days. "From Thomas?"

"Yes. From Thomas." He reached forth and handed the coveted post to her.

"Have you read it?" The words leapt from her mouth before she could stop them.

"It is still sealed."

She turned it over. How had she not noticed?

"I thought we could read it together."

How could she stand it? Would she be able to read it? Or even open it? Her hands shook as she maneuvered the envelope. And, try as she might, she could not work the slicer.

He put out a hand, and she slid the letter into it. "You read it out loud."

He took a seat next to her then opened the envelope easily and pulled out the paper within.

She leaned into his shoulder, fingers stretching forth to touch the writing. If she could, would it somehow connect her to Thomas?

Arthur watched her, his face drawn.

Was she so pitiful? No, she was a mother. A mother who missed her child.

After a few more moments, he cleared his throat and turned to the words scrawled on the parchment.

"Dearest Mother and Father,

"Your letter finds me in good health and well-encouraged by your prayers and words. I am in a small farm village of some eighteen families. I have contact with nearly all through my students. There are twenty-two students in my class. All seem eager to learn about Science, Math, English… every subject but religion. It is difficult. I incorporate God in all of my lessons, but getting through to them… that is different.

"Their religion may be the last piece of their culture they are holding to, and they are keeping a firm hold! They believe in a Great Spirit that created all things and presides over all things. It doesn't seem as if the Great Spirit and our God are dissimilar. I have my suspicions that the Cherokee may, in fact, be serving our God, but calling Him by another name.

"Perhaps you might write Andover Theological Seminary or the American Board of Commissioners for Foreign Missions and ask if they have any information on this topic. Or on the religion of the Cherokee.

"It is not as easy as I anticipated to form relationships with the people of this village. They are not trusting. But I believe if I am persistent, God will bless my efforts. I have one friend—my guide, Atohi, and have recently made a new acquaintance with the family of one of my students.

"Thank you for the news of Phillip and Emma and their families. I know Mother will be glad for the new arrival this Christmas! Hopefully, I can come home before the year is out. Until then, you are in my prayers. Keep me in yours.

"Sincerely, Thomas."

Silence stretched across the space as the last word seemed to echo. Arthur's eyes remained on the paper. Could she keep the reality of her tears from him? That was not likely.

A fresh flood of emotion overcame her.

"He sounds lonely." She dabbed at her eyes.

Arthur looked at her. "He sounds as if he's doing well. Perhaps having some adjustment pains."

Adjustment pains? Her son needed to be cared for. Loved. Not ostracized.

She sighed and pulled out her handkerchief. Were these the beginning tears of the torrent yet to come?

He put his arm around her. "Rest assured, all is well. Thomas has a good head on his shoulders. And the Lord goes with him. What was it you would tell the children? The Lord hems them in behind and before. He has never failed them. He will not fail our son now."

She burst into tears, pressing the handkerchief over her face, covering her shame. "I fear my faith is not that strong!" How could she be so weak? "I am a hypocrite. A Pharisee. I say those words, but don't live life believing that."

"There, there." He pulled her into his embrace. "That is not so. You have the strongest faith of any woman I know. We have weathered many storms together, and you will find that your faith will persevere through this one." Was Arthur speaking truth? Was her faith so strong through his eyes?

"I wish I could believe you." She laid her head against his shoulder.

"You don't have to. Believe God."

Senator Theodore Frelinghuysen climbed the stairs that led to his home. What a day it had been. What a month it had been. How was he ever to sleep with such a weighted conscience?

His wife would be waiting within. Sweet Charlotte. She shouldn't have to see him like this. In this melancholy over the goings on with his work. If only he were one such that could leave it at the office.

He paused and looked upon the door. Inside was the warmth of a secure home. His home. A place he could rely on. No one threatened to take it from him. Or would, in all likelihood.

Shaking his head, he continued up the steps. The burden was heavy. And he should bear it. He hadn't done enough.

As he reached the latch, he opened the door. Footsteps in the hall alerted him to his wife's faithful presence.

Sure enough, she rushed into the foyer. "My darling, you are home!" She grasped for his arms before he'd had a chance to even pull his jacket off.

Leaning down, he kissed the side of her face. Still, his body did not relax, could not. What right had he when others suffered? Others who had relied on him.

As she drew back, he saw a sadness in her eyes. She knew he held something back. With slower movements, she motioned down the hall from whence she had come. "Sit with me for a while."

He shrugged off his jacket. Most days, he went to his office and remained there until dinner.

But not today. The way she held to his forearm, the way she glanced back at him… he saw how desperately she longed for his "yes."

And he would give it to her. What a little thing to give the woman who would give him anything.

He nodded and moved to follow her.

She slipped an arm through his elbow and led him to the parlor.

As they entered the grand room, she called for tea. Curious. Teatime had come and gone. Then why did she call for it?

Dinner would be a couple hours coming. Perhaps she wished for something to wet his palate?

As she released his arm, he stepped across the room and deflated into his favorite chair, sighing deeply as he all but melted into the piece of furniture.

She sat on the settee nearby.

Should he avoid all talk of his troubles? Or would she rather speak of them? No, he must not burden her.

She broke the silence. "What concerns you so?" Her voice was soft.

He met her gaze.

Would he speak of it? Or could he dismiss her question? That may be the same as dismissing her. She was his partner. The wife of a senator.

"It is this Indian Removal Act." He measured his words.

Her features did not register any hint of surprise. Did she already know how it troubled him?

"It should never have happened." He rubbed a hand down his face. Would that he could wipe all worries away so easily. But he did not truly wish it. For as long as the Indians were in peril, he would bear the burden.

"You are not responsible for that. Can you not see that you did everything you could? To the very extent of what was even possible?" Her voice rose.

His eyes met hers. Was she so impassioned?

She looked toward the floor. "You did what you could." Her voice had dropped to more reasonable level.

"Yes," he said, leaning forward. "But that doesn't change the fact that while I rest comfortably in my home, safe, that thousands of Indians go to sleep, not knowing what the next days will bring." He dropped his gaze to the ground. Why must his heart be so in his politics? Because that's the kind man he was. He knew no other way to be.

"I thought you said this whole thing would be done peaceably. That there will be treaties, exchanges of land…" Her eyebrows moved together.

He met her eyes again. "I wish I could believe that is what will happen. But I do not have faith in our president's respect for the law." His brows rose.

"But President Jackson is bound by the law. He can't just willy-nilly go and do whatever he wants." She kept her hands in her lap.

He held her eyes but said nothing. Her faith in the presidency was endearing.

As he watched, her mouth twitched. Perhaps her belief was not as firm as she would have him think. The wife of a politician did not survive if she remained uneducated about the political machine. And he ached all the more for the loss of that bit of innocence. For as much as he wished he could promise her the American dream of checks and balances the forefathers provided, his hands were tied.

CHOCTAW TRAIL OF TEARS

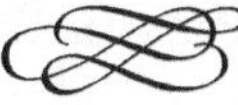

Adsila paced in her home's main living space. The bedrooms, partitioned off to the sides, were only big enough to hold their pallets. This larger area gave her more floor to pace. And pace she did.

Much had happened these last weeks. Too much to process. The Choctaw signed a treaty with the U.S. Government, and they would be removed from their land.

Tears stung her eyes. How could this be? What would become of her people?

Her little family had been helpless to do anything but read about it in the *Cherokee Phoenix*. Their world had changed. It was no longer safe. Even now, Father was at another council meeting. She could only imagine they discussed the ramifications of what all these happenings would mean for the Cherokee.

Knock, knock, knock!

The sound at the front door pulled at her.

Moving to open it, she wiped at stray tears.

She pulled the latch up and swung the door wide and found herself looking into the blue-gray eyes of Mr. Thomas Greyson.

Her heartbeat quickened, and her face heated. Her body wound tight as a spring, all too ready to strike at the closest target.

And he seemed to fit the need. Without a thought, her mouth coiled, perhaps into a scowl.

The man stood, breaths coming in gasps. His brows furrowed. What was his trouble?

Only then did she notice that he carried Tsiyi.

Her focus shifted toward her brother.

Tsiyi's face twisted.

She reached forth her fingers to touch his face. "Tsiyi!" Was he in pain? What had happened?

Moving a step back, she allowed Thomas to enter.

"He hurt his ankle playing with the other boys. I do not think it is broken." Thomas's words came in a calm, even tone.

A fire flared in her. Where did it come from? "I did not realize you were a doctor, too." Folding her arms, she planted her feet as Thomas passed her.

As soon as they left her lips, she wanted to take her words back. They were so harsh. But the bigger part of her wanted to offend him.

He paused.

Because of her words?

"I'm not. But I've seen enough of these kinds of injuries. If you'd like, I can go for the healer," he said, a bit abruptly.

She glared at him. How dare he speak to her like that!

Thomas stared back, his eyes like steel.

Tsiyi moaned.

Thomas broke their eye contact and looked at the boy in his arms. "I think Tsiyi may be more comfortable in his bed." He spoke with more gentleness, but there was still a slight edge to his voice.

She nodded then led Thomas farther into the house to Tsiyi's pallet. The cushioned surface was not much, but it was where her brother laid his head each night.

Thomas stepped past her, brushing her shoulder.

She jerked away. Why? He had not hurt her. But she behaved as if stung.

He laid Tsiyi on the blanketed surface with great care, placing a hand on the boy's shoulder. "You are very brave, young warrior."

She watched the exchange and fought the urge to let go of her anger.

His demeanor toward her brother was so gentle, so kind, so understanding.

But it wasn't enough. It didn't change the fact that his people lay in wait, watching, coveting her tribe's homeland. Ready to take what was not theirs.

Thomas stood then turned to face her.

"Shall I go for the village healer? Or for a doctor?" He lowered his voice, standing closer than she liked. It made her… uncomfortable.

All her nerve endings seemed to be firing at once. Still, she couldn't make herself step away.

"I can take care of my brother," she shot back, seething through her teeth. Her head swam. Why was she behaving this way? Did her anger truly burn this hot?

She thought of the Choctaw again. Yes, she had every right to be as angry as she pleased.

He grasped her arm and led her away from Tsiyi.

As they moved into the great room, she jerked away as if his touch burned. In truth, her flesh had heated several degrees, even through the fabric of her sleeve.

"*What* do you think you are doing?" she fumed, stomping her foot. How dare he touch her!

"Taking this away from Tsiyi." His breathing was ragged, but his voice remained calm. "I don't know what I have done to you, but this is a bit much."

"Then perhaps you should leave." She crossed her arms over her chest—as much to protect herself as to appear stern.

He threw his hands into the air. "As you wish." Without anything further, he made his way to the door, flung it open, and slammed it.

She gripped for anything solid. The top of a dining chair saved her. Sliding into its firm seat gave her the support she needed to let out a long, rough breath. There was a chill all of a sudden. Her hands moved over her upper arms, rubbing warmth into her limbs. Why did the room feel so empty?

Her eyes fixed on the door. Would he reappear? Come back to finish the argument? To further his point?

Nothing. The door remained as it was, slightly ajar after being slammed.

Running a hand over her hair, she attempted to clear her thoughts before checking on her brother. Yes, that's what she needed to focus on —Tsiyi. Not this white man who had come as a bad omen into their lives.

Walter Buckner sat in Senator Frelinghuysen's office, paper in hand. His current task—to take notes for the senator. He found himself in the senator's office more frequently of late. And it was Frelinghuysen who requested his presence. All in all, a good sign.

But something had nagged at him since that day Frelinghuysen had asked for his opinion.

He had tried to garner the courage to ask the senator about it, but never could.

What was he thinking? Frelinghuysen would probably tell him to mind his own business.

Frelinghuysen reached for his coffee. Had he finished his dictation?

It could be now. Or never. Perhaps. Maybe.

"Sir," Walter said, he wished his voice wasn't shaking. Had he actually done it?

Frelinghuysen arched a brow.

Dare he go on? Yes. "If I may, there is something I wanted to ask."

The senator sipped the warm beverage and then set the cup down. "Continue."

Walter looked behind himself. The door was indeed closed. They were alone. No one else would bear witness to what was probably an inappropriate question.

"You said before… um, last week… that you did not trust President Jackson to follow the letter of the law. I just wondered… that is, I thought… what did you mean?"

Frelinghuysen gave him a long look then took another sip of coffee.

"I meant exactly what I said. As you well know, the Indian Removal Act allows for treaties and agreements with the Indians regarding their land and their removal. We hope to *exchange* land west of the Mississippi River for their land. But I do not believe that is how things will proceed."

"Won't President Jackson have to abide by what Congress has passed?"

"Do you not remember what happened to the Creek Indians during President Adams' Administration?" Frelinghuysen set his cup down and steepled his fingers.

Walter nodded. "There was some kind of treaty dispute, and they were removed because they wouldn't leave." But it was a treaty dispute — surely the senator wasn't suggesting that President Jackson would forego the treaties and…

"The original treaty had been nullified, and a new treaty took its place that allowed the Creek to stay. The governor ignored the new treaty and had them removed anyway." Frelinghuysen's eyes seemed deeper in that moment, more serious. They held Walter's.

"Then why didn't the President send in the army to enforce the treaty?" The simple question came with a shrug of his shoulders. It seemed clear.

"He started to. But President Adams decided not to intervene because he feared a civil war. And, as he put it, 'the Indians are not worth going to war over.' If you've spent much time around President Jackson, you'll have heard the same kind of sentiment." The disdain was evident in the senator's voice.

"But you don't agree?" Walter said more than asked, eyebrows lowered ever so slightly.

"Do you?"

Thomas flung the door behind himself. It clapped and bounced shut. He was fuming! What was that woman's problem? Had he not been the good guy?

He brought Tsiyi home and offered assistance. What more could they ask?

And the way she spoke to him…

The flash in her eyes…

Those eyes…

He shook his head. *Don't start that!*

Glancing about his cabin for sanctuary… a safe haven for his mind, he landed on the bookshelf. Perhaps he could plan his next day's lessons?

Moving to his makeshift desk, he picked up the English textbook. He worked out sentences for the children to practice. They could write sentences about the fruits of the spirit.

Joy is being happy when life is hard. Peace is not the absence of conflict, but the presence of tranquility. Faithfulness is being firmly devoted to God. Love is an intense feeling of deep affection.

Intense feeling. He couldn't escape that phrase. What he felt around Adsila was certainly intense. Although 'affection' may not be the term he would use to describe his feelings. What word would he use?

Her features appeared in his mind's eye. Soon enough, he found himself dwelling on the contours of her face.

Shaking his head, he shoved the papers away. He stood and paced in the small space, hands hooked behind his neck, pulling his head forward. How could he clear this thing from his mind?

His satchel lay on the bed. He paused. Perhaps he could work on his latest piece. Yes, that would distract him.

Sitting on the mattress, he reached in and pulled out his whittling knife. Then he grabbed his most recent project—a bird. He had already roughed out the form.

He settled with his back against the wall and grabbed a basket to catch the shavings. Then he began to work his knife against the wood, and he soon immersed himself in the experience. The grain of the wood, slightly rough in his hands, was real and raw. As he breathed in the smell of the hewn strips, he remembered leaning against a tree, smelling the bark as his breath quickened.

He went back to that day when he watched the young Indian maiden in the stream. Adsila, her long, lustrous hair flowing as she moved, playing as if no one watched her.

Jerking himself out of his vision, he chided himself for letting his thoughts run rampant. He refocused on the wood block. And paused.

The bird's eyes had become eyebrows, the beak a slope of a nose, human eyes took shape, and the feathers became roughed out hair.

His hands shook. What was he going to do? How was he to get her out of his head?

He threw the block of wood against the opposite wall.

Pulling his feet onto the bed, he propped his knees up and rested his elbows on them, letting his head fall into his hands.

And he prayed.

Winter came. The air was much cooler and the wind brisker. Lillian Greyson bemoaned her son's sad situation—the poor conditions he lived in, and how he must be suffering in the cold.

Often, Arthur turned to his paper, raising it over his face to trick her into believing he was otherwise engaged and to leave him be.

She was not so easily fooled, but she let him be all the same. It would be best to leave him to his paper and her to her sewing and keep the peace.

On this particular day, however, it was from behind his paper, that Arthur sought out her attention.

"Look, my dear," he said, pulling the stack of papers to the side.

Still, he did not lower it. Not even an inch. What was that supposed to communicate?

"There's an article about the Indians."

"Oh?" Could it be about Thomas's Indians? "The Cherokee?"

"No, the…" He looked over the article again. "Choctaw."

"Oh." Not Thomas's Indians. She dropped her gaze to her sewing once again. When would she hear something? His letters had become less frequent. Was something wrong?

"It tells of how the president went about getting them to their new land. The columnist reports of how the Choctaws were migrated from their lands in Mississippi to new lands. The government, in accordance with the treaty, spared no expense to aide them. Five steamboats and forty government wagons along with food rations were only part of what Jackson's administration did to ensure the safety of the Choctaw Indians as they made their way to their new home. And though there was some amount of death due to sickness and old age along the way, thousands now enjoy the bounty of their promised land."

Why did he bother reading it? Could he not sense that she wasn't interested? He certainly wasn't concerned after anything to do with the Indians. Even as he read, he sounded bored. There was just the hint of forced enthusiasm you give for a child's bedtime story.

"Sounds all well and good, my dear. Seems as if the government has this thing under control." He raised his voice, speaking with confidence. As if that would reassure her. Still, this did not speak of Thomas's Indians. She cared very little.

"That's good, dear." She looked up from her work and offered him and small smile.

"If all the removals are this quick and easy, perhaps Thomas will be home before you know it."

Her eyebrows went up. She hadn't thought of that. That made sense.

"Either way, it's fine news." He pulled the paper back over his face.

Now? Just when she had become interested? She had no choice but to go back to her cross-stitch.

Gawonii picked up the most recent copy of the *Cherokee Phoenix*. He was not anxious for it. Some of the council members had already stopped by his farm and reported to him what they had read.

But he needed to see it for himself.

Holding the paper carefully, reverently, he made his way home. He would read this with his wife.

They would face whatever it said together.

As he entered his home, Inola stood near the door, awaiting his return.

A solemn look met his eyes as she greeted him.

She moved toward the dining table where two steaming cups of coffee sat in front of their dining chairs.

Gawonii settled into his chair and set the paper in front of himself. He reached for Inola, and her hand slid into his.

Then he began to read.

The whole edition discussed the removal of the Choctaw to lands west of the Mississippi.

"We were split into two groups. One to Memphis and one to Vicksburg. I was in the group that traveled to Memphis. We were to be transported by wagon from there to our new home, but flash floods made this impossible. The plan was then that five steamboats would ferry us to river-based destinations. But the rivers were clogged with ice for weeks. So, we remained in Memphis.

"Food ran low and there would be no travel for weeks. Sleet and snow covered us. Our daily ration consisted of a handful of boiled corn, one turnip, and two cups of heated water. Eventually, forty government wagons were sent to transport us to our new home. Nearly 4,000 of our number died on this journey from our ancestor's land to the new land promised to us. Our chief called it a trail of tears and death. Truly it was. The group into Vicksburg has still not arrived. We pray for their safety each day."

Gawonii finished reading and looked up.

Tears streamed down Inola's face, but she reached over and wiped at his cheeks.

Then he realized… he cried, too.

Thomas walked to the creek. He needed fresh water for cooking dinner and for his washbowl. A puritan book of prayers kept him company. The simple faith of the puritans refreshed him every time he opened the volume.

The movement of the stream alerted him that he drew closer, but he resisted looking up from the particularly entrancing passage.

He hit something solid, and cold liquid ran down his leg.

A woman's harsh admonishment filled his senses. "Watch where you're going!"

He all but dropped his book, apologizing as he tried to collect himself.

As close to the stream's edge as he was, the young woman must have turned just as he walked up. Had he caused her to lose control of her bucket? His gaze landed on her soaked skirt.

That must have been what happened.

Now having taken in the situation, he looked up to meet the eyes of the young woman he had intruded upon.

And met the deep brown eyes of Adsila.

"Do you always walk about with your nose in a book?" she asked with a sharp tone, shaking her skirt.

"N-no," he stammered. "I… I'm sorry. Let me refill your bucket." He stuck his hand out to reach for it.

Jerking it back, she spilled more water on herself. Then she spoke in Iroquois. Her voice was harsh, and her face appeared disagreeable. Whatever she said, it wasn't good.

She spun back toward the creek and bent down to fill the bucket.

He kneeled beside her, dipping his bucket in the stream as well.

"I truly am sorry." Why did these things keep happening? With Adsila? Was he doomed to forever disappoint this woman? "Not just for this, but for whatever I did to make you so mad at me."

She said something else in Iroquois.

"I really don't like it when you all do that to me." His voice came out rougher than he'd intended.

She stood straight up and fairly spat back at him. "There are plenty of things about your people we don't like." With that, she turned on her heel and walked away.

"What?" He fumbled. Why had she said that?

As quickly as possible, he was on his feet and chasing after her. "What is that supposed to mean?"

"You are close-minded," she said, still a few steps ahead of him.

He quickened his pace to catch up. "If I'm so close-minded, why is it that I was willing to listen to your father speak of your religion, but you won't give me the same courtesy?"

She turned on him and stared, folding her arms in front of her chest. What was he in for now? Another cursing in Iroquois?

He stopped, still several steps short of where she stood.

They stood staring at each other.

"Well?" she said.

"Well, what?" He tilted his head. Had he missed something?

She pushed out a sigh and rolled her eyes as if she were dealing with a small, annoying child. "I will listen. Speak."

He glanced from side to side. They were hardly in an appropriate place for such a conversation. "Here?"

"Is there something wrong, Mr. Greyson?" Something in her tone challenged him.

He crossed his arms. "I would prefer somewhere that's not in the middle of the path."

She let out another breath and took his arm, pulling him farther from the creek.

The contact took him by surprise, but he followed her.

They drew near a tall oak not far from the path.

Setting her bucket down, she settled herself next to the large tree trunk.

He looked down on her for a moment. Had she truly all but dragged him over here? Why? Because he had spoken to her challenge? Did she intend to sit and let him speak? Or would she bite back with heated comments at his attempts?

She raised a hand and indicated the patch of grass in front of her.

He lowered himself into a cross-legged position. Dare he try? If so, where would he start?

"It begins," he said on an exhale, "With God. He created the heavens and the earth…" He told her as briefly as he could about Adam and Eve and how sin came into the world. Then he continued. Telling her of Abraham and the promise, about Jesus, the promised Messiah, who came and died for our sins that we might once again commune with God and be righteous in His eyes.

She did not utter a sound as he spoke. Was it possible she listened?

This was the longest they had spent in each other's company without a harsh word.

He finished telling her about Jesus's resurrection, how He conquered death for all time, and that He would return one day to take those who had accepted His gift of salvation to heaven.

Still, there was silence. No thoughts. No questions.

Inclining his head toward her, he resisted the urge to rub his hands on his knees. Was it awkward for her, the two of them just sitting here now? What should he say?

Her voice cut into the moment. "There is a Cherokee legend about God, Ye ho waah. The story says that Ye ho waah came down in the form of man. Just as you say."

"I thought your Cherokee word for God was Uh-net-lahn-vee?" he tried the unfamiliar word.

"Unetlanvhi is the Great Spirit."

"I don't understand." He leaned forward, resting an elbow on his knee.

"The Cherokee believe in one God, Ye ho waah. But Ye ho waah consists of three 'god heads': The Great Spirit, Ye ho waah in the form of a man, and Ye ho waah."

"So, do you worship three gods?"

She shook her head. "No, Ye ho waah is one."

His heartbeat quickened and his pulse raced. "This is much like the Trinity"

She nodded. Could she see it, too?

"Then perhaps they *are* one and the same."

"Perhaps." She shrugged. "But I think the elders will find it more difficult to agree with you. Like Father, many cling to the last shreds of our culture."

Thomas nodded. His heart dropped. So heavy the sensation it made his stomach turn.

She shifted to rise. "I must go. Thank you for telling me."

He hurried to his feet. "Thank you for listening. And for telling me of Ye ho waah."

She nodded. Then turned and walked away.

As he watched her go, he wondered after these similar stories of Jesus and Ye ho waah.

When she glanced over her shoulder, his face warmed. She had caught him staring.

Still, as she continued along the path that took her farther toward the meadow, he was unable to tear his gaze away.

Walter Buckner sat, notebook clenched in his hands as he watched the Senate floor below. The movement of the senators as they spoke, even berated each other…it was like a dance. A political dance. Would he ever be suited for it? Or, in the end, did he care too much for his passions, his ideology to—

"Hey, Walter." The voice jarred him as someone settled into the seat next to him.

He turned toward the sound. Harry. What did he want? The man seemed somewhat obsessed with Walter. Why? They didn't agree on much of anything. Did he think Walter would further his political career somehow? That had to be it. But what did Walter possess that was of benefit to Harry?

Something to think on. Until then, there would be nothing gained from animosity.

"Hey," Walter whispered in reply, but he turned back to the action going on below their position on the balcony. No need to miss anything.

The senator from Tennessee stepped forward. He'd been waiting for this.

"What's happening?" Harry leaned in, his shoulder brushing Walter's.

"Shhh!" Walter focused on the senator, but his statement had been brief. And he now turned to sit.

Walter sighed. Though he'd wanted to hear the man, this wasn't the most crucial meeting.

He leaned toward Harry. "Nothing important. That new financial bill."

"Ah. Any discussion about the Indian situation?" Harry wasn't one to mask his point with his cohorts. Save that for the constituents. No matter, Walter preferred his directness.

"Some. Nothing of any consequence." He waved a hand and reached for his satchel.

"Senator Jamison said the president was rather pleased with the Choctaw removal. He hopes to model the others after it."

Walter stared at Harry. He couldn't be serious. Had President Jackson truly believed that went well? Did Harry agree this was appropriate progress?

"What?" Harry leaned back. Was Walter's gaze so intense? He didn't regret it.

"All those people, freezing in the cold... with barely enough food to eat? And what of the Vicksburg group? Lost in the Lake Providence swamps for God knows how long with that incompetent government appointed guide."

"Come now, Walter. Stop being so melodramatic. They're just..." His sentence trailed off. Did he not wish to speak it out loud? His prejudice?

"Say it, Harry, say it. 'They're just Indians.' That's what you were going to say, isn't it?" Walter's voice rose, and his face warmed.

"Calm down." Harry looked from side to side. Did he only care if they drew unwanted attention? "You've been listening to Senator Frelinghuysen a little too much."

If he intended to shame Walter with this, he was wrong. A lump pressed into Walter's throat. Could he speak past it? Surely his features reflected the color of the heat that overcame him. "And you've not been listening enough. You're out of touch with reality if you think what happened to those people was humane." He pounded his fist against his thigh, his eyes and face tight.

"I'm going to urge you to calm down one more time," Harry said, raising his chin. Was he as confident as he tried to make himself appear? Walter wagered it was a show.

"Or else?" Walter half laughed as he challenged his colleague.

"Or else, I'm going to leave." Harry puffed out his chest.

"No need." Walter grabbed his notebook and shoved it into his bag. "I'll go."

With that, he stood and made his way out of the Senate chambers, fuming as he went.

Thomas prepared himself for the school day. Leaning over the water bowl, he moved a blade across his face.

The door creaked.

He jerked his head toward the intrusion, nicking himself in the process.

Though he had been startled at first, he wasn't altogether surprised to see Atohi standing in the open doorway. He had no respect for privacy.

"Ah, pretty, pretty face!" Atohi's mouth spread across his features.

Smiling back, Thomas nodded. Tempted to ask the man to knock next time, he bit his lip. It would be a waste of breath.

"What brings you to my humble cabin at this hour?" Thomas

shifted his focus back to his water bowl and raised his blade once more.

"Good, strong cabin," Atohi argued. "Maybe small, but sturdy."

"Yes, yes." Thomas sighed, closing his eyes for a moment. Why did the man take everything so literally? "You are right." He lifted his gaze to catch Atohi's eyes. "That still doesn't answer my question."

Atohi arched a brow. "Come to see how school."

Thomas waited for him to finish. But the silence lingered. Perhaps that was the entire statement. What could he mean—how school? How is school? Maybe.

He swallowed and supposed so. "It goes well," Thomas said, making a final swipe with the blade before shifting to watch Atohi again.

The man eyed some of Thomas's whittling projects displayed on a small shelf.

"I enjoy the children, and it seems they are learning." Thomas closed the blade and set it down.

"Hope my son is good student."

"Mohe? He is an excellent student." Thomas splashed water on his face. The remainder of the soap dripped into the bowl, and all was removed with a thin towel.

"How you like life in village?" Now Atohi's dark eyes were fixed on Thomas. Such intensity.

"I enjoy it more every day, I think. I have made a new acquaintance." He dropped the towel by the bowl and quirked his mouth

Atohi's features contorted into a rather quizzical expression. "Acquaintance?" The word came out a bit awkward.

"Acquaintance... friend. In English, we use different words to describe friendships—close friends, best friends, and acquaintances— more distant friends."

"Ah," Atohi said, but he didn't seem to understand.

"The farmer that lives over the hill, not far from the creek. I think his name is..." Why couldn't he recall the man's name?

"Gawonii." Atohi rescued Thomas's troubled memory. "I know. I have heard."

"Heard?" Thomas's eyebrows shot up. What should he make of that? "Good things? Or bad?"

Atohi shrugged. "Why must be good or bad? Why cannot just be?"

Thomas rolled his eyes. Atohi could be so aggravating. "His son, Tsiyi, is in my class, but the daughter, Adsila, is not." His heart skipped a beat. Looking away from Atohi, he busied himself with his satchel. Did his features betray his interest? He hoped not.

"No. She is of age."

"Of age?" Thomas paused, turning back toward his friend.

"To be wife." Atohi smiled

"Ah." Thomas tried to ignore the slight twinge that ran along his spine.

"She will make good wife. Good with herbs. Maybe best garden in whole village."

"Really?" Thomas looked up from the books he was loading into his bag.

"Do not understand 'really'."

"It's a question that means…" Thomas started, but lost his words. How did one explain 'really'? "It's not important." He returned to his packing, but his thoughts were on Adsila.

Atohi's deep voice broke in. "I think it is time to go to schoolhouse."

Thomas glanced at his pocket watch and groaned. His students would be there before him.

School would not start for thirty minutes, but all his students came early. And if he wanted to be the first one at the schoolhouse, which he preferred, he had to get there thirty minutes before school started.

"I thank you for your visit." Thomas nodded at his friend as he rose to his full height.

Atohi nodded. "Wife expect you to dinner tonight."

"Tell her I'll be there."

His friend nodded again and stepped out of the cabin, leaving Thomas rushing to pull himself together.

Adsila pulled her blue dress from its place in her nook. Tugging it on, she readied herself in a hurry. Her hands moved over the folds of the thin material, but her thoughts drifted to her conversation with Thomas the day before.

Father did not talk much about Ye ho waah in human form. This story about Jesus was new. Could it be true? All of it? Could there be sin in her that she must be saved from? Or was this only for the white man? She did not feel bad or evil. Wasn't she a good person? Did she truly need saving?

The more she thought on it, the more questions arose. But, she pushed those thoughts to the side and focused on readying herself for the day.

Mere moments passed before she stepped into the great room, hair braided and face washed. She moved to the dish cabinet, pulling the small door open to reveal the modest plates.

Mother brushed past her, carrying steaming food to the table. She continued on to the door and, swinging it open, yelled for Father.

Tsiyi limped toward the dining room table, the uneven rhythm of his footfalls pulling Adsila's attention briefly from her task.

Offering him a small smile, Mother pulled his chair out and spooned food onto his plate as soon as Adsila set it in front of him.

"Your ankle should have healed long ago. If you wouldn't insist on playing so!" Mother clicked her tongue against her teeth.

He nodded, tilting his head down, his shoulders tucked.

Mother looked to Adsila. "You've been wearing that dress quite a bit lately."

Adsila's hands flew to the pleats at her waist. Why should she be favoring any dress in particular? If anything, she had trouble not over-wearing her red dress. *Perhaps that's it.* She had focused on not wearing her red dress as much and started grabbing for the blue one.

Mother turned and heaped food onto Father's plate.

Shrugging it off, Adsila filled her own plate. Then it struck her—this was the dress she wore the night Thomas Greyson came for dinner. He had said 'nice dress.' At the time, he meant to comment on having seen her wearing the deerskin dress earlier that day, but…

No, she was overthinking this. He was not the reason she donned this dress with greater frequency.

The door opened.

Father, coming in from the field.

He sat, and they began their dinner ritual.

Still, thoughts of the dress and why she might be wearing it more often continued to nag her.

Pushing his pen across the paper became tiresome to Senator Frelinghuysen. Was it truly the only thing left for him to do? This battle. This overwhelming battle seemingly became bigger by the week. And no one else, it seemed, would step forward to help him and the few senators who would stand against President Jackson on behalf of the innocents.

But if writing letters was all that was left to him, then that was what Frelinghuysen would do. What he had done. For the better part of the day.

Charlotte had left that morning for her myriad of meetings. What was it today? The booster club? Church fundraiser? Lunch with friends? He could not remember what kept her busy these days. But he heard the front door open and shut moments ago.

In his eagerness to speak with her, he summoned a maid and sent her after Charlotte. He hoped she would not be overtired.

The lightest raps possible sounded on his door. How had he not heard her on the steps?

"Come," he called.

He remained hunched over this last letter. It would only take one more moment to complete.

Pushing the door open, she stepped within.

A thick pause filled the space. She did not often come into his office. In fact, he could number them on one hand. Perhaps she was uncertain.

He opened his mouth to reassure her, but she breached the silence before he could.

"Darling?" Her voice only just above a whisper.

He turned, wishing to offer her a smile. But his features would not make one.

She did not move. Was she holding her breath?

"I'm glad you're home." He stood and crossed the space to greet her with an embrace.

She wrapped her arms around him, losing her breath. Still, she remained rather unyielding. Had this summons unnerved her? It had been unlike him. Was she so concerned?

"I understand you had quite the morning." He pulled back and looked over her. There was tension around her eyes, but she managed a small smile.

"Yes, it was. But you..." She seemed to gain some confidence. "You're home!"

As well perhaps he should not be. Would he best serve his constituents and the Indians at the Capitol?

Her features dropped. "Please, tell me what has happened, Theodore."

"I do not wish to weigh you down with the details of—" Why had he summoned her? To brighten his day? To worry her? Or to indeed share these very things with her? If not, then why?

"But it burdens you. Let me share that load."

How could he protect her if he bared all of what had occurred? Let her believe the papers. But she was his wife. Who better to understand? Hadn't they promised to walk these hard roads together?

He took her hand and led her toward his desk. Drawing her to the seat nearby, he sat in the desk chair he had earlier vacated.

His heart thumped loud in his chest, but he worked to remain calm. He had made his decision.

"I have not been completely honest about what's happened with the Indians." He measured his words.

"The Indians?"

"Yes. You must have read some things in the paper about the removal of the Choctaw."

She nodded slowly.

His stomach turned. "I tell you, Charlotte, that's not how it was."

"Then tell me." Her voice sounded small. Was she ready for these truths?

His eyes focused on hers. He then described what he knew of the conditions of the trip and the Choctaw's journey, of the sickness, and of the death.

As much as she worked to remain as still and calm as she could, tears made small rivers on her face. But she let him continue.

He did not stop, could not stop, until he had finished. By then, he had begun to question his decision to share with her.

"How can God let something like this happen?" She wiped at her eyes.

"He put us in place to prevent this. To be the voice of the orphan and the widowed. Of the disabused and mistreated. And I failed." This was not about him. He would not make it about him. Keeping his features strong and firm and set, he let this be about what it was. A chance to stop this. A lost chance.

"Theodore, you can't think that. You did everything you could."

He shook his head. Of course, she would want to comfort him. "It's about to happen again."

"Again?" Her eyes were wide, glassy, as they settled on him.

He slid his chair closer to hers. "The Creek Indians still living in Alabama have appealed to President Jackson. They are asking, well, pleading for protection from the state government."

"What is Alabama trying to do?" She blinked a few times.

"They are attempting to get rid of tribal governments and extend state laws over the Indians. Their goal, of course, is to get the land. Somehow, some way."

"Won't the president help them? They are citizens, aren't they?" Her voice was stronger than he would have expected.

"Not technically." He lifted a hand to emphasize the last word. How had he and the others not seen this coming?

"I thought the Indians had been told that if they became civilized, they would be the same as citizens."

"Yes, but not *technically* citizens." The way she looked at him pierced his heart as if she'd shot him with an arrow.

"That won't stop the president from helping them, will it?" Her eyes glistened anew.

"Charlotte, there's something you need to understand about President Jackson. He wants nothing more than to see the Indians—all Indians—abolished from our lands by whatever means necessary."

"Lord, may it never be!" She jerked back as if she had been slapped.

"Yes, we need to pray. And pray hard. We need the Lord to show us His hand, His will."

"Let's pray now!"

"Yes."

But as they bowed their heads, Frelinghuysen could not help the small doubt that crept in. Would prayer do anything? Was God even listening?

Thomas cleaned the children's slates. A mindless task, it gave him the chance to think on other things. Was he reaching the young Cherokee? Would he? What kind of impact could he have on this village if the people despised him so?

The floor creaked in the direction of the door.

Jerking his head, he set eyes upon Adsila.

She stood in the doorway, her gaze sweeping around the empty classroom.

His breath caught. Why had she come? To see him? No that wasn't possible. For Tsiyi? Yes, that must be. To help Tsiyi hobble home.

He cleared his throat. "Mohe went with Tsiyi. Did you not pass them?" Maybe she *had* come to see him?

Her eyes met his. They were intense but her features were tight, betraying nothing. "I came another way. By the stream."

She did seem to enjoy being near the creek.

Silence fell between them. A somewhat uncomfortable silence.

Thomas set down the slate he had nearly finished cleaning and turned his body toward her.

"Thank you," she said, spinning and stepping through the door.

"Adsila," he called, maneuvering around his desk.

She halted and half-turned. Facing him, one of her eyebrows rose.

He paused. Was that all the response he would get? Letting out a breath, he continued, "I wondered if you thought any more about our talk."

"Our talk?" Her brows furrowed.

"About Jesus. About his sacrifice."

"Oh." She looked away. Was she thinking on it?

He held his breath, praying she did.

"No." She turned her face toward his again.

What? How had she…? He caught her eyes.

She peered at him, almost into him. Was she waiting for his response?

Pushing aside his disappointment, he attempted to keep his voice even. "If you decide you want to talk about it, or have questions, my door is open."

Her face contorted. "But your door was closed."

Should he laugh or cry? Just like Atohi, so literal. "It's an expression. It means 'I'm always available to talk'."

She searched his features. Was she not sure he spoke the truth?

After a few moments, she said, "I see. But there is no need. I have no questions. No talk needed."

His brows met, but then he sighed. "Just… I am here if you do." He threw his hands up and turned back to his desk. Picking up a slate, he wiped at the chalk marks. She would be gone soon enough. What had kept her here this long was a mystery to him.

"And what makes you think you have all the answers?" There was an edge to her voice.

When he looked up, he fought to keep his surprise from showing. She had come several paces into the room. How did she move so stealthily?

Keeping his voice in check, he said with an even tone, "I never said I have all the answers." He continued to work on the slates, but he found it difficult. Why? Because she now stood a mere three feet away? "I only think I can answer some of the questions you may have about our talk."

She arched a brow. "Oh? And if *you* have any questions..." She paused. Was she searching for her words? "You can ask someone else."

How dare she take that tone with him? What nerve to scoff at his well-intentioned offer! And he had only ever approached her with the kindest of manners. What had he done to deserve this?

"Don't worry," he shot back, thrusting the slate he held to the desk. "I will."

He abandoned the cleaning altogether and, coming around the desk again, closed the gap between them. Why was he letting her get a rise out of him? How was it that she could draw such intense emotion out of him?

"Good. Because I don't care what you think!" Her eyes flashed.

His breath quickened. Was the room spinning? But she remained at the center of it all: her and that blue dress. How was it that every time he saw her, she wore that blue dress? The same one he commented on that night he dined with her family.

He shouldn't, but he leaned closer. Their faces were inches apart.

She didn't pull away, but her hands curled into fists. Was he having the same effect on her that she was on him? He could barely see straight. And he was certain his heart would thump right out of his chest.

The heat between their bodies was stifling. He had to resist the strong urge to crush her to himself. No, that would not end well.

He lowered his voice until it was not much more than a whisper. "If you don't care what I think, why do you keep wearing that dress?"

Adsila opened her mouth.

Nothing came out.

He stared into her eyes. This was dangerous.

Too dangerous.

Her voice rang out between them. "Because I only have four."

He pulled back. "Oh."

Had he imagined everything? It had nothing to do with him? Naught but the product of a limited wardrobe?

He stepped back.

She let out a ragged breath. Had she been holding it?

When he looked at her, she caught her lower lip between her teeth.

He drew himself away and turned to his desk, his back to her. Leaning one arm on the classroom wall, he took several deep breaths. Only then had he truly regained control.

"Adsila, I..." he started as he turned.

But she was gone.

TROUBLE FOR THE UPPER CREEKS

Atohi came upon the small house over the hill and near the creek. He waved at Adsila tending to her herbs in the side garden as he walked by.

She smiled and waved back then turned her attention back to her plants.

As he approached the door, he landed his hand on it three times.

A moment later, Inola greeted him. "Atohi, it is good to see you," she said as she wiped her hands on her apron. "How is Yona?"

"She is well, but growing quite large as her time nears."

"It won't be long now, and you two will share sleepless nights again." Inola winked.

He smiled. "I came to speak with Gawonii, but I didn't see him in the field."

"He went into the center of the village for the paper. You know how he is. Should be back soon, though. Come in." She moved to the side and welcomed him into her home. "I'll make some coffee."

Atohi nodded as he stepped through the doorway. He always enjoyed this particular home. A mixture of the most pleasant smells always filled the rooms of this house. The cook that inhabited this home was the best in the whole Cherokee nation.

Inola bustled about, warming water on the stovetop and setting out cups.

He took a seat at the table and watched her move about the kitchen as if it were the most natural place. His own wife could be called a decent cook, but her true place was among the animals of their flock. Yes, Yona found herself most at home tending to the cows and chickens. Her cooking just did not compare to Inola's.

When the water bubbled, having reached its boiling point, Atohi's mouth watered. He could almost taste the hot beverage he would be graced with.

Creak.

The door protested as Gawonii entered.

Atohi glanced back at his friend, but Gawonii's attention was on the paper, his brows furrowed.

Inola's features shifted, her concern on display. "What is it?"

Gawonii closed the door. Did they not wish Adsila to hear?

When Gawonii looked toward his wife, his eyes landed on Atohi. His eyebrows shot up, and a smile touched his lips.

"Ah, Atohi, how are you?"

"I am well. And you?" Atohi hesitated. Something weighed on the man.

A great sigh released from Gawonii. "We are well but not at all pleased by the news we receive these days." He raised the paper into the air.

"It is sobering. I haven't had a chance to read today."

Gawonii shook his head as he sat. "Reports of the Seminoles and the Creek." Gawonii opened the pages wider. "The Seminoles are at Payne's Landing on the Ocklawaha River for treaty negotiation."

"Treaty negotiation?" Atohi's breath caught. "Will all just give up their land? What about the Cherokee?"

Gawonii's jaw was set, his eyes hard, as he said, "I won't. The land is part of my soul. I will stay and fight."

"Don't talk like that." Inola blotted at her eyes with the edge of her apron.

"We must talk like this." Gawonii hit the paper. "The Upper Creek

Indians have earlier this month signed a treaty. Their land will be divided into allotments."

"Allotments?" Inola seemed to not understand.

Atohi was glad she asked, for he was uncertain he could see it.

"Each Creek will own his allotment and can sell or exchange it as he pleases," Gawonii said. He did not seem pleased about it. But why would he be?

"I don't trust the white man to be fair." Atohi narrowed his eyes. "They are devious."

Gawonii remained silent.

The door flung open, and Atohi's attention was drawn to the intrusion.

Tsiyi stepped into the house, Adsila not far behind him.

She shook dirt from her skirt, but her eyes were wide, her forehead wrinkled.

Inola rose, glaring at Tsiyi. "What are you doing home? It is the middle of the school day."

Tsiyi shrugged. "We were at recess, and three men with painted faces came. They talked with Mr. Greyson. He told us to go home. So, we did."

Adsila's face paled. As if the blood had drained from her features. She rushed out.

Inola looked after her for a moment but turned back to Tsiyi. "These men, what did they look like?"

"They were Cherokee," the young boy said. "With paint on their faces."

"Tell me of the paint." Gawonii's eyes were serious.

"Black across their eyes. Red streaks down their cheeks. And white on their foreheads." Tsiyi bit his lip and frowned. "What's going on?"

Atohi glanced between Inola and Gawonii. He put words to what they all knew to be true. "War paint."

Adsila rushed into the schoolhouse. Overturned desks and chairs filled the room. Papers and books were scattered everywhere. Where was Thomas? Had they…?

Stepping farther into the room, she swallowed to keep from vocalizing her concern. Her knees trembled as she moved forward. Would they hold her? Closing her eyes, she breathed in. She had to be stronger than this.

The sound of another breath, drawn in, this one ragged, gave her hope. He was alive!

Her gaze moved around the space. Where was he?

As she came close to the chalkboard, she spotted his limp form, slumped against the back of his desk.

"Thomas?" Her voice shook. *Stronger. You must be stronger.*

A weak groan was his only response. He made no move to so much as turn in her direction. He was still. Too still.

"Thomas, please look at me," she said, fighting the fear welling within. She took tentative steps toward him.

Pressing a hand to the floor and grasping for the top of the desk, he struggled. Was he attempting to stand?

"Thomas!" She rushed for him. Ducking under an arm, she helped him rise.

The guttural cry he emitted caused her stomach to knot. Did she truly care so much?

Would he now face her? She looked at him, but could see only a portion of his profile.

He passed a few labored breaths.

How could it be that they pained her, too?

Turning his head, he caught her eyes.

As much as his gaze tempted her, she could not keep from examining the wounds marring his features. Blood seeped from the corner of his bruised lip. A red gash over one of his eyebrows stretched to his hairline. Swollen patches on his jaw promised bruises in the days to come.

He attempted to turn away. Was her stare too much?

She gripped his shoulder and he grimaced.

Were there bruises under his clothing as well?

She jerked her hand back. Had she hurt him?

Still, she could not help herself. She needed to see him. Lifting fingers to his jaw, she turned his face back toward her. "Thomas, what happened?"

He shook his head and looked down.

"Please." She stretched her hand across his cheek, urging him to look at her once more. "Tell me."

"So fast." He let out a breath. "It all happened so fast." His eyes held hers. "And I don't even know who they were."

Her heart sank. The attack was no mystery. Tsiyi had spoken of Cherokee in war paint. Who else could it have been? Cherokee traditionalists on the warpath, seeking revenge wherever they could find it.

She frowned, working to keep her anger out of her features. While it was true that white settlers were brutalizing her people needlessly, it didn't give these men the right to beat Thomas.

But then...

Her resolve melted.

Thomas *wasn't* responsible.

Not for the poor treatment of the Cherokee. Not for the Indian Removal Act.

None of it.

Her eyes met his again, and the close proximity of their bodies became uncomfortable. She took one step back.

"Adsila?" He searched her eyes. "Do you know something?"

"I..." The words wouldn't come. Many emotions coursed through her, none that she could put a name to. But not one of them spoke of hate. How was it that she didn't hate Thomas after all? Rather there was something more in her heart she didn't understand. Something warm. And unnerving.

She found her voice. "Let's get you cleaned up."

Taking his hand, she grabbed the cloth he used to clean the slates. Careful to take slower steps, she led him out of the schoolhouse and toward the creek. Drawing him to sit down by the stream alongside her, she faced him. And, dipping the cloth into the cool water, she brought it to his lip.

He startled and pulled back, but leaned toward her again and allowed her to press the cloth to his wound once more.

She continued to work, wiping all traces of blood from his face.

He stared into her eyes as she did so.

This, too, she found both pleasing and unsettling.

After she cleaned the last cut, she leaned back. "There," she said, as she let the cloth fall into her lap. Her eyes, no longer occupied with his injuries, found his. Could she read his thoughts? How was it that she found herself so fearful of her own?

Thomas cleared his throat.

"Thank you." He reached forward and touched her hand.

She looked down at their overlapping fingers. How could she face him with her next words? "I am so sorry… for what happened."

He ducked his head. Was he attempting to catch her eyes? "Why? You are not responsible."

She looked at him. So kind. So gentle. "But it was an act of my people. Taking out their anger for the white man on you." Tears stung her eyes.

"Do *you* think I am responsible for what is happening to your people?" His voice was soft and kind. Too kind.

And she knew. In that moment, it was clear. He had known about her anger toward him. Despite her tears, she turned to meet his eyes again. But she saw no accusations there, only sympathy.

"No." And she believed that with every part of her being.

He exhaled, closing his eyes for a moment. When he opened them, he spoke, "You are no more responsible for the actions of your people than I am for the actions of mine."

She nodded, basking in his grace. He had every right to turn her earlier anger toward him back against her now. Only he didn't. And then she understood why she needed Jesus. While it may be true that her life was full of good things, there were things in her life and in her soul that were sinful. Her anger toward Thomas was but one example.

She needed God's forgiveness.

She needed His grace.

Thomas's face twisted, and he held his side.

"What is it?" She leaned forward, laying a hand on his shoulder.

He held up a hand. "Just a muscle cramp."

"We must get you to the medicine man."

"I don't think…"

She gave him a look she hoped invited no argument.

He nodded his surrender.

Lillian Greyson moved about the dinning space. She couldn't help but smile. For she was well pleased. Everything seemed to be going her way. So far, two Indian groups had signed treaties, and one more was in progress, according to Arthur. It seemed as if her son would be home soon. Imagine—Tommy returning, the prodigal son. He could find a church here, court a girl, settle down…

But they would not focus on that this night. Tonight would be about Phillip. Her eldest had accepted a promotion to partner at his law firm. Such exciting news! Phillip, Clara, and their two children would be dining with her and Arthur tonight.

She returned her attention to the task at hand—the table arrangements. The room looked splendid. Everything was ready.

And just in time. They would be here any minute.

"Go tell Mr. Greyson it's almost time."

A nearby housemaid nodded and moved off on her errand.

Just then, the door chimed.

She would prefer to be in the parlor to greet her guests. But they would catch her in the hallway.

It would be just as well she meet them at the door.

Stepping toward the entrance, she listened as the butler welcomed Phillip and his family in.

"Dearest Phillip!" Lillian came around the corner with open arms.

"Mother!" Phillip accepted her embrace.

She couldn't help but think of Thomas while embracing Phillip.

Not only because of how much her two sons favored each other, but perhaps it was where her thoughts were most often of late.

Was he warm? Being cared for? Did he have friends?

As she pulled back from Phillip's shoulder, she pushed thoughts of Thomas from her mind and shifted her attention to the children around her.

"Come, give Grandma hugs." She leaned down and extended her arms.

Two brown-haired children stepped to her.

As she rose, Clara laid a hand on her shoulder. "How are you, Mrs. Greyson?"

"Quite well, thank you. And you're looking well"

"Thank you. I'm trying a new hairstyle." Clara seemed somewhat timid. Why did she always have to act that way? It wasn't as if Lillian may bite her.

"It's rather… unique." She hoped her voice did not betray her true thoughts. Clara's hair looked ridiculous. Far too elaborate for any everyday style. The young woman might as well have been going to see the queen of England in that up-do. Curls everywhere. And Lillian wagered about a thousand pins to keep it stable.

"Ah, there's the man of the hour!" Arthur said from the top of the stairs.

Lillian shot him a look as he descended. Why must he insist on that old out-of-date coat? Before meeting anyone's eyes, however, she found her smile again.

"Grandpa!" the children called.

He pulled them into his arms as he stepped onto the bottom stair.

"Perhaps we should move into the parlor where there's more room." She put a hand on Phillip's arm and allowed him to escort her in that direction.

Everyone followed suit and fell in line.

As they entered the parlor, the children ran to their corner. Lillian always made certain there were games and toys put out for them. The adults would be more able to enjoy the sitting area and converse freely until the butler called for dinner.

The men launched into talk of politics. Why must they speak of such boorish things?

Lillian smoothed over her skirt and turned to Clara. Must she attend to her with that hair?

She searched for something to say. Anything. Did they have something in common? If nothing, Lillian had good breeding. There was that to fall back on. "What is new with you?"

"Nothing to speak of."

Will she not assist me with this conversation making? Is she as dull as she seems?

Then she spoke again.

Thank the Lord!

"The children take up much of my time. And with Phillip's promotion, I would like to think we might see more of him... but I doubt that will be the case."

Fill her day? The children? That certainly couldn't be so. Didn't they attend some sort of learning institution? "What fills your day while the children are in school?"

"I do enjoy painting and sewing. And I keep up with the house and correspondence with my family. But I wish I had some other outlet." The last word came out a bit shaky.

Dearest God in heaven, the woman was hopeless! Must Lillian hold her hand? "You should come join me at the women's booster club. It would be a good opportunity for you to get out of the house and into the community." As soon as she said it, Lillian regretted it. Maybe inviting Clara into her own booster club was a mistake. There were others.

"That sounds like something I would be interested in."

Wonderful. Now she would be stuck. Lillian looked away as she was certain her thoughts were on her features.

"How is Emma and her little addition?" Clara asked.

Now this was a subject Lillian loved. "Oh, the new little one is absolutely delightful. But I know Emma is tired." She wanted to speak further, but perhaps she best not.

Clara nodded.

Another silence.

Clara excused herself to check on the children, and Lillian turned toward the conversation between the two men.

"I read that seven Seminole chiefs went to inspect the new reservation before signing a treaty," Arthur said.

"I bet all of Washington D.C. is holding its breath. None of the other tribes have been so bold." Phillip let out a stiff a laugh.

"I don't know that President Jackson has anything to worry about." Arthur spoke with a more serious tone. "What are the Indians going to do even if they don't like what they find? They can't realistically stay here forever." Arthur stressed the word 'realistically.'

"What do you mean? It's their land. Why can't they stay as long as they please?" Phillip's confusion played on his face.

"It's not that simple. Did you read about the treaty the Creek Indians signed?"

"Yes. I thought it was a fair treaty. It gave the Indians a chance to decide for themselves and their families if they wanted to sell their own land." Phillip's tone matched Arthur's.

"Have you not also read that squatters and land speculators are defrauding the Creeks out of their allotments? There's been fighting and all manner of violence breaking out because of it."

Phillip raised a brow. "And what is the governor doing about it?"

Arthur shrugged. "Nothing, as far as I know. No reports of any intervention by the governor or the state militia. And President Jackson is taking a hand's off approach to this one, it seems."

Fighting. Violence. This didn't sound good to Lillian. Not one bit.

"How will this affect Thomas?" Phillip threw a hand up.

"Thomas?" Lillian interjected, a lilt to her voice.

"I was just wondering what affect all this business with the Indians will have on Thomas where he is," Phillip explained.

"He's with the *Cherokee*." Arthur gave Phillip a sharp look. "We've heard nothing of the *Cherokee* in the news."

"That's right." Phillip nodded toward his father. He then turned toward his mother. "I'm sure Thomas is doing well. Have you heard from him lately?"

That was a relief! Lillian settled herself back in her seat and smiled. "We heard from him a while ago. He *is* doing well. He wrote to us of his students and the connections he is making. We're so proud of him."

"That's great, Mother. I'm really glad to hear he's thriving."

The butler entered the parlor just then and announced dinner.

"Shall we?" Lillian stood, hands clasped to hold them steady. All this talk, and her poor Thomas…

Arthur stood. "We shall." He reached for Lillian's hand and escorted her from the room.

Dinner awaited them.

Thomas was fine. Warm. Happy.

Then, why the trembling hands?

Lillian swallowed the lump in her throat and held tight to Arthur.

Adsila leaned back, angling her body toward the sky. The heat of the sun covered her skin. Closing her eyes, she sighed as the rays bathed her. She soaked up the light much as her plants did. Would it rejuvenate her the same? Couldn't she just sit here forever? Why couldn't life be as simple as her garden? Without complications?

But it wasn't.

And she couldn't pretend it was.

Mother and Father must not realize how thin the walls of their small cabin truly were. Their words penetrated her solitude. Would she rather not know?

Her heart poured hot liquid. Tiny rivers formed on her face.

Yes, she mourned for the Choctaw, the Creek, and even more… for what may happen to her people.

The wind lifted her braid slightly. Would it carry her fears away?

If only.

She exhaled into the wind.

Oh God!

Could He hear her? She had never prayed to the Christian God.

God, are you there? Do you care about my people? Didn't you care about the Choctaw? The Creek?

No answer.

Thomas says You care, but You allowed them to be...

What? What words to put to it?

If You are almighty and all-powerful, could You not have stopped it?

Thomas's voice came to her, "God has a plan in all things. We don't always understand, but if we look for it, we can see His hand."

Is that true, God? Could this be Your plan?

A shudder shook her shoulders.

If so, I'm not sure I want any part of You. A good God would not allow such suffering.

"God is unchanging. God is love. God is good," Thomas's voice continued in her head. "We cannot lean on our own understanding. Our perception is imperfect."

Could Thomas be wrong? A part of her wanted to believe, but what she saw around her didn't fit the idea of a loving, merciful God.

Thomas had said God was big enough for her questions. She gazed toward the clouds.

Help me understand. If You truly are who Thomas says You are, help me understand.

A man cleared his throat behind her.

She jerked her head around, nearly losing her balance. She caught herself just short of falling face first in the dirt.

Thomas stood by the fence, a half grin on his face. How long had he been there?

"Thomas! I..." she said, trying to stand up. Had she been praying out loud? What had he heard?

"I didn't mean to intrude." But his smile widened to cover his entire face.

Her features warmed. He must have heard everything.

Once the dirt was beneath her feet and her dress smoothed, she raised her eyes to meet his again. "I'm sorry, when did you... where did you...?"

She couldn't even form a sentence. Swearing briefly in her native language, she cursed her tongue-tie.

"Not long."

His eyes were bright. Amused?

"I didn't wish to disturb you. You seemed so peaceful."

She folded her arms over her chest and looked toward the ground. Couldn't she become a bird and fly away?

"But I didn't want to eavesdrop either." He tilted his head and caught her eyes. "Honest."

She glanced at what a picture he made, hunched over and head cocked to the side. He looked like his body was disjointed. A little laugh escaped her lips.

He straightened and chuckled, too. Did he know what a sight he was?

Either way, it felt good to share a laugh.

"You're not intruding." She stepped toward him, maneuvering through the small gate to stand next to him. "I was just thinking."

He nodded, but his gaze drifted to something in the distance. Where were his thoughts?

"Did you need to speak with my father? I can fetch him." She turned in the direction of the house.

"No," he said, placing a hand on her arm.

She glanced at the place where he made contact. Why did his touch heat her skin so?

He pulled his hand back. Did he think he had offended?

"I, um, came to talk to you."

"Me?" What would he need with her? While they'd had their share of interactions, it was always a result of them being thrown together. Single men only sought maidens out for one reason.

"I need to ask a favor." He shoved both hands in his pockets.

What kinds of favors did white men ask maidens for? She leaned against the fence post. Her stomach turned.

"I need to be away. Only for a few days. I wondered if you could… if you wanted to… if you'd be willing to… take up teaching at the school? Just until I get back."

A knot pinched in the pit of her stomach. "You're leaving?"

His gaze leveled on her, his blue eyes darker than she had ever seen. Was he weighing some decision?

Finally, he spoke. "The state of Georgia has passed a law that prohibits white men from living on Indian land without a state license."

She shook her head. State law? What could this mean? Keeping white men off Indian land? Wasn't this a good thing? Except... except it would mean all the missionaries, the teachers; any aide would be forced to leave.

"One of the missionaries, Samuel Worcester, believes this law is a way the state is taking power from the Cherokee Nation. Passing a law to tell them how to manage their own territory. Twelve of us missionaries are going to New Echota to protest."

"You and other white men are going to protest your government for the sake of the Cherokee?" Her eyes widened. There was a strange sensation high in her chest. Not unpleasant exactly.

"Of course." His eyes searched her features. "What they are doing is not right. Your people should be allowed to govern yourselves. The Cherokee have a governing system. It's not as if it's anarchy down here."

The tingling in her chest intensified and filled that space until it seemed it would burst she was so... happy? But why did the knot in her stomach continue to tighten?

"So, will you?" His eyes were bright, his voice soft and low.

"Will I what?" *What had he asked me again?*

"Will you take charge of the school while I'm gone?"

"Do you think I am the most qualified?" Her brows furrowed. "What about Atohi?" She could not be the most suitable replacement.

"Not the most qualified? I think you could teach the children a lot about herbs and gardening. You have the best English in the village. Besides, Atohi's wife will deliver any day now."

Her face heated all the more. Such compliments! But he was right about Yona.

"If you are certain, I will accept." She managed to make her mouth broaden into a smile she wasn't sure she felt.

"I am certain." He placed a hand on hers.

And it came—that silence in which they just stared at one another. What was he thinking? Drawn into those blue-gray eyes, she found it difficult to think. And, try as she might, she could not tear herself away.

Thomas disrupted their gaze by turning and then pulled his hand away.

She gripped the fence to keep from swaying toward him. Did he notice?

"Thank you, Adsila. I am much relieved to know I leave the classroom in good hands."

She offered him a weak smile. Her thoughts and emotions were too tangled for anything more. "When will you leave?"

"Three days from now."

The knot tightened. It was unbearable now. She placed a hand over her middle.

"Could you come to the schoolhouse tomorrow? It would give me a chance to tell you where we are in math, reading, and science."

She nodded, afraid to speak, afraid of what she may say.

"I'll be going, then." He turned.

What was she going to do? Could she let him walk away? Her heart thundered. And her throat tightened as his steps carried him away from her.

"Dinner?" she called.

"What?" He spun, an eyebrow quirked.

"Would you like to stay for dinner?" She let out a long breath.

He smiled. "Love to."

Walter Buckner moved pen across paper. He busied himself answering constituent mail. Not his favorite part of the job, but it was necessary. The senator's staff must not forget the men whose votes got Frelinghuysen here, and, by extension, them.

The Indian issue was often mentioned. Some wanted Frelinghuysen to support their removal, but many who voted him in because of his political bend, encouraged him to keep fighting for their Christian duty to the Indians.

As this political debacle continued (there was no other word for it), the more Walter was sure it would forever tarnish the reputation of Jackson's presidency.

Someone brushed against his desk. He glanced up. Mason, Frelinghuysen's secretary. What could he want? The man was always stirring up some kind of trouble in the office.

"Here's some more letters." He placed a stack of opened envelopes in front of Walter.

"Thanks." He made great effort to not look, but continued working on his current correspondence.

"If you ask me… I think you're taking all of this a little too…"

Walter looked up, his predicament forgotten. What was he trying to say? "A little too—?"

Mason jerked back. "I don't know. Seriously?"

"Seriously?" Walter's voice rose.

"I know this is a stepping stone for your career. So, you have to take it seriously. But you've taken this whole Indian thing too far."

He stood. "That's because it's a *serious* issue."

Mason glanced around. Were others watching? Walter didn't care.

"Isn't it enough that it weighs the senator down?" Mason shrugged. "Do you have to carry such a burden, too?"

"I think that not enough people are taking it *seriously*." Walter turned to grab his jacket.

"What do you mean?"

Walter wasn't having it. Spinning back toward Mason, he let the heat of his anger burn in his voice. "People are dying. By the *hundreds*. And here we sit in our comfy offices, sipping coffee, worrying that we might be taking things too seriously."

Mason held up his hands. "I was just trying to help."

Walter's volume dropped, and his voice calmed. "I know. I just think we all need a good dose of reality. It's not enough and too much all at the same time, you know?"

Mason looked up at him, his blue glassy eyes so completely devoid of any deeper thoughts on the matter. "No. I don't."

He grunted. "Maybe it's just me."

"Maybe it is." Mason shrugged again before moving off toward his desk. "Maybe you need a day or two off. The stress is getting to you."

"Maybe." He was done trying to convince him.

Thomas gazed at the men in the room around him. Many of them knew each other. Being new to his placement, he had yet to become acquainted with the other missionaries in this field. But he took comfort in the knowledge that they were here for the same reason. One shared purpose.

As he continued to sweep the area with his eyes, a man approached him. The man's long nose was not fit for every face, but with his dark eyes set deeper into his features, and wide, thin mouth, it seemed right. When the man neared Thomas, he stretched out his hand.

"Welcome to New Echota. I don't believe we've met." The wide mouth broadened into a smile.

"I don't believe we have. I'm Thomas Greyson." Thomas slid his hand into the man's firm grip.

"Samuel Worcester." The man gave his hand a hearty shake. "I've heard good things about you, Thomas. You showed a lot of promise at Andover."

Ah, Andover. The finest Theological Seminary in the United States. At least in Thomas's opinion.

"Thank you, Mr. Worcester. It is an honor to meet you. I've heard plenty about you as well."

"Please, call me Samuel."

Worcester seemed friendly enough, but his dark eyes were rather intense.

"How are you finding your field?" Worcester broke the moment of silence between them.

That's interesting. Jumping right to the meat of it. "I am adjusting well, I think." How much should he share with the man? They were brothers in their mission, after all. Perhaps Worcester could give him some advice. "I have found the Cherokee rather resistant to anything resembling new religion."

Worcester nodded. "I encountered similar challenges early on."

Then the man could help him! "How did you overcome them?"

The man shrugged and offered Thomas a small smile. "You have to be patient. And prayerful. Remember, it is God Who works on the heart. You simply bear the message."

Thomas nodded. Worcester was right. "I have had an interesting conversation or two with one of the maidens in the village. She enlightened me to some of the Cherokee beliefs. About Ye ho waah? Is there any possibility that the God they worship and our God is one and the same?"

Worcester's brows met. Was he thoughtful? Or concerned?

"I have wondered the same thing. Unfortunately, I have no answer. Either way, it is best they come to a correct understanding of Christ." Worcester's eyes lingered on him. They seemed to peer into his very soul.

"I understand," Thomas said, his words measured. But he couldn't help but continue. "This maiden, Adsila, seems to be slowly coming to that understanding. I cannot be certain, but I believe something is happening in her heart."

Worcester's gaze remained hard and after some moments, softened. "I should caution you against any entanglements with the maidens in the village. It may be best that you work with the men and children. Then let them spread the message to the young women."

Thomas's brows furrowed. "I don't—"

"Just a thought." Worcester lifted a hand and laid it on Thomas's shoulder. "Now, someone had best call this meeting to order. And I suppose that would be me. It was good to meet you, Thomas. May God continue to bless your work."

With that, Worcester stepped around Thomas and moved toward the front of the room.

He took to the raised platform and, speaking in a loud voice, called for everyone's attention.

But Thomas could not focus. He was deep in thought about Worcester's words. Was he getting too close to Adsila? There had been looks, glances, touches… but nothing sinful. He had to admit there was a stirring within himself. But was it wrong, as Worcester suggested? He and Adsila were both unattached. Or did Worcester refer to the fact that she was Cherokee and he was white? Surely not.

Shifting his attention, he tried to take in what Worcester was saying. The man spoke of the plight of the Cherokee, of which they were all aware. And of the recent law. Then he opened the floor for suggestions.

"I think we should protest in the capitol!" one man shouted.

"But what kind of message would that send?" another responded.

"We ought to go about this peaceably," a tall red-haired man said.

"Jesus wasn't too peaceable about running the merchants out of the temple!" the first man replied.

"I don't think we should encourage any level of violent protest," the second man inserted.

"What's violent about standing at the capitol stairs with signs?" the first man spoke out again.

"You know those types of protests aren't apt to stay calm. They aren't viewed with high regard," the man with the red hair argued. "What about a petition or a resolution?"

Several voices spoke at once then, many in agreement.

"What's to say the governor won't just throw it in the trash?" the first man brought up.

"What's to say he won't?" the man with the red hair shot back.

Things became more heated, and Worcester raised his arms. "Gentlemen," he called.

Everyone quieted.

"It seems we have two choices: a verbal protest at the capitol or a written protest in the form of a resolution. And I think we should put it to a vote."

Mumbles surrounded Thomas, but a general state of agreement rose above the din.

Worcester called for those in favor of the verbal, physical protest.

Only four raised their hands.

He asked for those who supported the resolution on paper.

The remaining seven raised their hands, including Thomas. He in no way supported anything that could be misconstrued as violent.

And so, it was done.

Worcester drew up the resolution and all penned their names to it. They then prayed over the petition and were dismissed.

Governor George Rockingham Gilmer sat at his desk. A handful of his staff assembled around him, prepared to do his bidding. On his desk sat a resolution, signed by twelve Cherokee missionaries. It enraged him. His face burned hot. How dare they oppose him!

"Sir," his chief of staff spoke up. "Shall we take the resolution before the Senate?"

"I think it needs to go before the House," another staff member said.

"Or maybe forward it on to the president," someone piped in. "Let him take the political nose dive for it."

"No," Gilmer said, his voice growing louder. "No, no, no, no, no. This is the *law* and they *will* abide by my laws! If they won't get a license, arrest them. Arrest them all."

Thomas waved an arm over Adsila's plants. "Thank you for teaching us more about your plants." He couldn't help the smile that spread across his features as he gazed in Adsila's direction. Did he imagine it, or did her cheeks color when her eyes met his?

The children clapped.

He didn't wish to disengage from their interaction just yet. "And thank you for teaching us so many things these last several days."

Adsila turned toward the class and bowed. Then she stepped to the side, creating distance between them where there had been little.

His heart dropped. Did it show? Perhaps it was best he focus on his students. They had gathered at the front of the room where they had a better view of the plants. "Where does the plant get water?"

"The rain," one student replied.

"That's right. Does rain always fall calmly from the sky?" He stretched his arms out and looked toward the ceiling.

"Sometimes there's a storm," another, older student replied.

"Does the plant still need that rain?" Thomas ran his fingers over the leaves, grazing the foliage.

"Yes," several students said together.

"Does the plant understand what a storm is?"

The class fell silent.

His gaze wandered over the faces of his pupils. Their curious eyes watched him with interest. He glanced in Adsila's direction as she, too, quirked a brow. Was she just as eager to know his point?

"No," one student shouted.

"What about us?" He shifted his focus to the younger boy who had spoken. "When God sends a storm... a difficult time perhaps, do we always understand?"

There was silence.

"No. We won't. But He will also send rain, or blessings we need for growth, in the midst of that storm. And we must endure the storm to receive the needed rain. Just like the plant."

Dark eyes glared at him. Dare he continue? He must.

"We can know two things in this—" He lifted two fingers into the air. "God is with us through the storm, and He has a plan to grow us."

Blank faces stared back.

A sigh escaped his lips. Was he getting through to them? Would he ever? He pressed his lips into a smile. "That may be enough for today. Let's return to our seats and gather our things."

The children turned and made their way to the rows of desks as instructed.

He looked across the open space separating him from Adsila. What was that in her gaze? Pity? Understanding? Her thoughts, as usual, were difficult to discern.

Whack!

The door to the schoolhouse flew open, and a handful of soldiers filed in.

Thomas stepped in front of Adsila.

The Cherokee children moved toward the outer walls of the schoolhouse, huddling there together as far from the intruders as possible.

"Gentlemen," Thomas said. Did his voice betray his uneasiness? "You have entered a schoolhouse. Full of *children*. This is no place to conduct your business."

The men moved down the center of the room, marching in line, intent on their purpose. What was that exactly?

Thomas held his arms out and stepped forward. Could he distract these men from doing harm to his students? Adsila?

"Trust me, Mr. Greyson," one of the men said as he stepped out of the group and toward Thomas. "We have no interest in the Indian children. Just you."

"Me?" Thomas dropped his arms. At least Adsila and the children would be safe.

"You are in violation of Georgia law, and we are here to arrest you," the man said in a gruff voice, stopping just short of where Thomas and Adsila stood.

Adsila's arm wrapped around one of his.

Why would she make such a bold move? Was it possible she cared?

Another soldier came forward and took Thomas's other arm.

"Adsila." Thomas turned and looked at her. "Please, take the children away from here."

She opened her mouth. Her eyes glistened in the simple light rays coming in through the window. So full of life. But she soon sealed her lips and released his arm.

As she stepped around him and spoke in Iroquois, he wished for the words she almost said.

But she was lost to him as she moved toward the door and the children scrambled to follow her, surrounding her as they did so.

The soldiers, for their part, barely afforded them a glance.

"Thank you," Thomas said to the militia's leader, once Adsila and the children were out of the schoolhouse. "For waiting. I will come with you willingly."

"Yes, Mr. Greyson, you will," the man said, a gleam in his eye.

Lillian Greyson loved the interchange between Emma and Mr. Knightley. He scolded her quite thoroughly. But even so, he cared for her. So deeply. How could she not see it?

Someone drew in a deep breath over her.

She jerked back. Had someone trespassed on her silence?

Arthur stood no more than three feet away, staring down upon her.

Hand over her thumping heart, she had half a mind to scold him. But she took a few breaths and tried to calm herself. Then it occurred to her how strange it was that he was not in his office. He never came to the parlor unsummoned. Never. Had something happened? "What brings you to the parlor at this hour?"

He sat beside her and lifted the book from her hands. Laying it aside, he grasped her hands.

Something *had* happened. Her pulse raced, and her head swam. The room spun.

Dear God.

But there was no way to know what had happened.

Still, it must be serious.

"What..." Her voice came weakly. She swallowed. "What is it?"

"Lillian, it's Thomas." His words were measured, his tone calm, yet it did nothing to soothe her.

"Oh, dearest Lord, it cannot be! Not my Thomas!" Her hands flew to her mouth. How could God let it be? That He would allow harm to befall her child? She swayed to the side.

Arthur gripped her shoulders and held her upright. "Calm yourself, Lillian! Let me finish. He is well."

The words penetrated the fog surrounding her brain.

"He is well?" She met Arthur's eyes once more.

He nodded. "Yes. No harm has come to him."

"Then what...?" Her mouth now dry, she couldn't make herself swallow. The words became lost.

Arthur studied her then drew in a slow breath. "He has been arrested."

"Arrested?" One hand rose to her chest.

Her husband's hands on her shoulders tightened once more. Was he fearful she might faint?

She gripped for the lapels of his jacket. "Tell me."

He quirked a brow. A moment of indecision?

"Please, I must know." She forced her features to remain set and stiffened her spine.

Loosening his hold, he rubbed her upper arms. "The state of Georgia passed a law about white men living on Indian land. Apparently, he refused to acquire the proper license."

Her shoulders slackened, and her body became weak.

Arthur's eyes widened.

She firmed her posture and cleared her throat. "W-why?"

"I don't know the details. Phillip has made plans to go to Georgia and do whatever he can to assist in Thomas's defense."

Phillip? Yes, that was the best plan. Phillip would make things right.

"I'm going, too." The statement came out stronger than she'd expected.

Arthur tipped his chin down. Was he so disbelieving of her abilities? Perhaps her near-faint earlier was not the best way to recommend herself. "Come now, you must see that is impossible. The best thing we can do for Thomas is stay here and pray. He doesn't need us distracting him right now."

"I wouldn't be a distraction. He needs his mother." Her voice rose, and her fingers gripped at his shirt.

He pulled her hands loose. "Lillian, I won't allow it. We will not speak of it anymore." His tone became harsh and biting.

She quieted but she could not stop the tears that betrayed her.

He spoke, this time his voice gentler as he wrapped an arm around her shaking shoulders. "I know this is hard for you, darling. It's difficult for me, too. But we have to trust Phillip. We have to trust God."

Theodore Frelinghuysen laid the newspaper in his lap, the coarse material of his pants grazing the backs of his fingers. Incredible.

"More tea, dear?" Charlotte's voice broke his concentration. She sat across the parlor, eyes raised from her sewing.

"No, thank you." He drew the paper up once more.

How was it that Jackson's re-election campaign came into full swing? Even more so, he touted himself as a hero? The Republicans, on the other hand, painted him as a self-appointed king—a man who knew no boundaries to his power. And respected no limits.

Was this truly what disturbed Frelinghuysen? Or perhaps it was the emphasis of the campaign and the focus of everyone's attention these last few weeks: the banks. Absurd.

"Something troubles you?" Charlotte's needlepoint now lay by her side.

He jerked the barrier between them aside. "This presidential campaign."

"You mean to say *Jackson's* campaign." Her brow rose. How had she guessed him so well?

Nodding, he set the papers on the table next to him and lifted his teacup.

"I noticed an interesting cartoon the other day. What was it? Something about a hickory stick." Her brows knit across her forehead causing wrinkles that did not disappear completely when she calmed her features. "Oh, I wish I could remember."

"Hmmm." Sipping the now-cold tea, he wished he had requested a fresh pour.

"Do you think the people will re-elect him? Even after his cabinet members resigned over Mr. John… oh, what's his name?"

"John Eaton," Frelinghuysen said flatly. What did Charlotte know? He had been careful not to speak of it at home. Best to protect her as much as he could.

"Terrible business, if you ask me. Shameful!"

Still, he knew of which she spoke. How could he not? The affair between a married woman and a man Andrew Jackson had appointed to his cabinet could not remain secret. The couple had insisted they were only friends until her husband's death. But the two married much too soon for propriety's sake following the man's death.

"Then again, President Jackson's marriage was quite the scandal." She picked up her thread and needle as she leaned back into the sofa.

Frelinghuysen remained silent. How had his wife become so well informed? Jackson's wife, Rachel, had married him before the divorce to her first husband was final. This, too, he supposed, was too much common knowledge for him to think Charlotte ignorant.

"The White House, I say, is full of scandal."

He stood and moved to the window. His eyes searched the gardens beyond. The greenery of summer delighted him on most days, but not today.

At times, Charlotte walked the line of being a gossip. He wanted neither to encourage nor upset her by pointing it out.

"Theodore? Is everything all right?" The rustle of clothing told him she shifted behind him. He imagined she set her work aside once more.

"Yes," he called back to her. "Everyone is just caught in this whirlwind—the banks, the President's Cabinet, even his wife. I only wish there were more to be done for the Indians. Perhaps if more people were concerned…"

He didn't finish and she remained silent.

"It seems we've all moved on to the next issue, while they still suffer."

"You can't make people care, Theodore." She spoke in a soft voice. Did she even care?

"I know." His gaze dropped toward the ground. Spent. "But I wish I could make people aware."

Adsila made her way home after a long day at the school. It wasn't that the children wore on her, but something else weighed on her shoulders. Perhaps even on her heart.

Was it the reminders of Thomas scattered throughout the small building? Her thoughts were on him when she taught, when she cleaned, even as she walked to and from the schoolhouse. And at night, she did not have peace. She could not clear her mind of worry over how he fared.

She poured all her energy into Thomas's students each day, giving the children everything she had. Just as Thomas would want her to. But she couldn't talk to them about God. Not like Thomas had.

Often, she recalled what he had said about storms and rain. Was God growing her through some sort of trial? If only she saw His hand more clearly. Her heart ached. Why must she struggle so? Why must her people? Within the next few months or years perhaps, the Cherokee faced removal from their land. How would it come? By force? Would they resist?

And her friend, Thomas, was… somewhere. Maybe in pain. Suffering because he stood up for her people.

The familiar sights of her father's farm and her own garden were now in plain view. How had she closed in on home without awareness?

Moments later, she opened the door and entered the small house.

She came face to face with Mother and Father, nearly smacking into them. Had they been waiting on her?

Her eyes scanned the large room behind them. Tsiyi was nowhere to be found.

"Adsila," Father said in a low, solemn voice. "Please, sit."

"Has something happened to Tsiyi?" Her heart raced. He had left the schoolhouse an hour or more before she had. There was little doubt he made it home before she did.

"No, Tsiyi is fine. Please, sit," her father repeated, pulling out a dining chair.

Her pulse throbbed in her wrists. Something wasn't right. Still, she stepped forward and slid into the chair across the table from where Mother now stood. The *Cherokee Phoenix* lay haphazardly on the table. Should she reach for it? Instead she sought her Father's eyes.

"What is it?" She gulped. Could she swallow her fear? "What's happened?"

"It is Thomas Greyson." Father's gentle voice did little to soften the news.

Her heart sank. Tears pricked at her eyes. She looked to Mother. Would there be strength there? Hope?

The older woman's face was downcast as well.

"The missionaries have been convicted and sentenced to four years of hard labor at the state penitentiary in Milledgeville." Father's gaze remained on Adsila, his words coming slowly.

All the warmth drained from her face. She pressed words forth, yet nothing but a whimper came. Her mouth was dry, but her eyes were full.

Mother laid a hand on Adsila's arm.

"How?" Adsila squeaked out. Was that even her voice?

"It will be as the Great Spirit wills it," Father said. His eyes reflected a kind of sadness she didn't expect. Did he care so much about Thomas?

This couldn't be right. How could the Great Spirit...or God will such a thing? Still, she knew what Thomas would say — she must have faith. She would only see God's hand if she had faith.

May it be as You will, God.

WORCESTER V. GEORGIA

Dearest Mother and Father,

Do not be concerned about what you read in the papers. I know you may have seen Thomas's conviction and sentence. However, take heart, I have good news. The governor issued pardons to the men. Samuel Worcester, who seems to be the leader of this venture, urged nine of the men, including Thomas, to take the pardons. He and another of the missionaries wish to appeal to the Supreme Court.

But that is no matter for you to concern yourself with. Thomas will come home with me as soon as we clear up some legalities and can arrange train passage.

Your loving son,
Phillip Greyson

Atohi listened as his wife sang to their infant daughter. He hoped the small girl would sleep soon. He longed for a few moments with Yona. Time with her seemed far too scarce these days. Hadn't they known it would be like this? But with Mohe already seven years of age, it had been some time since they'd had a new baby. Many things had been forgotten.

Yona stepped from their partitioned room and smiled at him.

"She sleeps," Yona whispered. A smile for him upon her lips.

He, too, felt the corners of his mouth rise as a weight lifted. Yona crossed the room and sat beside him.

Her hand grazed his.

Flipping his over, he intertwined their fingers.

"What is happening?" She nodded toward the paper sitting on the table beside him.

He shook his head. "More politics. More trouble." She didn't need to know.

"And what of your friend Thomas Greyson?"

Turning away from her, his brows furrowed. She must not see the concern in his eyes. "He was convicted but accepted a pardon. He will be safe."

"Will he return?"

He turned and faced her. Despite his efforts, there was sadness in the deep brown eyes that stared back at him. "I don't think he can. Not without a license. And I do not think the state will grant him that after he participated in the protest."

"Too bad." When Yona spoke, it was smooth and melodic. It sounded like a song to Atohi. He could not forget how this drew him to her in their younger years. "Mohe will really miss him."

He narrowed his eyes slightly. Did she bait him? Her gentle expression spoke affirmation.

"Mohe is not the only one." He pressed her hand.

"He had become a dear friend." She reached for his cheek with her free hand. "But you will manage."

"Yes, yes." He waved her off with his other hand. "But that is not of what I speak."

"Then who?" A thin eyebrow rose.

Truly there was none more becoming than his Yona.

"Adsila." He spoke in a hushed tone as if he shared a great secret. Indeed, he did.

"Adsila? What concern could she possibly have for Thomas Greyson?"

"They have developed a... friendship." He chose his words carefully.

"Are you certain that is all?" Her words were sharper than he had expected.

He thought for a moment, his mind flashing to conversations with Thomas and the looks passed between the missionary and Adsila. "I am not certain of anything."

"It would be best if that *was* all." The singsong quality of her voice had all but vanished.

She spoke truth. It would be better if nothing further developed. Adsila and Thomas were from two very different worlds. Two worlds that were quite at odds now.

But he could not deny the heat he had witnessed.

"Come," his wife said as she stood. "Let us retire and sleep while we can."

He could find no argument. And so, he allowed her to pull him to his feet and lead him to their bedroom.

The train chugged into the station and screeched to a stop. Thomas's body jerked, people all around him rose, but Phillip continued to look over his paper. Would they wait for the aisles to clear before gathering their things?

Thomas stretched out his arms and legs, releasing tension from his muscles. His limbs warmed as blood flow increased. Turning his attention out the window, he looked for his family. Who would have come to the station for him?

The crowd thinned, and Phillip put his paper away.

Thomas grabbed for his bag, and they got to their feet. His legs seemed almost spring-loaded, wanting to go faster than he was able. He stilled his shaking hands, running one across his chest as if that could calm his racing heart. Was his whole body filled with nervous energy? It had been so long since he had been home.

He followed Phillip through the dusty train car and down the stairs. His nerves eased once he set foot on solid ground. They continued on, moving about the platform. All manner of reunions carried on around them.

"Thomas!" His name was shouted from off to the right. He turned to see his mother rushing toward him.

She fell into him, pulling him into a fierce embrace.

"Mother, I'm here. I'm fine." He squeezed her close then released her.

"I know, I know," she said, handkerchief in hand, already dabbing her eyes, dotted with tears. "It's just that I've missed you so!"

She pulled him to her for another hug.

A hand clapped his back.

He flinched under the weight of Father's greeting.

"Glad you're home, son. We've been praying for you." Father's voice was firm, but had an almost imperceptible shake to it.

"Thank you." Thomas turned from his mother's arms to face his father. "It's good to be home."

A number of well-wishers pressed in.

Emma, his sister, was the next to catch his attention.

"And who is this little one?" He reached out a finger for the baby in her arms.

"This is our little Joseph," she said, beaming.

"How are you, Joseph? Is Mommy getting any sleep?"

A tiny hand captured his finger.

"Some." She smiled at her younger brother before throwing her free arm around his shoulders and drawing him near. "It *is* good to have you home. You've been missed."

He hugged her back and whispered, "We must talk soon." He could always talk to her. About anything. And he did have quite a few things to share.

Pulling away, he spoke to everyone, "I have so much to tell, so much to share of my adventures."

"And share you shall, dear," his mother said, stepping toward him again and hooking an arm in his. "Once we get home and get you settled."

He couldn't deny that her plan sounded like a good one.

"Come, you are all invited to dine with us. Our Thomas has completed his mission to the Cherokee Indians and is home to stay."

"Completed?" Thomas tucked a hand inside his jacket.

Mother continued as if she hadn't heard. "Now, come along, Thomas. Let's not linger."

With that, the entourage led Thomas to the waiting carriages.

Walter Buckner could not help the skip in his step as he took the steps up to the Capitol building two at a time. Even if someone pinched him, he would hold firmly to the dream as reality.

For when the Supreme Court met yesterday, they had finally made a decision on the Indian issue. How would the decision be looked upon throughout the years to come? For certain, it would be seen as justice come forth. What would it mean for him? For his descendants? How could he know? But what it meant for the Indians today was life altering.

Moving down the familiar hallways, he approached Senator Frelinghuysen's section of the massive structure. And, without pause, Walter went straight to the senator's private office. His feet did a sort of jig as he knocked on the door. Would he be able to contain himself? No matter the implications of this decision, he must not present himself in an unprofessional manner.

"Come in." Frelinghuysen's confident voice filled the space. Was it quieted at all by the barrier the door presented?

Walter shrugged and entered the smaller space.

The senator looked up from the papers on his desk and offered Walter a small smile. Or rather what he interpreted as a smile. There was a slight upturn to one corner of the man's mouth and a tilt, though almost imperceptible, of the eyebrow on the same side of his face. Was he amused?

"Good morning, Mr. Buckner." He motioned toward one of the seats across his desk.

Walter sat but soon shifted, playing with his hands. Could he not be still? It seemed as if some manner of tiny bug crawled about through his limbs. They did not itch. No. Rather, they teemed with energy.

Frelinghuysen just stared. The smile, or rather semblance of a smile, had vanished. In its place was an expression that betrayed his barely contained annoyance. Had something vexed the man? Had Walter intruded?

"Did you need something?"

"It's just that I was… um… see, I heard that…" This was not going well. He drew in a breath. "I was terribly excited, overcome to tell the truth, about the Supreme Court's decision yesterday."

"Oh?" Frelinghuysen's brows furrowed, and there was a slight lilt in his voice. "*Worcester v. Georgia?*" Did he speak in question?

"Yes! Imagine what it will mean for the Indians!" Walter leaned forward. Surely that would spark something in the senator.

The man's silence prompted Walter to lean farther. So much so, he almost lost his balance and his seat.

Frelinghuysen either did not notice or pretended not to. "It's difficult to say."

"Difficult to say?" Walter shot straight up, his back as stiff as a rod. "Why wouldn't it mean good things? After all, Judge Marshall even stated that the Indian Nations are to be treated like, well, nations. That they should be dealt with as nations deal with other nations. Doesn't that mean the states no longer have power over Indian territory?"

"I suppose that is true." Frelinghuysen words lingered.

"And won't the president's hands be tied? He'll *have* to make treaties with the tribes just as the Indian Removal Act says." He made abstract gestures with his hands as if to emphasize his points.

Frelinghuysen met Walter's eyes. There was nothing fatherly or kind in the man's gaze now. "Have you not learned, yet?" The senator leaned over his desk, lowering his voice.

What did he say? Walter moved forward once more. Did he imagine it, or was there something darker in the man's voice?

"The president's hands are never tied." The senator's voice, edged with seriousness and heavy with warning, caught Walter.

A moment later, he sucked in a breath. Had he forgotten to breathe? The situation couldn't be as the senator said. It couldn't be. "But… we have a system of checks and balances…"

There was no change in Frelinghuysen's expression. His brows lay low and his eyes pierced Walter's outer defenses. What could he see?

At last, he spoke. "The Supreme Court, young sir, doesn't have an army."

Thomas leaned back in his father's leather chair. The material was smooth, but he did not favor the texture. Yet he had been drawn to this high-backed chair almost every day since his return. Why? While the library continued to invite him in, there were other places to sit, others covered with thick cloths. Why then would he choose to persist with the treated animal skin?

He did not consider himself so offended by the use of animals. Though perhaps it did feed his aversion to the chair. Had not God put creatures great and small on the earth for man's use? But not man's abuse. Man could be wasteful. Then again, the Cherokee used the whole animal. They had a purpose for every part. And they showed respect even as they took from the creature.

Maybe…

Was that it?

Did the leather remind him of the Cherokee?

Of Adsila?

Her face appeared in his mind—her features soft, wistful.

What was he doing?

He must not allow himself to daydream in this direction. Nothing existed between them. Nor would there be.

No?

"Thomas!"

Who called for him?

"Thomas?" The masculine voice became louder.

Phillip.

No doubt he neared the library. He must have guessed where Thomas would be. There had been a period of no less than three years during which Thomas earned the nickname "Bookie" from his older brother. It had been well deserved.

Glancing around, Thomas noted there were three books open around him and one in his lap. Had he pulled so many to read at once? He hadn't changed.

A shadow fell across the opening in the doorway, and Phillip's head appeared around the large oak frame. "There you are."

"I didn't realize I was hiding." The corners of Thomas's mouth rose. He caught his brother's gaze.

Though Phillip didn't return the smile, there was a sparkle in his eye as he stepped farther into the room. "Hide, you might have tried. Hidden well, not at all, Bookie."

Thomas closed the volume in his lap. It had not provided the answers it promised. He resisted the urge to stretch his arms, instead, indicating a seat nearby.

Phillip shook his head. "I can't stay long. But I felt it was my duty to share some rather good news." He made a slight bend at the waist toward Thomas as if speaking down to a child. Would he ever see Thomas as a grown man?

Thomas brushed his rising frustration aside. It wouldn't serve either of them. "Whatever could have made you rush over here?" Had he news of the court case? Had something been decided about the

Cherokee? Would they be removed soon? Ejected from their homes while he was forced to remain here—?

Phillip spoke, breaking into Thomas's thoughts. "A ruling came down in *Worcester v. Georgia.*"

"Oh?" Thomas's forehead tightened as his brows rose. He gripped the arms of the chair. Rampant emotions were difficult to keep in place. Was his face the mask he hoped?

Phillip watched him, his own features unreadable. What could Phillip gain from Thomas's? "The court ruled that only the national government, not the state governments, have authority in Indian affairs."

Thomas turned his head. The words made sense, but what were the ramifications? Could he return? "What does that mean?"

"In other words, Georgia cannot impose laws in Cherokee territory. The law prohibiting you from living among the Cherokee is void." Phillip made a slash with his arm.

"Then, I can go back to my village?" Thomas stood, no longer concerned with containing his emotions.

Phillip's brows furrowed.

What had he seen?

Thomas dropped his arms to his sides. "That is… good. For the people."

An awkward silence fell between them.

"And the missionaries."

"Yes," Phillip said, measuring out his words. "I suppose it will be good for them."

Thomas met his eyes. "And for me."

"You?"

Tilting his chin down slightly, Thomas set his features. "Of course."

Phillip did not speak. What was he waiting for?

"I intend to go back to my post."

"Why?" Phillip crossed his arms. His features contorted. Was he so concerned? "These people are marked for removal. There is nothing you can do to stop it."

"Maybe. Maybe not. But I can share Jesus with them until that time."

Phillip's gaze held. How could that man's stare be so intense?

"It's what God called me to do."

"Are you certain that is all?" One of Phillip's brows arched.

What did he imply? Did he suspect there was a more base reason Thomas wished to return? Heat crept up Thomas's face. He opened his mouth to chastise his brother, but bit back his response. Was Phillip right? Did he want to return because of his mission to the people or because of a hope for something with Adsila?

He stepped back and looked down, testing that thought. Had she given him any reason to think there was potential? Perhaps. But there was no promise. The reality remained that they were quite different. And they had drastically different outlooks. Besides, she did not want a relationship with Jesus. That was the long and short of it.

Thomas met Phillip's stare once more. Only this time, with more confidence. "I must return for the sake of the Gospel. To carry His name and His word to the people who need it."

Phillip nodded. "It's what you truly want, isn't it?"

Thomas's jaw was set as he bobbed his head. He pushed all thoughts of Adsila from his mind.

"Then I support you one hundred percent." The hard edge to Phillip's gaze softened.

"I am grateful." Thomas stepped toward Phillip. "You don't know how much."

"Just don't make me show my support by being in the room when you tell Mother." Phillip landed a hand on his brother's back.

Though his voice was light, Thomas knew all too well how serious he was.

Mother's heart could be rather tender. It had been difficult the first time he left. But God would be with her, give her peace, and comfort her. She had to understand that he had been called. She *would* understand. Wouldn't she?

Frelinghuysen pushed a breath out through his teeth. The final numbers came in. Not even close! Not at all.

Andrew Jackson would retain the Presidency. By a landslide.

As he sank into a nearby chair, Frelinghuysen put his head in his hands.

What was he going to do?

The American people had spoken.

They supported Jackson and his policies.

How could they not care that he thumbed his nose at the law and did whatever he darn well pleased? In fact, it seemed the people *wanted* a president that behaved in such a way.

The people couldn't be so blind, so ignorant to the goings on of Jackson and his administration.

They *had* to care.

But Charlotte was right... Frelinghuysen couldn't make them. Perhaps a majority of Americans were nothing more than sheep. They would even follow a wolf to his lair for the slaughter.

As long as he spoke the right words.

Where were the Christians? The people who were supposed to speak out? To use their votes to oppose all manner of deceitfulness and treachery?

Or was he truly alone in this?

The morning had come—crisp and new. But for Adsila, it didn't seem as bright and sunny. She took the quicker route to the schoolhouse. The one that did not take her by the creek. It was no use. Not even the sight of the teeming water could improve her mood today. Nothing, it seemed, would turn out well.

Father intimated this morning that a faction was forming within the Cherokee nation. And this group wanted to sign a treaty with the U.S. Government. Trade their land for whatever pieces of silver they could get. Started by a man named Ridge, the growing faction had taken on the name 'Treaty Party.'

Adsila's whole being ached. A growing weight in the bottom of her stomach made her nauseated. Would her people not stay and fight? What would become of them? After centuries of surviving, independent and proud, would they succumb to the jingle of a few coins?

As she approached the schoolhouse, she straightened her back and squared her shoulders. Nothing good would come from her melancholy in front of the students. They needn't know. If they didn't already.

Stepping into the one-room building, she set her things down and prepared the classroom and herself for the arrival of the students.

It wouldn't be long; she would have only a few minutes to herself. Her mind escaped to the same thing it always did when she had a quiet moment— Thomas.

Where was he? What was he doing? She had been relieved to hear of his pardon, but it saddened her that he would not be able to return.

When had it happened? These feelings for him?

She did not know, but she could not deny the ache in her chest when she thought of him. And now she would probably never see him again. Still, she wished him well. She truly did. He should be happy where ever he was.

Adsila pulled herself from her musings. Her students would be here soon. Shifting papers on the desk, she could not help but let her hand linger on the worn wood. Thomas's hands rested here once.

She closed her eyes and let her memory trace the lines of his face.

The door creaked.

Her eyes opened.

The first of her students nodded in her direction and made their way to their desks.

And so, it begins...

She stood as the children found their seats. Over the next several minutes, the classroom filled as Adsila forced herself to focus. Once all were accounted for, she secured the door, and they went through the morning routine before she launched into her first lesson.

When Adsila first realized that she had landed this teaching job as a permanent placement, she became determined that she would teach the children things that would be practical. Many of them would be farmers. Some would keep sheep. So, their lesson today would be on sheep and other livestock.

"What do we know about sheep?" She watched the children from the front of the class.

"They smell funny," one student said, contorting her face.

"We use them for clothing," another shouted out.

"We are like sheep," an older student tried.

"What?" Adsila wrinkled her nose.

"Mr. Greyson says that we are like sheep," the student attempted to explain.

Now, Adsila was quite confused. "I don't understand."

"Mr. Greyson told us that we are like lost sheep. And that Jesus is like a shepherd who will leave the whole flock to find one lost sheep."

"Leave a whole flock to find one lost sheep? That doesn't make much sense." What was this nonsense? Surely the student misheard Thomas.

Another of the more advanced students spoke up. "That's what we said. He told us that this is how much Jesus cares about those who don't know Him."

Adsila stared; she didn't know how to respond.

No so for the students. The first student continued.

"He used another example." The student came to the front of the class and stood beside Adsila. Holding up one hand the student said. "This hand is me."

She laid the hand flat, palm up, and placed a small book of poems on top of her hand. "And this book is my life. Written on the pages is everything I have done and said, good or bad. My other hand" —she held up her other hand— "represents God." She tried to put her hands together, but the book was in the way.

"God cannot commune with me because my sinful deeds are in the way. God cannot commune with sin. Now this hand is Jesus" —she grabbed one of Adsila's hands— "All we, like sheep, have gone astray, every one to his own way. But God has laid on Him"— she transferred the book onto Adsila's 'Jesus' hand— "the iniquity of our sin."

She put the book down. "Now we are free to commune with God." She put her hands together and even interlinked her fingers.

"I see," Adsila said. "Thank you." Her thoughts raced. Why would Jesus leave heaven to come find her, a 'lost' soul? If what her students had just told her was true, it was because He loved her deeply. Had He come and died so that she could be in communion with God? So that her sin could be paid for? If so, she truly did need Jesus. She needed salvation.

Atohi stepped through the door and into his home. Why had Yona summoned him? Not that he was ungrateful. He relished the break from his work in the field.

As he entered, he sought out his wife. What had happened? Was she well? Had Mohe gotten in trouble at school? Was the young one all right?

As his eyes adjusted to the dimmer recesses of the cabin, he saw the reason for her interruption of his work, and his thoughts calmed.

Yona and Inola fawned over the infant in the nearby great room.

Gawonii was at the dining table, sipping coffee. Another steaming cup sat to his right.

Atohi smiled and took his seat, dragging the warm beverage closer.

"To what do we owe this visit?" Atohi's words were out only moments before the cup's rim met his lips.

"You will have a good dinner tonight." Gawonii's eyes gleamed as he smiled and looked toward his wife.

"Ah," Atohi said, already salivating. Inola's cooking had long since been heralded as the best in the village. What had she prepared for them? Not that it mattered. Anything she made would be delicious.

"You seem tired, my friend." Gawonii clapped him on the shoulder.

Atohi nodded. "I sleep too light. And I wake every time Yona rises to feed."

Gawonii looked down and his shoulders shook. Contained laughter?

No offense meant, none taken. Such was the way with friends. Gawonii perhaps remembered his own days with young children.

His eyes lifted as he took another sip. "Have you read a paper in the last week?"

"No, I am out of touch with the happenings of the world. What goes with the Cherokee nation?" Atohi met Gawonii's gaze. Had something of importance occurred? Gawonii wouldn't have spoken of it unless there was news.

"There has been a split of the Cherokee nation."

Atohi swallowed his sip of coffee with difficulty. "A split?"

"No one has told you? There has been formed the Treaty Party and the National Party."

Atohi stared at his cup. How could he look at Gawonii and not show his concern?

Gawonii leaned forward. "The portion of the Cherokee who wish to make a treaty with the U.S. government formed the Treaty Party."

Atohi looked to Gawonii and narrowed his eyes. "I had heard of this group. Before."

"Chief Ross canceled the national tribal elections this year because of all the dissension."

Atohi's eyebrows shot up. What a big move for the Principal Chief to make. Daring even. The man who sat over all the tribes and their chiefs had made a risky decision. Would it prove a good one?

"Wise. I think. Much has happened. Too much is at stake."

Atohi nodded. His fingers ached. He loosened them. Had he been gripping the cup so tightly?

"The national council threatened to impeach the Ridges. But..."

"What?" Atohi's widened his eyes.

Gawonii glanced at the women.

They were engaged in what appeared to be light-hearted conversation.

The older man leaned even closer to Atohi, so he did the same.

"Murder." Gawonii's voice deepened as he whispered.

Atohi's vision blurred. "Murder? Not Chief Ross..."

"No." Gawonii shook his head, looking back toward the women.

Had Atohi's remark disturbed them?

Yona and Inola continued to chatter on.

Gawonii scooted his chair closer. "A prominent member of the Treaty Party — John Walker."

Atohi could not have pulled his gaze away from Gawonii's if he had tried, the man's eyes were so intense. "Did they discover who—?"

"Not yet. But now the Ridges have formed their own council and insist on having their own elections. A man, William Hicks, now leads the pro-treaty council."

Atohi's head swam, but he would not let his features show it. He pressed his mouth into a straight line and lowered his brows. "This is not the time for such nonsense. It is enough we have to fight against the white man. What chance do we have if we don't stand together?"

Gawonii eyes were solemn. "I do not see the way forward. But I believe it will become much worse before we see good. If there is to be better at all."

Thomas stepped into the parlor. He heard the light breathing of his mother within the darkened room. Only the early light of dawn lit the room. All was quiet and solemn. If he didn't know better, he would have thought she was sitting up with the dead.

The door creaked as he closed it, and her head jerked in his direction.

Seeing it was him, she lowered her head once more.

"Mother?" he said, his voice barely above a whisper.

There was no answer.

"Mother, talk to me," he said, a bit more insistent.

A whimper came from her direction, and her shoulders shook.

Crossing the room, he knelt in front of her and gazed up into her downcast eyes.

"Mother, don't be sad." He took her hands in his.

"How can I not be sad?" Her voice broke as she spoke.

"How can you ask me not to follow God's will for my life?" He widened his eyes and frowned. Was Mother not as committed to God's mission as he thought?

"How can God take you so far away from me? And put you in harm's way?" She reached a trembling hand toward him.

"Did you, yourself, not teach me that God is not always safe, but He is always good?"

She bit at her lip, tears flowing down her face.

"Mother, you know I have to go." Could he go and leave his mother like this? Dare he not? He must follow God's direction. And Adsila…

She nodded.

"I don't want us to part like this."

She looked away, pulling her hand back to put it to her own face.

"Please, don't make me leave you like this."

She sniffed a couple of times and wiped away the tears. Then she faced him with a brave smile.

"I am so proud of you, Thomas."

"I know." He leaned forward and slid his arms around her.

Her body shook again. "I'm sorry. I am trying to contain myself. I am."

"It's okay. Your tears don't upset me. As long as I know I have your blessing," he said into her shoulder. His heartbeat thundered, but his trust was firm in God. All would be well.

She pulled back and took his face in her hands. Her gaze caught and held his for several seconds, and then she pressed a firm kiss on his forehead. "You have it, my darling boy. You have it. Go with God!"

Walter Buckner crumpled the fine stationary in one hand as he set his head in the other. Tightness filled his chest and pressed up into his throat and, with it, heat. He shut his eyes. Perhaps it would keep him from finding a target for his anger.

Anger.

An emotion he thought he could control better.

And why had it taken him by storm now?

Not because of disbelief. Should he be surprised by such tidings? He wasn't.

This almost living being pushing to get out, stirred by the words written upon delicate paper, found its reasoning in an offended sensibility. Or perhaps an offended pride.

The letter came from Harry.

His *friend* saw the need to let Walter in on something that everyone else had been talking about.

President Jackson had written to one of his representatives, John Coffee. How the president's private correspondence had become known by others in the Capitol, Walter did not know. Why it was now knowledge of his own, he did not care. Would that he did not know at all.

Still, he found himself unfolding the cream-colored paper and reading the recitation of the president's words: '...the decision of the Supreme Court has fell stillborn, and they find that they cannot coerce Georgia to yield to its mandate.'

Walter's hands shook.

So, Jackson thought the Court's opinion was just that—their opinion. And, since they had no power to enforce it, what did it matter?

Senator Frelinghuysen had been right, President Jackson did not intend to enforce or even respect the Supreme Court's decision.

Had this letter been made public weeks ago, would it have affected the election?

Walter's stomach turned, and he tasted bile. There was little doubt in his mind that the American people would not have cared.

This couldn't be happening.

Not in the United States of America.

How would history remember this moment?

Remember Andrew Jackson?

The children ran out of the schoolhouse. Recess — another part of the day Adsila both looked forward to and dreaded. Left alone with her thoughts again, they often drifted to Thomas. Could she not control them? No matter how determined this would not be the case anymore, a random object in the classroom had her stuck in a daydream once more.

Not today. She had to learn more about this Jesus. Running a finger along the volumes on the small shelf, she picked up a Bible Thomas had left behind.

But where should she begin? Was this a book you started at the front? Or from anywhere you chose?

Perhaps she best open it at the beginning. And go from there.

The first of the Bible read easily enough. God created everything. But where was Jesus? The first man's name was Adam, not Jesus. Surely Jesus would come soon. Instead a serpent came and led the man and woman astray, the purity of the garden was destroyed.

Adsila's stomach growled. Perhaps she should eat her meal before recess ended.

She grumbled and put the Bible aside.

Checking her braid, she pushed all thoughts of the Bible away for later and moved toward the door.

The voices outside became louder. Much more so than they should have been.

Was there some sort of commotion?

Rushing to the window, she peered out.

The students were in a huddle.

A fight?

Grabbing up her skirts, she rushed into the schoolyard.

Pushing through the students, she worked her way to the center of the crowd.

"Stop! Stop that now!" she called as she pulled students off of students.

She was almost to the center. When she discovered the culprits, they would learn the consequences of breaking her rules.

Suddenly, a man, not a schoolboy, stood from his crouched position.

Thomas Greyson.

Her heart stopped beating for a full five seconds. Then it was as if it would burst from her chest.

"Thomas!" She rushed to embrace him, throwing her arms around him.

He caught her, sliding his arms around her after a few seconds.

She breathed in the scent of him. Relished the feel of him. Wait. Where were they? Had she just thrown herself at him? This is not what they were to each other. And in the schoolyard? In front of the children?

Peering sideways at her students, she loosened her grip.

The children stared.

She released her hold on him and stepped back. Her face burned.

"Mr. Greyson," she said, smoothing her skirt. "I am… glad to see you."

Some of the children giggled.

Thomas shot them a harsh look. Then his eyes were on Adsila. "And I you."

She glanced away. When had his eyes become so intense? "The children have missed you so much."

"They've been in good hands." He smiled broadly.

Her face warmed all the more.

A couple of the children whispered to each other.

"As you know, *Mr.* Greyson," she said loudly, as she glared at the group of students. "Recess is over."

The children groaned.

"But we would love if you would join us for the rest of today's lessons." She smiled.

Whispers of 'oh, please' were heard as the students clamored closer.

"I would like that very much," Thomas said, gazing at his students.

The children cheered.

Gawonii took his place in the sacred semi-circle. This council had been meeting for many, many years now. The faces of his counterparts were familiar, as were their families. Even their struggles through the years had been known to him. They were every bit his people as if he were chief.

They talked amongst themselves as they waited for Chief Unaduti to call them to order.

But Gawonii did not participate in any of the many conversations. His gaze moved about the semi-circle, and he wondered after the future of these men. Would this council remain? Would their sons take up these seats? Would Tsiyi discuss the issues of his people as Gawonii did? Or would this, too, be stripped from them?

"Friends." Chief Unaduti spoke loudly, though his voice alone would have been enough to draw their attention. "I have summoned you for many reasons. Some of which you are already aware. You have read the *Cherokee Phoenix,* as have I. The seven Seminole chiefs sent to scout the land out west have returned. They say they were forced to sign a statement that the new land is acceptable. But it is not good land which they offer for the fertile land they wish to claim."

There were grunts around the group, but none dared speak. Chief Unaduti had not finished.

"Fighting between the white man and the Seminole has become so terrible that some of the Seminoles in the Apalachicola River have been persuaded to go west. This is the government's doing."

Now the voices renounced the government as many were no longer able to contain their ire.

"White devils!"

"They are devious!"

"They will get what they want."

"But they will pay!"

"We must make them pay."

"The Seminole warriors will not stand by."

"There will be war!"

Gawonii continued to sit and watch his fellow councilmembers, his brothers. He understood their thoughts, their anger. But he could not own it.

Chief Unaduti held up his hands.

All voices halted.

"We cannot control the government or the Seminoles. We can only decide what our course will be."

"We must refuse a treaty at all costs!"

"Never shall we give in!"

"This is our land, our fathers' lands. We will not give up!"

"They will never take my land."

"Send men to the National Council. They must know what we think!"

"Yes, Chief Ross must make the right decision for our people!"

"I have faith in Chief Ross."

"I have word." Chief Unaduti spoke again. As his voice rose, all others ceased.

"Chief Ross has sent word. It is his desire that we stand our ground."

The air was thick. Gawonii sensed many emotions in the silence. Were they those of his brethren? Or his?

"But there is a growing faction within the Cherokee that would have us sign a treaty."

Now the men spoke out again.

"Traitors!"

"Let us hunt them down!"

"They do not speak for the people!"

"No, the National Council speaks for us."

"This is no way to settle anything!" The chief spoke in a boisterous voice. "We must stand together or we will fall. Who here will stand with us and hold firm to our lands?"

Every hand went up. A few slower than others.

But Gawonii's hand shot up. There was renewed confidence in him. But the rushing beat of his heart seemed curious. Invigorated? Or maybe... just maybe... could he be afraid?

The chief nodded. "Then it is settled."

Thomas stayed at the schoolhouse until the last student packed up. Trusting Adsila with his class had been the right thing. His faith had not been misplaced. As she gathered the remaining things from around the classroom, he couldn't help but watch. Even in the short time he had observed, he saw what a gifted teacher she was.

How was it that so much about her manner could have changed in the short time he'd known her? From the fire and passion at their first meeting which, unfortunately, had been directed at him in anger. And that anger had lingered between them for quite some time. But something had softened. There were moments he was certain. As when she embraced him before...the memory warmed him to his core. What *had* changed between them? He was unsure.

Thank God for the turn. He now saw a different side to her. She wasn't all flare and fire; she was caring, compassionate, and patient. A woman who loved her people and cared about their well-being. Had that been the source of her passionate anger all along? It certainly laid a foundation for her passionate teaching.

She gave everything she could to the children.

That much was obvious.

He hadn't been able to do anything but stare as she gave final assessments and assignments to the students as they left minutes ago.

She was beautiful. Any warm-blooded man could see that.

But there was something more to her beauty. Something that went beyond what the eye could see. A grace, a peace, a... what? He couldn't name it. Not yet, anyway. But their earlier embrace haunted him. Why had she done that?

The last student walked out the door, and Adsila turned to face him.

Her eyes settled on his. Calm. Serene.

Had she noticed him staring?

"I believe, Mr. Greyson, that the class is yours again."

He straightened and nodded. "I am sorry to have to take it back. They will miss you."

Her lips curved upward. "Don't be. My plants and herbs have gotten the worst of me. They need serious tending." She turned her head to the side in an exaggerated way. "Besides, I grow tired of these children. So many questions."

"Ah." He chuckled. "If that is the case, I will be all too happy to take them back."

"Very well." She bobbed her head once then looked toward the door. "Shall we?"

Must their time together come to an end? How could he resist it? Prolong their interaction? Ask her why she threw herself into his arms?

But he found no reason to linger in the classroom or the courage to face the question he desperately needed an answer to. "We shall."

He lengthened his step, sliding past her and reaching for the door. With slow movements, he swung it open, but his eyes were on her as she stepped near to pass through the doorway.

What would she do if she were to see him transfixed on her features? How would he explain it?

Pulling his gaze away, he secured the door behind them.

When he turned, she was grinning at him. "I…"

"May I walk you home?" This was a boldness he wasn't sure he understood. Not from himself. For a moment, Worcester's words of warning rang in his head. He pushed them to the side. There was no sin in his actions.

She watched him for a moment.

Could she see his indecision? Or was she caught in her own?

Then she nodded.

He joined her at the bottom of the schoolhouse stairs and, when she turned toward the meadow, matched his steps to hers.

They walked for several minutes in silence until they came to the place where the path separated. Either they would walk by the creek or take the shorter route across the hill.

"By the creek?" Thomas's heart thumped louder than he wished, and he held his breath.

"All right," she said, her voice almost hesitant.

Did she not wish to spend more time with him? Had he misunderstood? Was she just being polite? He couldn't make himself speak as they walked, and sweat trickled between his shoulder blades. Why must this be so difficult?

He glanced at her, but she watched the ground. As if sensing his eyes, she looked at him. And he smiled at her and turned away. How awkward.

In minutes, they were by the creek.

"May we stop for a few moments?" Her tone had become soft.

"Of course." His voice broke, and his face heated.

She turned toward the creek, and he stole another glance at her, watching as she gazed over the bubbling stream.

She closed her eyes.

Was he intruding? Was this some sort of private time with her thoughts?

He closed his eyes. If only he could stop sweating. For certain, his shirt was starting to cling to his back.

But as he stood and let the stillness of the moment wash over him, he became more aware of the small sounds around the creek—the rush of the stream, the birds in the distance, the sound of water gently flowing over rocks, and the rustling of leaves.

"I am ready, Thomas, to accept Jesus."

His eyes shot open. He had been so tuned in to these small sounds, her voice sounded magnified. Had he heard her correctly? "What did you say?"

She turned to face him. "I know I need Jesus."

He enveloped her in his arms. "Adsila, that is wonderful news!"

She didn't respond at first, but eventually reached up to place her hands on his shoulders.

Something stirred in his chest. Something deep. Something powerful. He had to pull away.

It took everything in him to do so.

"This will change everything for you. Eternally. You don't know how excited I am!"

He searched her eyes. The sensations that began in the center of his chest continued to spread. And his body seemed rather heated suddenly. "How… I mean, I know we talked about Jesus, but we never spoke again…"

She smiled. Was she so unaffected by their closeness?

"The children. *Your* students taught me about God. And He… God has been working on my spirit."

His mouth broadened, and he found his focus on God. Praise the Lord, somehow he did.

"Shall we pray together? Right now?"

She was silent for several seconds.

Was he pushing? For his own reasons? Oh, God, what was he doing?

Her sweet voice broke into his thoughts. "Yes. I am ready."

"Are you ready to pray for yourself? If you can, I think it's important the words come from you."

Her brows furrowed. "I have never prayed like this before."

"Prayer is just a conversation with God. The only difference between talking with Him and with me is that you can't see Him."

"Will He talk back?" Her voice shook. Was she so nervous at the thought of an unseen God talking back?

He tried not to laugh. "Sometimes."

"It might scare me if He does," she said, her eyes widening.

"Trust me, it won't. It will fill you with love and peace."

She nodded. Did she trust him so much? It filled him with emotions that confused him. And a pride that probably shouldn't be his.

He drew in a breath and let it out. He could do this. He could. "All right, let us open the prayer to God, the Father. And we are in confession, which basically means we agree with God about our sin, and that we need forgiveness." He tilted his head forward and closed his eyes.

She started speaking, her words slow and almost cautious. "God the Father, I agree with You that there are things in my life that are not good. In fact, they are bad. They are sinful. I am sorry for these things, and I need Your forgiveness."

"We receive forgiveness through Christ's blood shed on the cross, remember?" He kept his words soft.

She nodded even though her eyes were closed.

Still, he couldn't help but admire her features as she prayed. *Father, help me.*

"God, I accept Christ's blood for my sins. I believe He died on the cross for my sins."

He focused with all he had on God and how important this prayer was. "The Bible tells us in Romans that if we confess the Lord our God and believe in our hearts that God raised Jesus from the dead, we shall be saved." And he forced his eyes to remain closed. *God, keep me.*

"God, I confess Jesus as Lord. And I believe You raised Jesus from the dead for my salvation. I accept Jesus as Savior. I thank you for saving me. I thank you for forgiveness. I thank you for grace. I thank you for Jesus."

When he opened his eyes, she still had her eyes closed. They soon opened. She looked up at him and smiled, tears glistening.

He reached out to brush them away and was overcome with the urge to brush his lips against hers.

Not now. Not yet. Not in such a spiritually charged moment.

Had he not been warned that a single man should not pray alone with a single woman?

"Praise God," he said softly. Perhaps it was only because his heart was so full of praise. Or perhaps it was to pull his mind off her lips.

Her eyes danced in the ever-waning sunlight.

Waning sunlight? The sun had started to go down. Surely her parents would begin to worry after her.

"It's getting late. We best get you home." He drew his hands back.

She nodded.

They walked toward her home and spoke a little of spiritual things along the way.

She did not bombard him with questions, for which he was thankful. Concentrating around her proved problematic.

As they neared her home, she slowed and turned to face him once more. "This is where we should part."

He nodded. Why couldn't he walk her all the way home? But he respected her enough to say farewell as she wished. As she shifted to face him, his heartbeat thudded in his chest.

Loud.

Too loud.

She had come to mean so much to him. Did she feel the same?

She moved closer, taking one of his hands in hers.

Now his pulse thundered in his ears—a call to boldness. He pulled her hand to close the distance between them.

The warmth in his core turned molten.

Drawing her face to his, he planted a gentle kiss on her lips.

She responded to him immediately, pulling him deeper into their embrace.

Still, he dare not let the kiss continue for long. He had not lost his senses completely. No, it was best not to linger in that dangerous position.

Yes, a few moments longer and he would be lost to her.

SEMINOLE WAR

Walter Buckner sat on a bench outside the Capitol, he took another bite of the sandwich that had long since lost all flavor. But he didn't mind. His attention had been on the notes splayed out to his side, causing him to turn that way, his body angled somewhat awkwardly.

Frelinghuysen's proposed bill.

He took in a breath and let it out. It had become difficult to focus on the words. Who cared about financial bills when this issue with the Indians was still so fresh?

Yes, of course Frelinghuysen cared. What was it then? Had he been cornered? So politically cut off that no other options remained than for him to move on? No doubt he would leap at any opportunity to assist in the Indian crisis… but nothing had been forthcoming.

So, Walter, like Frelinghuysen, must remember that the people still depended on him. He forced his mind back to the notes.

A shadow darkened the papers.

Who?

Walter turned toward the intrusion.

Henry Corbell. A smile spread across the entirety of his face. "Walter! Taking lunch outside?"

"Yes, I have to get out of the office every now and again." Sweeping the papers up, he shoved them into his bag.

He started to rise, but Harry plopped into the now empty space on the bench.

Walter could still go. He should, in fact. But he didn't wish to be rude.

"How are things with old Frelinghuysen?"

Walter nodded, looking forward, keeping his gaze on a spot in the distance. "Fair to good."

Though he couldn't see Harry's face, he swore the man's smirk was audible. "Truly?"

"Yes." Walter faced him.

"At least he's given up on his grumbling after the Indian removals." Harry leaned back and watched Walter.

Was he playing Walter? Trying to trick him into revealing something? Walter turned toward the Capitol Building, away from Harry, and took another bite.

The silence between them was too short. Shuffling sounds indicated that Harry shifted. Walter sensed that his friend had leaned forward.

"You know the Cherokee are next."

Walter could not help himself. He spun a little too quickly, and Harry jerked back at the sudden movement.

But Walter had not the presence of mind to enjoy the momentary lapse. He had to know of what Harry spoke. "What do you mean?"

"President Jackson appointed Reverend John Schermerhorn as treaty commissioner to deal with the Cherokee problem. You must have heard that he's been authorized to offer $4.5 million for the Cherokee to remove themselves."

A cavern opened in Walter's chest. $4.5 million seemed like so much money. But for the land they would be vacating… it was a farce. They wouldn't accept it. Not willingly.

"That's pitiful compensation for that land, and you know it."

"I hear talk that some of them are agreeable to leave."

Could it be true? Had the Indians decided to give up and go? Had they lost all fight? Or did they believe they were on their own? With no hope? No help? But Senator Frelinghuysen had done what he could. And all of it came to naught.

Harry shrugged and leaned farther forward, his elbows on his knees and his eyes forward. "What choice do they have? They either agree to the terms, or President Jackson will *strongly* encourage them to agree."

Walter's gaze leveled on Harry. He ached to speak, to contradict Harry's pronouncement of the Cherokee's doom, but there were no words. Harry was right. Once Jackson set his sights on removing them, they would be next.

"Charlotte!" Frelinghuysen rushed down the stairs. Where had the time gone? How could he have let himself lose all thought of the hour, pouring over maps. "Charlotte!"

He reached the landing and turned. Where was she? Had she gone out on an errand? It couldn't be. Tonight was too important.

Charlotte stepped from the dining hall, rubbing her hands in a cloth. Had she been tending to the work herself? "The table is set, darling."

Frelinghuysen allowed himself a deep breath. "Good." He moved toward the parlor. Yes, the maids had prepared everything according to his instructions. Casting a long glance at the front door, he fidgeted with his necktie and pulled at the hem of his jacket.

These were not the typical dinner guests they expected. No, they were far more important. Their visit had not been long foretold, but it had been greatly anticipated.

For tonight, the chief of the Cherokee Nation, John Ross and another Cherokee representative, John Ridge, would visit Frelinghuysen's home. His fingers trembled slightly as he pushed them through his hair, smoothing back the thick waves. What would come of their time in Washington, D.C.?

As Frelinghuysen understood, this man, John Ridge, did not quite see eye-to-eye with Chief Ross. In fact, the man led a sort of dissension, a group in favor of making a treaty with the U.S. Government.

A split in the Cherokee Nation. How had tensions within affected their ability to mediate and negotiate beyond their borders? With the U.S. Government?

They had rejected the first treaty attempt at Red Clay. How had that impacted the rift between the so-called Treaty Party and the rest of the Cherokee Nation? It certainly hadn't resolved the split.

Was the internal outcome of that treaty failure the reason Chief Ross had brought John Ridge? Some attempt to bridge the gap between the two groups?

The purpose of their travels to Washington, D.C. was to open new negotiations. They had already met with President Jackson earlier that day, and Frelinghuysen could hardly contain his eagerness to learn the details of that interchange.

Just then, the doorbell chimed. Moving to the entry, there was a rustling of clothing behind him.

He turned.

Charlotte came alongside him.

A smile pulled at his lips. It warmed him to have her by his side. He grasped her hand briefly.

The butler stepped in front of them and opened the door.

Two haggard men, both with gruff expressions filed into the house.

As the first man entered, Frelinghuysen attempted to decipher who was who. This man was shorter, had a smaller face with a rounded nose and kind eyes. Was this the chief? Ross's father had been of Scottish descent. So this man did seem the more likely of the two to be the chief.

John Ridge, however, tall with angled features, had all the markings of a full-blooded Cherokee. And he was younger than Frelinghuysen had expected. He couldn't be more than thirty.

"Come in, Chief Ross, Mr. Ridge. You are most welcome in my home." Frelinghuysen extended his hand.

Chief Ross shook it. "Senator, please, call me John." Then he glanced at the man nearby. "Perhaps 'chief' will lend itself to less confusion."

Frelinghuysen smiled. "Chief." The man was warm and open. But he seemed displeased. His countenance dropped, except when he conversed directly with Frelinghuysen.

John Ridge stepped forward and offered his hand as well. "John Ridge. 'John.'"

Frelinghuysen shook his hand with equal fervency. But the man hesitated. Why? He was pleasant enough in his address, but there was an abruptness to his character.

"Please, call me Theodore. And this is my lovely bride, Charlotte."

"It is good to meet you." She put forth her own hand to exchange greetings.

The footman and butler helped the two men out of their overcoats.

"Let us adjourn to the parlor." Frelinghuysen offered his arm to Charlotte and turned toward the far hall. They would have more privacy there. Not as many ears listening.

Once they were all seated and had assured the maid they were no longer in need of anything, Frelinghuysen could hold his tongue no longer. But he forced himself to pace his words.

"How was your meeting with President Jackson?"

The men exchanged a look.

Ross's gaze turned back toward Frelinghuysen, his eyes darkened and his brows furrowed. "Then you do not know."

"Pardon?" Frelinghuysen fought the urge to lean forward.

"The president refused to see us." Ross maintained his posture, but his hands wound into fists. "I thought you would have heard…"

"I'm not privy to all that makes its way around the Capitol," Frelinghuysen grumbled. Perhaps he had been left unaware because of the grudge many carried. Why did so many find him difficult? Because of the strong stand he took on certain matters? Shouldn't they all take a side and stand strong? For the sake of those who relied on them? Who voted for them? But his peers seemed to think he was committing political suicide. Thus they did not wish to be associated with him.

"We were turned away and told to deal with Schermerhorn."

Ridge's words were partly ground out. "Which is what we should have done in the first place."

"Now, John," Ross warned. "This is neither the time nor the place for another of these discussions."

Ridge bowed his head and said nothing further.

Another of these discussions? Had the two men dabbled often in such discourse? What did they argue about?

The room fell silent.

"You alone have opened your home to us." Ross's tone was even.

Frelinghuysen could not disguise his surprise. His features morphed to display his thoughts. Had the president not made accommodations for them?

"I suppose we must find some inn or—" Ridge started.

"Of course not. You will stay here."

Charlotte made a small sound. Was she worried after the preparations not made? The reaction was understandable and, thankfully, nearly imperceptible.

"Senator, that is most gracious. But we cannot impose." The lines on Ross's face softened. "It is not a hardship for us to stay in one of the many hotels—"

"I will not hear of it!" The force of his voice surprised even him. Frelinghuysen took a breath and calmed himself. "You are diplomats from an allied nation. I insist you be treated thusly. Allow me to offer my home as a poor substitute for the fine accommodations you should have received."

Ross smiled, and even Ridge's lips turned upward.

"We thank you for your hospitality." Ross leaned forward. "It will not be forgotten."

Thomas rubbed his arms as he waited for Adsila. He stood at the very spot he had been when he first noticed her playing in the creek. This would be their place. They could meet here, far enough from the prying eyes of their students and the villagers. And, most importantly, in secret from Adsila's parents. Not that he enjoyed being secretive, but he understood the need to be quiet about their relationship. For now.

"Have you waited long?" A gentle voice spoke from behind.

He turned.

Adsila stood only steps away. How did she do that? Come so near without making a sound?

"No." He reached for her, his arms enveloping her.

The warmth of her body melted any lingering cold in his.

"But I would wait forever."

She rose onto her toes and pressed a kiss to his mouth.

After several seconds, he prudently pulled back.

"Adsila," he whispered and pulled her closer, burying his face in her hair. If she would let him, he would hold her like this forever.

It was several moments before he felt her body begin to shake. Leaning back, he examined her features. Tears filled her eyes.

"What is it?" His eyebrows knit together, and his heart ached. Had he done something wrong?

"I worry about my people. And my family." She looked down. To hide the depth of her emotion? Did she still not trust him?

He pulled her to himself again, trying to soothe her with soft words. What had made her so concerned? Why had she become overwhelmed so?

"Please, tell me what's happened." He rubbed a hand across her shoulders.

She turned her face toward his. "There's been a treaty."

"A treaty?" He jerked back.

She stiffened.

This was no time for him to give into his own emotions. He needed to have a care for hers. Moving hands over her arms, he softened his voice. "But I thought the Cherokee had decided to stay and fight."

"That man… Schermerhorn, only invited the pro-removal council members and had twenty-one proponents of Cherokee removal sign the treaty." Her eyes were deep in that moment. And sad.

His forehead creased. "Then it can't be legal." How could it?

"I don't trust the whit—" She stopped herself and leaned into his chest, hiding her face.

He kissed the top of her head. "Say what you mean to say."

She gripped the front of his shirt. "I don't trust *some* white men—the ones sitting in the Capitol, making decisions least of all."

"Even of those men, Adsila," he said, careful with his words. "I guarantee not all support what the majority are doing."

Nothing. No sound. No movement.

Nothing.

Did she doubt him?

"Not all white men, as you very well know, want your people gone or forcibly removed. I have to believe that there are at least one or two good men in Washington that seek your betterment."

"If you say it is so…" Even as she spoke, there was hesitation in her voice. "I will trust you." Her final words seemed only somewhat more resolved. But she leaned into him again. "Even so, the majority is what matters. So, what are we to do when this treaty goes before Congress and they call for our removal?"

What indeed? The prospects were grim. He swallowed hard and stroked her hair. "We will deal with that when it happens."

"What recourse will be left to us but to fight or be removed?"

Neither seemed like good options. What would he do? As he held her, he looked at the horizon.

"You and your family could escape." He looked down as if to look at her.

"Escape?" She jerked back. "Where would we go?"

"We could go to Charlotte. My parents would give us safe haven until we could figure something out."

"That's crazy," she said, making a sound that was between a laugh and a cry.

He rubbed her arms. It seemed clear to him. This was the only way. How could he convince her? "No, it's quite reasonable. But it's not something we have to decide now. Just keep it in your mind." He pushed a stray hair off her face, tucking it behind her ear. "In case we need a plan."

"All right." When she leaned into him again, he enveloped her in his embrace.

"I will always take care of you." Why had he said that? It seemed a big commitment to make. Especially now. Considering...

But as he held her and ran the words over in his mind, he knew he had meant it. He would do whatever he could for her.

Always.

Senator Frelinghuysen chatted with Chief Ross and John Ridge as they neared the Capitol. Another treaty had been drawn up for the two men to review. Frelinghuysen volunteered his office for the potential signing. There was one interesting point: several Cherokee had already signed it. How had this happened? Weren't Ross and Ridge here to do the negotiating?

Frelinghuysen tried to hold back his skepticism, but he could not help the darkening of his mood. Still, something about the whole thing intrigued him. If the Cherokee would be peaceably removed, that may just be for the best.

Removal loomed. It would come. That was inevitable. The choice remained whether they stood and fought or relented and signed a treaty.

And, as much as he hated to side with Ridge in this, Frelinghuysen began to see his side of things. A treaty might be in their best interest. It could well be their only option at this point. Staying and fighting would only bring great loss.

Everyone in Washington, D.C., and in the whole of the United States, had become all the more leery of the Indians since the Dade Massacre. It did not paint them in the best light. The Seminoles had ambushed an army company of 180, leaving only three alive.

Yes, it intimated the army.

Yes, it made them nervous.

No, it did not help matters here in the political scene.

The ride to the Capitol was quicker than usual, as they proceeded with all due haste. Stepping from the carriage, they made their way into the massive structure. Frelinghuysen did not have to scan the area to know that many curious gazes were upon the small group as he led them toward his office. At least some of these glances were simply that—curious. Some, however, were darker, more menacing. Either way, he wasted no time getting the two men to the more secure space.

Frelinghuysen made quick introductions between his staff and the two men. He then requested coffee be brought in as they awaited the arrival of the treaty. At last, he ushered them into his private office where they were freer to converse.

Several moments passed, in which they talked of things of little consequence, before a knock sounded on the door.

Frelinghuysen swallowed. Was this the treaty? Would it bring hope? Or devastation?

"Come." His voice seemed weaker to him. Did the others notice?

Ross and Ridge turned their attention to the door. Perhaps they had not.

Mr. Buckner slid through the narrow opening in the door.

Frelinghuysen straightened in his seat. Best to present all business. "Mr. Buckner, what can I do for you?"

The young man looked at the two Cherokee men but averted his eyes quickly. Was he intimidated? Or, like others in the courtyard— condescending? But when he spoke, his manner was respectful, and he seemed almost hesitant. "Mr. Parsons, one of Reverend Schermerhorn's staff, is here with the treaty."

"Send him in." Frelinghuysen stood.

Ross and Ridge also rose.

A man, lanky and bespectacled, came in with a rolled document. He paid little mind to the inhabitants of the room, granting them little more than a cursory glance as he cut through the room to the desk. Leaning over the flat surface, he unrolled the awaited papers. Again, without so much as a greeting.

"Thank you, Mr. Buckner." Frelinghuysen smiled at the young aide. This man, who had for months now taken a particular interest in the Indian issue, perhaps earned a closer seat. "Feel free to stay."

Buckner made a gallant effort to push down his excitement, but it was written on his face.

Ross and Ridge moved to the desk and looked to the document.

"Five million dollars?" Ross exclaimed. "That doesn't add much to the previous offer."

"See here," Ridge argued, pointing to something in the wording. "They added another half million for educational funds. And we're getting official title to the lands west of the Mississippi River." His eyes bored into his counterpart.

Even Frelinghuysen could sense the intensity of that gaze.

Ross stared at him, mouth agape. "How can you think this a fair agreement?"

"And how can you be willing to sacrifice lives? You want to stay and fight? This is the best we're going to get. Mark my words, after this, it will be forcible removal. Is that what you want?"

"You know it's not." Ross spoke sternly.

"Then what are you after?" Ridge asked, throwing his arms up.

"I want my people, *our* people, to be treated fairly. Just as any nation would be. That's what the Supreme Court says and that is, in fact, what is laid out in the Indian Removal Act. It does not allow for forcible removals."

Ridge leaned toward Ross. "That has not stopped President Jackson from forcing the Creeks west," he whispered harshly. "Think of our people. Think of their lives. We can make a new life. We can *survive*. And we'll have a chance with this money."

Ross was silent.

"And what of these other Cherokee that agreed to these terms?" Ridge slapped a hand against the signed portion of the document. "They represent the will of the people."

Ross looked over the signatures. "No, they don't. These are all from your Pro-Treaty Council. That is not a fair measure of the will of the Cherokee!"

"Listen to me," Ridge pleaded.

"No!" Ross moved a hand to shove the paper away as he moved back from the desk. "I will not sign it."

The room was quiet. One could measure the breaths each man took.

Ridge broke the silence. "Well, if you won't. I will!"

Ross glared at him, eyes hard. "You have no more authority to speak for the Cherokee Nation than the names on that paper!"

Ridge took up a pen and signed his name at the bottom. He looked at Mr. Parsons. "There's my signature for whatever it's worth."

Ross's eyes narrowed. "Traitor! You're all traitors, and you will be dealt with accordingly."

"Perhaps it is *you* who are the traitor. *I* am thinking of our people's best interest."

"But you have no authority. The Cherokee have entrusted me to look out for them, and that is what I intend to do. Excuse me, Senator Frelinghuysen, Mr. Buckner," Ross said, nodding. "But this room has just become a little too stifling."

With that, he took his leave of them.

Frelinghuysen looked after him with a heavy heart. What was right for the Cherokee people? He did not know. But fighting amongst themselves was certainly not it.

Spring was in the air. Life was new. The days were longer and brighter, but not everyone relished the feeling of the bright sun or the colorful blanket of flowers stretched out on the earth. For all was not well. The Council members trudged home to their families with hard news.

Gawonii's steps were slow as they moved up the path to his home.

As he neared his family's cabin, he stopped and looked over his farmland and homestead. This place. This land. How long had his father's fathers kept it? Would not the very concept of owning the earth or any part of it seem strange… foreign even, to those men of another time?

Bending forward, he grabbed a handful of the loose dirt. He held it for a few seconds, letting the warmth of the soil and the grittiness of it fill his senses. Spreading his fingers, he then watched as the deep brown specks escaped.

How fitting.

For that was exactly what was to happen.

Their land, this piece of earth they had known for generations as home… would soon be lost to them.

Must he be the bearer of such tidings? See the downcast faces of his family as they came to realize what it meant? If only he could take an arrow for them. Die as a brave warrior defending his people. But that option had not been presented.

He forced his feet to move again, marking his way toward the cabin. Toward this conversation he would wish away if there were any other way.

Yet he would not run from his responsibility. The chief had spoken, and Gawonii would respect the decision of those chosen to shoulder such a heavy burden.

Stepping inside, he remembered what the small cabin represented —the home they had carefully built and made into a comfortable place for their small family when the tribe had given up living in tents. It was the only home Tsiyi had ever known. What would become of it? Of them?

Inola stood by the stove, busying herself with dinner. She had always been a good wife. Steady as the river's current and sure as the sun each morning.

Adsila sat at the family's table near Tsiyi. Did they talk of school-work? The world as they knew it was whole and perfect as of yet. But he would shatter that.

Looking up from Tsiyi's work, Adsila noticed him first and smiled.

Such innocence. She'd had her suspicions, but they had quieted.

He struggled to force the corners of his mouth upward and, in the end, failed. Then he felt Inola's eyes. Turning toward her, he managed a small smile after great effort.

It did not wipe the concern from her face.

As he walked to the table and placed a hand on Adsila's shoulder, he raised an arm to Inola and curved his hand.

She dropped her spoon and crossed to him. Her eyes glistened. Could she guess what news he brought?

Wrapping an arm around her, he drew her closer. The feel of his wife in his arms gave him great comfort and strength. That he needed greatly.

"Father, what has happened?" Adsila's voice shook.

"Tsiyi, you need to—" Inola spoke, her tone uneven.

"No," Gawonii said. "This time, Tsiyi stays."

Inola fell into her chair, a small whimper escaping.

Gawonii sat beside her, taking her hand in his. Could he give her the same measure of unspoken support she had given him? He searched her eyes.

They were sorrowful.

She knew.

He swallowed hard, keeping his features set. A brave face for his children. Turning toward Adsila and Tsiyi, he spoke. "The Treaty of New Echota has been ratified by Congress."

Inola wailed. Then the tears came.

"I... I don't understand." Adsila appeared as stunned as she sounded. Her eyes were wide and her mouth had fallen agape. "Chief Ross and the National Council told Congress it was a fraud. That it did not represent the will of the Cherokee people."

Gawonii shrugged. How could he speak truth and show respect? Did he owe them any? No longer. They were no longer an authority in his eyes. If they did not concern themselves with the truth, he would not concern himself with how his children viewed them. "They do not care."

"But how..." Adsila's body shook and tears welled. "How can this be?"

She truly was so innocent.

"Because they make the laws," Gawonii said evenly.

"What is the Treaty of New Echota, Father? Why is Mother crying?" Tsiyi appeared frightened. He had not been party to any of the goings on. Had he not even heard mention of it at all?

There would be no sense in softening the reality of it. Not with what Tsiyi would face in the coming days and months. He must be prepared for the harshness of it now. "It means we, the Cherokee, are agreeing to leave our home."

"But I don't want to leave. Where will we go?" Tsiyi's voice broke.

"I know, my son." Gawonii place a hand on his shoulder. "But we have no choice. They say we must go west of the Mississippi. Some Cherokee want to stay and fight."

"Will we fight, Father?" Tsiyi blinked several times. Did he struggle with his tears? Not wish to show them? Trying to be strong even now? "What about Mother? Adsila? Will they fight, too?" His voice broke with the last sentence. Perhaps he did not like the idea of his mother and sister fighting.

Gawonii held his response for several seconds. He did not wish to admit defeat, but he did not want to give them hope where none existed. He didn't want his wife and children to fight, to face the sword of a soldier. But he didn't wish to go west either. Either way, it was best his family have a better idea of what it came down to. "I don't know."

"Those may not be our only choices." Adsila's voice strengthened.

Gawonii and Inola jerked their heads in her direction.

What could she mean?

"What do you speak of?" Gawonii's brows rose. Was there hope?

"Thomas… Mr. Greyson has offered to take the four of us to his parent's home in North Carolina. Just until we figure out what to do." The words rushed out of her. "It would be safe there. No fighting. No one looking for us."

Gawonii looked at his wife for several moments. Was she wondering as he was? Why the offer for just their family? Why not others? Had more occurred between his daughter and the missionary than he knew? He was not blind to their close friendship or even to their budding attraction. But he did not think it had developed beyond that.

Tsiyi opened his mouth.

For certain what he would say would venture into conversation best left alone for now.

"We must take all things into consideration," Gawonii said. "Now, no more talk of this. We must turn our minds to more pleasant things. Like what Mother has made for supper."

Adsila and Tsiyi were obedient despite their obviously troubled hearts. They nodded and cleared the table.

Inola moved back to the stove.

And Gawonii watched them. His heart still heavy for his little family and the decisions they would have to make. But perhaps for at least for one more night, they could just enjoy being together at this table.

Walter Buckner locked the door to the senator's offices. Heaving a sigh, he made his way down the long hall that would take him out of the building. The days passed slowly, but the weeks seemed to go by so quickly. Had it been six years since the Indian Removal Act passed?

He shook his head. That couldn't be right.

But it was. Six long years.

Everyone else had moved on long ago.

Yet he still clung to some shred of hope for the remaining Indian groups—hope that they would be treated fairly, that their removals would not be so tragic.

But then war had broken out with the Seminoles, and there came dissension within the Cherokee tribe. Dissension that President Jackson would certainly take advantage of.

Stepping into the temperate evening air, Walter was nearly blind-sided by a man rushing out of the shadows. Immediately on guard, he stepped one foot back, bracing himself. Then he put up his arms to shield his face.

"What's wrong, Walter?" a familiar voice said. "Oh, sorry. Didn't mean to jump out at you like that."

Walter let his arms fall and found himself looking into the face of Harry Corbell. "Jeez, Harry, cut a guy a break! I thought you were… well, never mind. What do you want?"

"I've only been waiting out here an hour to tell you that Senator Jamison has a space on his staff." Harry beamed. "And I recommended *you*."

Walter gave him a sideways look. "But I already have a job."

"Come on, Walter, you can't be serious! Look at what's happening. It's time to jump ship while you still can."

"I don't know what you mean." Walter started moving down the sidewalk again.

Harry kept step with him. "This obsession with the Indians has got to stop."

Walter tossed him a stern look.

Harry slowed a little. "Okay. Let's say you care. That's great. But it's a lost cause! Even you must see that. The Seminoles will soon be over-powered, the Cherokee are on the move…"

"The Cherokee are what?"

"Well, *some* of the Cherokee are on the move. The rest will be soon."

Walter stopped. He understood then. The faction of the Cherokee nation that supported the treaty had left. The rest would stand their ground.

He hung his head. It would mean more lives lost.

"So?" Harry said, raising his hands, palms up.

"So… what?" Walter looked back toward his friend.

"Do you want the job or not?" Harry dropped his hands to his side, and his voice went flat.

"No," Walter said, distracted.

"Fine." Harry waved him off and started walking again.

"Why do you care so much anyway?" Walter called after him.

Harry turned. "What do you mean?"

"About me. Why do you care so much?"

Harry shrugged. "I think you're a good guy. And I think you're being led down the wrong path. I'm just trying to help."

Walter was silent for a moment. "Thank you. I mean it. I appreciate your consideration. But I have to be able to live with myself, whether I have a political career in five years or not."

"Five years? Try one!" With that, Harry turned and walked off.

Thomas stepped onto the same train station platform he had so many times before. Most recently with his brother. This time was different. So vastly different. For now, he ushered his beloved Adsila and her family to safety.

He had not anticipated how many new experiences there would be for them on the journey. First, there was the novelty of the wagon ride and then the train. Lord of all that is good, the train. It had frightened Tsiyi, but he had been brave. His wide eyes peered about him as his white knuckles clung to his mother's dress. Adsila sat perhaps a little too close to Thomas.

He felt alive and nervous at the same time. And he wanted to draw her even closer. Her parents' constant watch gave him pause. No, he did not wish to risk deepening her parents' curiosity as it was.

A part of him wondered what would be so bad about them knowing. There was nothing impure or inappropriate about anything he and Adsila were doing. Still, Adsila resisted letting them know just how connected she and Thomas had become.

But now they had arrived in Charlotte, and he would have to decide what he wished his parents to know. He had considered the question and had not come to peace with an answer.

Raising a hand, Thomas helped Adsila, then Inola off the train steps. Gawonii helped Tsiyi down, lifting him easily. They had dressed in their best clothes for the journey. But what they had to offer was far less than what would be expected in society here.

People were definitely staring. Was it because of their attire? Or because of their ethnicity? Thomas couldn't say. Perhaps for both reasons. Had the people here ever seen an Indian in person? From the open mouth stares they received, he doubted it.

How much of this was Adsila sensitive to? Did she notice? Did she care?

He glanced toward her.

Her eyes were downcast. She glanced up every now and again to see the horrified stares and quickly looked back down again. Was she offended? Hurt?

Drawing closer to her, closer than he probably should, he whispered, "Don't let it bother you."

She peered up at him. Her eyes displayed her disbelief.

"You are not the problem. They are."

She turned her face so he couldn't see her features.

He looked across the way. Her parents were taking it all in as well.

Drawing even closer to Adsila, he lowered his voice. "You are perfect in God's eyes. Lacking nothing."

Her chin lifted, and her eyes caught his.

"And so you are to me."

Gaze glistening, she raised her face even more. Her lips parted, but she did not speak. As her attention cut to her parents, she took a step back from him, but looked into his eyes once more.

His heart thundered in his chest. How was it that she could always do that to him with just a look?

Gawonii, Inola, and Tsiyi stepped to where Thomas and Adsila were. Thomas indicated that they should step farther away from the train then he strained his eyes, seeking out his own parents. Where were they?

And so, their travel-weary group stood in the middle of the train platform as he hunted for any sign of his mother and father. Not helping the spectacle they appeared to be making.

At last, he spotted them.

They stood off to the side, as if hesitant about the whole affair. Were they, too, affected by the reactions of the people around them? Or did they share in the trepidations of the society folks?

Their son was a missionary. Certainly they did not harbor such prejudices. Waving, Thomas motioned them over.

At length, they did move in his direction. What held them back?

As they neared, Thomas stepped forward and enveloped his mother. "It is so good to see you!"

She hugged him back with some stiffness. "And you, darling. Welcome home."

As Thomas pulled back from the awkward embrace, he moved toward his father, who only nodded.

"Welcome home, son."

"Thank you."

A silence fell between them.

"I suppose these are your guests?" Mother looked at Adsila's family.

"Yes." Thomas moved closer to them. "My friends." He made quick introductions around the group.

Father put his hand forth and shook Gawonii's then Inola's hand. Mother followed suit.

The whole thing seemed rather awkward, and an uneasy feeling settled in Thomas's stomach.

"We thank you," Gawonii said. "For hospitality."

Father's face was a blank.

"Of course," Mother responded, her voice tentative as she spoke. "We are glad you have come to stay with us."

There was silence again.

"Perhaps we should make our way to the carriages?" Father suggested.

"Yes," Mother agreed, turning toward Gawonii and Inola. "It will be a short ride to the house." Then, with nothing further, his parents moved off.

"Please." Thomas indicated the direction his parents went. "This way."

Adsila, who was nearby, groaned.

Thomas understood, she was likely none too excited about another form of transportation.

"I know we've been traveling for a long time. This will be like the wagon. Then we can rest and be still for a while."

She looked at her parents and brother and spoke briefly in Iroquois. They looked at each other before nodding and following Thomas out of the train station.

As they walked, he reached out and brushed his hand against Adsila's.

In most times, she would hook a finger with his for a moment. It was their way of communicating their attachment. Though, in that moment, she pulled her hand away.

This was not going well.

Atohi fumed as he stepped into his house, slamming the door.

The baby startled at the sound and let out a cry.

Yona stood, bouncing the small bundle lightly. She had been settled in her favorite nursing chair. Had he disturbed the baby's meal?

"What troubles you?" Her features cringed.

"A man comes to each house in the village." He dumped his things in a chair by the door.

"What does he seek?" Her brows came together as she continued soothing the infant.

"I do not know." He moved about the cabin. Where was it? Had Yona put it away?

"What is it?" She all but cried. Was she so exasperated? She had been a bit emotional since the young one's birth.

"My hunting knife." Opening a cabinet and pulling out the cutlery tray, he moved his hands over the utensils, looking for his most prized weapon.

"I put it in my trunk." She moved past him to fetch it.

When she returned, he pulled it from her hands and slid it into his belt. Then he pulled his shirt over the hilt and blade, hiding it from view.

Her eyes widened. "What are you—?"

He held up a hand.

Hoof beats sounded in the distance. But they came closer.

The man approached. Yona, the baby… they must not be found.

"Go! Into the bedroom." He maneuvered her in the direction of their partitioned off room. "And try to keep her quiet."

"Please," she whispered. "Don't do anything mindless."

His eyes met hers. Could he communicate his love for her in a look? As he did when they were young and in love? If it were possible, he did so.

Her gaze softened. There was a sadness there that tore at his heart.

But they would get through this. Alive.

Of that, he was determined.

"Do this. For me." He prodded her further with a wave of his hand into the only space she and the infant could be hidden from view. "Stay."

She nodded, moving into the curtained off area.

The baby quieted.

Whatever Yona did to calm the young one had worked.

It wasn't long before a knock landed on the solid wooden door.

He could not help the snarl that marred his features as he faced it. "Who is there?"

"U.S. Army General John E. Wool. I must ask you to open the door, sir."

He paused but for a moment, looking back toward the bedroom. Then he proceeded with a hand hovering over the unseen hilt of the knife.

The first thing Atohi noted was the man's uniform. U.S. Army indeed. What could they want? Were they here to remove them? What would he do to stop them if that was the case? What would they do to him?

"How may I help you?" Atohi kept as much confidence in his voice as he could muster.

"We are here to round up the Cherokee for removal."

Atohi felt sick. He would defend his family, would defend their land. And he would for certain lose his life doing so. He reached for the hem of his tunic.

"We have government provisions for all who are willing to go."

Willing to go? What was he saying? "My family not willing."

The man became quiet for a moment. Then he sighed. "I wish I could say you were the first and only. But nearly all have said the same."

This man sounded truly saddened by this. What was it to him?

"We will not go."

There was silence again.

General Wool nodded and turned.

Atohi watched him walk away. Relief poured through him, thick like molasses. He would not fight this day. He would not die this day.

Moving toward the partition that separated him from his wife, he sought the comfort only found in her.

As he neared, Yona pushed the curtain aside and stepped out of the bedroom, rushing toward him.

"What will happen to us?" The words fell from Yona's mouth.

He placed his hands on her arms. "We will stay strong."

"Mother?" Thomas stepped into her rooms. The maid had summoned him, telling him only that his mother requested his presence on a matter of great import.

"Come in, Thomas," she called.

Dare he venture further in? His parents' rooms had been largely off limits to him for many years now. He couldn't remember being in his mother's chambers, but he had been told that as a boy, he would run through in the wee hours and wake her.

Still, she called for him; he knew better than to not follow her direction.

Taking another step, he noticed his father sat in the small, carefully arranged sitting area.

"Father," Thomas acknowledged him. "Mother, you asked for me?"

He offered a smile despite the nervousness filling him, the twisting of his stomach that warned him to be cautious.

Mother did not return the smile. "There is a matter we need to discuss." Her eyes were hard, serious.

He frowned as a wave of dread overcame him. Why should he feel this way? There was no sin in him. What could they possibly need to speak with him about?

Mother motioned for him to sit across from Father, and he took the seat without hesitation. In that moment, it was as if he were a teenager, fearful of punishment from some rule violation.

Except he wasn't. He was a grown man. And he had done nothing wrong.

He cleared his throat. "I wanted to say again just how grateful I am that you have provided sanctuary for my friends. It means a lot that you have taken them in."

"I suppose we should be thankful you didn't bring the whole tribe with you." Father smirked.

Mother shot him an icy look.

Thomas frowned. Was there some truth behind his father's joke?

Mother turned back to him. "You know you are always welcome here. It is your home, after all." She lowered her chin such that she peered at him as if he *were* a schoolboy. "And we are happy to accommodate your *friends*."

What could that mean? These were his friends. Except...

Surely they couldn't know about Adsila.

Warmth drained from his face.

His parents exchanged a look.

"Let's get right to it," Father said, sounding almost bored. "No need to beat around the bush, so to speak."

"Y-yes. Of course..." Thomas leaned forward. More from the pinching pain in his stomach than from an eagerness to get anything into the open.

Another meaningful look passed between his parents. Were they gauging who should start?

In the end, Mother turned to Thomas.

His eyes met hers.

There was no hint of kindness there.

"I saw you." Her words were sharp. Accusing.

"S-saw me?" was all he could manage.

"Yesterday. On the stairs. With that girl." Mother's lip had an almost unnoticeable curl to it.

Where had that come from? Was this not the woman who had taught him about God's love for everyone?

"Well?" Father's deep voice cut through Thomas's thoughts.

On the stairs... What could Mother have seen?

Then he remembered. It had to have been this past evening when he and Adsila said goodnight. Thinking they were alone, he had leaned in and pressed a light kiss to her lips.

Why had his mother been watching? Had they been keeping an eye on them? A pang shot through his chest. Why? Did they not trust him to make good decisions? Did they not, in fact, believe that God created all man equal? He lashed out with the only defense that reached his tongue. "Were you spying on me?"

"Of course not!" Mother jerked back, hand on her chest. "Can a woman not turn a corner and use her own eyes to see what's happening in her home?"

Thomas looked toward the floor. His face warmed. But why should he feel embarrassed? So, their secret was out.

But then there was the other thing...

How long before Adsila's parents would know?

"You must stop this at once." Father's voice rose.

"What?" Thomas's gaze moved over his parents. What were they saying? That he could not pursue Adsila? Why?

"Thomas," Mother said, her voice softer. "You must see that you cannot continue this relationship. It's just not right." She paused and leaned forward. "It's not kind."

"What are you implying?" Thomas stood.

"Come to your senses, boy! She's an..." Father halted, turning. His features were red and hot. Fists pressed against his legs. The anger he held in check boiled so close to the surface.

But Thomas would not back down. He couldn't. He narrowed his eyes as he glared at them. "A what, Father? An Indian? Is that what you were going to say?" How had he never seen this prejudice in them? It was as if his eyes were opening for the first time.

Silence fell. A thick, tense silence.

His father would not look at him.

Mother appeared stricken, but her mouth was drawn and she kept her chin up.

"And just what does that have to do with anything?" Thomas ignored the warning signs, the choices he had to douse the fire lit in his spirit. He wanted answers.

"Now, let's all calm down and talk about this rationally." Mother stood and reached for Thomas's arm.

He jerked it away. "No, I want to know what you two are trying to say! I don't remember the Bible mentioning the words 'white men' anywhere. I remember that Jesus died once for all. Not for all white men."

Not even his mother would meet his gaze. He should stop. But he was a man possessed. "Or didn't you know, Mother, that Jesus wasn't white? That's right. Neither was Moses, or Abraham, or any of them! No, they were dark-skinned Semites."

Then he shifted his attention to his father, who now shook with fury. "And, you, Father... You cling to your precious ideals of the government and the republic. What about 'all men are created with inalienable rights'? What of that?"

"Thomas, please!" Mother started to break down.

"Please, what?" What did they want from him? A good boy that would follow their ideals?

"Lower your voice and calm down." Father's words came through clenched teeth as he peered through narrowed eyes at Thomas.

"I will *not* calm down! How can I when you dare speak this way of the woman that I love!"

"The woman that you what?" Mother grasped for Father's arm, allowing him to help her sit.

"That's right! I love her. And I'm going to be with her as long as she'll have me."

"Thomas, you can't mean…" Mother seemed pale. Was she going to faint?

Thomas could not withhold the truth from her regardless. "Yes, I'll stay by her side and stand with her come what may."

Mother swooned and wailed. For herself? Or for him? He could not be certain.

"So, you've made your choice then?" Father's voice cleared, but did not calm.

"Yes. If that means we need to leave, we will."

Mother sat up. "Let's not do anything so rash. No one is going anywhere. We said you could stay, and we do not intend to ask anyone to leave."

Father looked away. Was he displeased with Mother's pronouncement?

"Please, Thomas! Please say you'll stay." Her eyes watered as she begged.

Thomas held his tongue. He wanted to blurt out that they would leave as soon as they could get packed. But that was not wise. They had nowhere safe to go, and it would only create a greater distance between him and his parents.

"We will stay."

Mother let out a breath. "Thank God!"

"But you would do well to remember that this is my life," he said gently. "And if I am to make a mistake, it is mine to make."

Mother nodded, biting her lip.

But his father looked away, his gaze stony.

CREEK WAR OF 1836

Arthur Greyson settled into his chair in the parlor and reached for his pipe. As he did so, he looked into a dark corner of the room. A place where a shadow fell. Did he notice the lone figure there? The one who had been in the parlor when he came in?

The elder Greyson jumped up. His face paled as if he feared a ghost lurked beyond his vision. "Good Lord, who are you?"

"It is I." Gawonii stepped forward.

Arthur squinted his eyes in the dimness. Could he then make out the shape of the Cherokee warrior's face?

"Oh. You scared me!" Arthur placed a hand over his heart.

Yes, it should be that he and his people were in fear. Not the other way around. Instead, Gawonii offered a slight smile. "Did not mean to. Only like to look out window."

"That is one of my wife's favorite views as well." Arthur settled back into his chair.

The wife... Lillian... had a good eye. This view of the flowers was beautiful. Adsila planted mostly foodstuffs—things they could use. Not many flowering plants. "Garden is nice."

"Thank you. I'll pass your compliments along to the gardener." Arthur pulled out the morning paper and opened it.

Gawonii grunted. Gardener. They did not work their own land. How curious. He came to sit on the large, rather wide seat near Arthur's chair. "News?"

Arthur lowered the paper. "Yes, this paper has the current news of the day. Do you have a paper in your village?" The man smirked. Was he doubtful? Thought the Cherokee so uncivilized?

"Yes. *Cherokee Phoenix.* Good paper. Miss it."

"Oh." Arthur's features betrayed his surprise.

Gawonii enjoyed the moment.

"If you'd like," Arthur offered, opening the paper wider, "I can read to you. Fill you in on the news, as they say."

Gawonii allowed an eyebrow to rise. Would this paper be different? How so? "Yes. Thank you. Would like very much."

Arthur cleared his throat. He looked over the paper for several moments. Then he turned a page. Did he think Gawonii incapable of understanding some things? Just as the Cherokee was about to reconsider the man's offer, Arthur began to read.

"Secretary of War Lewis Cass has dispatched General Winfield Scott to end the violence in Alabama by relocating the remaining Creek Indians to west of the Mississippi River. Cass feels that..."

End the violence by relocating the Creek. It read as if the violence had been caused by the Creek. Gawonii grunted.

"Did you have something to add?" Arthur asked, already seeming a little guarded.

What to share? What to keep for his own consideration? Did any of it matter? Could he change even this one man's opinion? He sighed. "They go to force Creek to relocate. Creek not go willingly."

"What makes you say that?"

Did the man not see it? "Creek fight for land. They not wish to go."

Arthur tilted his head and seemed to consider it for a moment.

Could he not see the truth of Gawonii's words? The Creek fought for their land. Only as white speculators and squatters moved in on their land, had there been violence. Only as the Creeks had enough of the white man encroaching on their land had they risen up.

The elder Greyson looked back at Gawonii. "But was that the best course of action? Bands of Creeks on the warpath burning homes and farms? Good Lord, they even burned a whole town to the ground."

Gawonii shook his head. "Creek asked for peace. Asked president for peace. For help. No help. Must do things how they know." How could he make this man understand? It may not be right. But it was the only way they knew.

"By displacing families?"

Gawonii bristled at the comment. "Creek families displaced by squatters." And they would separate Gawonii's family, too. The government's intervening had already caused him to be separated from his village, his people, all he had ever known.

Arthur nodded. "I wonder why President Jackson wouldn't intervene. Wait. The paper had given some reason… what was it? Ah, here it is… too close to election time to be taking sides." The man's words started with such confidence, but trailed off. Almost as if even he saw how hollow the reasoning was. Did he?

"I just want an end to the fighting." Arthur sighed, meeting Gawonii's eyes.

"I, too. Cherokee want peace. Creek wanted peace. But peace maybe not come… for either."

Arthur gazed at him for a long time.

Could it be that the man and he came to an understanding?

When Arthur spoke, his words were quiet. "I hope you find that peace."

Adsila strolled among the flowering gardens of the Greysons' home. Her hands itched to dig in the dirt and bring forth life from the earth. But these were not her gardens. These were not her plants. And the owner of this garden did not even take the pleasure of creating in it. No, a laborer tended to this garden. *Absurd!*

Looking over the blooms, Adsila wondered about the practicality of such a garden. Truly it was beautiful to behold, but only for a short season in this climate. What of the herbs? The plants that would season the dishes coming from the kitchen or assist in soothing wounds?

A crunching sound came from around the corner ahead. Footsteps falling on grass.

Who was intruding on her solitude? She looked toward that side of the grand house.

Thomas appeared.

Offering him a smile, her stomach fluttered. Thomas returned her gesture, taking the steps to close the distance between them.

"I knew I would find you in the gardens."

"Yes, they are lovely." She hesitated. Why? This was not for her to judge.

"But not what you would make."

She shook her head. "It is a beautiful place. I just don't see much point in it."

He nodded. Had he too come to see that the way their peoples viewed these things was quite different? "I'll be sure to pass your compliments on to the gardener. And to my mother."

Adsila's heartbeat quickened. And her breathing became fast. "You wouldn't dare!"

He reached forth and took her hand, chuckling. "Of course not. I'm only teasing."

Letting out a breath, she allowed herself to relax. Then she turned her attention to the feel of her skin against his. She longed for him to take her in his arms and...

She became aware that they stood only a few feet away from the large window overlooking the gardens from the family parlor. Someone might see them!

Pulling on her hand, she attempted to free herself from his grasp.

"What's wrong?" His eyebrows furrowed.

"Have you lost your senses? Someone will see!"

"I think, dearest Adsila, that it doesn't matter if they do."

Was he out of his mind? What would their parents think? She was not ready to face them. Would his parents accept her as his choice? Would her parents think her out of her mind? Too much had transpired. The removals, the awkwardness between the two families, the fact that their relationship would be to the disapproval of their families... it was too much.

"Thomas, I'm not ready for your parents to find out... I..."

"They know." His features were set, calm. How was he so calm?

"What?"

They confronted me yesterday. They know. And I think we're deluding ourselves if we think that your parents haven't figured out."

All of a sudden, she struggled to breathe. There wasn't space in her lungs for the air she needed. No, not now. She fought down the wave of panic threatening to overtake her. Breathing in and out slowly, she normalized the rhythm of her respirations.

Could it be true? Could they already know? Why would they remain silent? But she knew why. Because it was a dangerous relationship, but they loved their daughter and didn't want to see her hurt. Besides, what could they say to her?

Wanting to hide her emotions, she looked away until she could push them down.

He gripped both her shoulders, turning her toward himself. "Don't shut me out," he said softly.

She looked at him and made no further effort to hide the tears that came.

He stepped closer and wiped at the trails the tears made. "Please, tell me."

"It's everything. My parents... this is a life they cannot lead. No matter how hard they try. They are not made for this. We are simple people."

"This," he said, waving an arm, "is only for a little while. We can find a small farm somewhere and settle there."

"It's more than that. This place, this house, even these gardens... they're a reminder."

"Of what?"

"A reminder that they escaped. That they... *we* abandoned our people."

"But you didn't. You only did what you had to in order to protect your family."

Her face contorted. "And it's chipping away at their souls! I can feel it!"

His features softened. "Because it's chipping away at yours, too, isn't it?"

She nodded. "You don't understand. It's bigger than us. Much bigger. It's about our people."

He pulled her closer. Enough so that his forehead rested on hers. "But I have to keep you safe. I cannot risk what might happen if we go back."

She ran hands up his arms. "What about my people? I don't think we can live with ourselves if we abandon them for good."

He pulled back. "I don't understand. You'd rather die with your people, than live free?"

Adsila searched his eyes. She desperately wanted to say, no, to tell him that she wanted to be with him… wherever he was.

But it wasn't true.

While she may want to be with him, she could not do so by turning her back on her people.

Returning to Cherokee land would probably lead to nothing but heartache and tribulation for her family, they needed to face it *with* their people. To stand and fight with all they had in them… together. And together suffer their fate.

"It's not what I want, Thomas. Please understand that. It's what I *have* to do."

He looked at the ground for several seconds. Was he so conflicted? By what? Did he struggle between his care for her and his attachment to his parents? Or was it the risk of what awaited them in Georgia? In all truthfulness, they would not be treated well. They may be returning only to die.

But when he raised his face to hers, he was resolved. "Then I will go with you."

Theodore Frelinghuysen sat at his desk, a war within him. Hadn't he known where he stood on this issue? He had. And he stood firm.

Only now he wasn't so certain. After his encounter with Chief John Ross… now having made the personal acquaintance of a Cherokee, he wanted to protect his friend.

It didn't change his belief about the necessity of the things he had done. He would fight against the Indian Removal Act just the same if given the opportunity.

But could he support them to stay and fight in the face of such risk to their lives? He grimaced. How had he been so blind?

Was it possible to convince his friend to see reason? His people must go. And must do so peaceably. Chief Ross had to know nothing would be gained by standing their ground. Only loss.

He grabbed for paper. Leaning forward, he dabbed the quill in ink. The tip hovered over the parchment for a few seconds as he hesitated.

Why? Did he question the criticality of his action? Or the letter's reception?

It mattered not. Whether or not Ross looked kindly upon the senator's words did not change the need for him to write them. To do something. To try.

Dear Chief Ross

There, he had started. But how was he to broach this subject? He wished to remain cordial, though he took the side opposing Ross on this matter.

I hope this letter finds you and your family well. How are things on Cherokee lands?

Balling up the paper, he then tossed it toward the waste bin. Such nonsense. Nothing would be gained with small talk. Ross and his people were in an emergency situation. They had no time for fine words of no import. He must say what he needed. Nothing more, nothing less.

Dear Chief Ross,

Please know I write this with a friendly hand. But I must implore you, once again, to consider a peaceable solution to the impending confrontation with the U.S. Army. It is coming. Of that, we can be assured. It may have reached your ears by the time you receive this, but I will share of the recent peaceable relocation of the first group of Chickasaws.

Mr. John M. Milliard led the relocation effort. The Chickasaws were gathered in Memphis, Tennessee, on July fourth with all their assets and led across the Mississippi River without incident. They then merged with the Choctaw Nation and, as I know it, are living well—free from the problems they experienced previously in Arkansas.

Do not read this and think that I have decided to support Indian removal. I continue to be as loud a voice as possible against such atrocity. But I see what lies before you. The army has been handed down orders to assist with relocations. And I daresay state militias will be assembled to also assist in the efforts. There may be thousands of soldiers on your doorsteps within the year.

Please, listen to reason. For the sake of your people, consider a peaceful relocation.

Sincerely,
Senator Theodore Frelinghuysen

Frelinghuysen pushed the paper away and moved a hand across his face. Was this what he intended to say? Or was there more?

No, he wanted... needed to be as concise as possible while expressing his support and concern for their safety.

He reread the words. Yes, they best suited what he wished to convey.

Folding the letter, he slid it into an envelope and sealed it.

Then, laying his hands over it, he said a brief prayer that it would find a reasonable man in Chief Ross.

Lillian Greyson sat alone in her family's parlor. Years upon years of happy memories lay within these four walls. Voices echoed within the confines of the room as the scenes of holidays and grand evenings past unfolded in her mind's eye. Her children were always center stage. None more so than her vibrant, fun-loving Thomas.

But he was no longer a child. And no longer willing to remain safely in her embrace.

No, he refused to find contentment with her any longer. His future, as far as he was concerned, lay with the red-skinned girl. The one who, even now, prepared to take him away once again and walk him directly into the mouth of danger.

Lillian didn't try to stop the angry tears.

The door creaked, but she made no move to wipe her tears nor make herself presentable. She didn't care.

After some long moments of silence, she glanced toward the opening.

The silhouette of her husband stood in the doorway. "Lillian?"

"Yes?" Her voice broke.

"Why are you in here alone? In the dark no less?"

She looked away. He wouldn't understand.

He let out a breath. And a grunt.

Yes, frustrated. She could have guessed as much.

"Surely, we must go to Thomas. He can't be serious!"

She tucked her hands into the folds of her skirt. No, he didn't understand. Thomas was quite serious. What use was there in trying?

"Why are you moping about?" Arthur ground out. "Come now, we must talk sense into him."

She shifted her head, looking back toward her husband. "He will not stay."

"He must at least listen to reason," Arthur said firmly.

"You know, as well as I do, that he will follow his heart." Her words were spoken softly, and she watched as he drew near.

"Come now. Let us go together. We must stand united. Or do you wish him to go?"

Her mouth dropped, and she furrowed her brows. "Wish him to go? How can you say that? Of course, I don't! But this… this *girl*… she has bewitched him." She searched Arthur's eyes.

The reflection of his emotions there surprised her. Or had her words taken him aback?

She jerked away. "He believes this is his calling. And he will follow it to the bitter end." She choked on the last word.

"You can't think like that." His voice was strained. Was he becoming so impatient? She cared not. He would do well to tread carefully.

She leaned forward, almost nose to nose with him. "I know it's *true*! His mind is made. His heart is set. And there's nothing I can do to change it."

"I won't give up that easily. I refuse." Arthur backed away from her and straightened his jacket. "He's my son, too. And I will not stand by and watch him march to his own demise." Arthur's voice rose.

A knock sounded on the already opened door. Arthur whirled around and she shifted to see around her husband.

Thomas stood, tall and well postured in the pressing light. How long had he been there?

"I've come to say farewell."

She longed to rush to him, pull him into her embrace and refuse to let go. Even if he wouldn't allow it, she would keep him safe from the harsh world he insisted on facing headfirst.

"Thomas," Arthur began, "Let's talk for a moment." He indicated an empty seat nearby.

"I'm sorry, Father. But I've decided. I must go where God leads."

"Surely God would not want to put you in harm's way." Arthur held up his hands.

"Nothing in Scripture leads me to believe that His plan will necessarily keep me safe."

Arthur blinked.

"Listen… just for a few moments." She hoped he might agree to a levelheaded conversation. Perhaps they could speak truth then. "We just want to talk."

"But I don't wish to have a heated discussion and leave with high, tense emotions. Please, let us part like this."

"Your mother and I are rather concerned—" Arthur started.

"I understand. And I would be surprised if you weren't. But you have to let me go."

"So, you can chase after this—" Arthur's voice rose once more.

She thanked God that Arthur bit his tongue and didn't finish that sentence.

Thomas's eyes darkened.

Then Arthur spoke again. "We can and will do everything in our power to keep you safe!"

Thomas sighed. His features lightened. Had he given up on this discussion? "What will you do?"

"I forbid you to go." Arthur's face reddened.

No! He hadn't said that. She stood and rushed between her husband and son, but Arthur waved her off, moving her to the side.

"But you see, Father, I *am* going. You can't stop me." Thomas took a step toward the door.

"If you walk out that door…" Arthur stumbled over his words. "So help me, you may not walk back through it!"

She wasn't hearing this. A cry escaped her throat. Couldn't Arthur take back what he had said? Yes, that would make it all right. Turning toward her husband, she shook her head and raised a hand to him.

"That is your choice. I must make mine." With that, Thomas

nodded to her and then to his father one last time and made his way out.

Lillian couldn't move. This could not be happening. Her son had just removed himself from her home. Where would he belong now?

Something weighed on Thomas. But what? Adsila heard him and his parents speaking loud words to each other the day they had all left the Greysons' home in Charlotte. Even from the foyer, she and her parents had overheard the vocal exchange. But what had led to such anger or the words flung, she did not know. What had upset them?

She slid a hand to set on his.

He flipped his hand to capture hers and offered a weak smile.

Perhaps that was all he had to give.

He sighed. A deep, heavy sigh.

How she wished she could take some of the weight he carried!

Looking at their hands clasped on his knee, she noted how different they appeared. Her small brown one lay secure in his larger white one. She *did* feel secure with him.

Though this train carried them closer to an uncertain destiny, she felt more at peace and more in her place than ever before.

Yes, she would face her fate with her people and with Thomas by her side.

"Thomas," she said, mindful of her volume. Her parents need not hear, but she must be loud enough to be discernible above the train's movements.

He arched a brow. A signal to continue?

"Thank you." It surprised her when her voice caught with emotion.

"For what?" His brows furrowed. Was he so unaware?

"For rescuing me. For understanding. For taking me home. For coming with me. And… for telling me about Jesus." At the mention of His name, she became all too aware that her parents faced an uncertain fate without the security she had in Jesus.

How was she to tell them? To help them believe?

They were so stuck in the old ways…

Thomas squeezed her hand. "I would do anything for you." His voice had a deep, husky quality.

It was true. He loved her that much. But did she love him back? She turned it over in her mind. But it was too much for her heart to comprehend. Too much clouded her thoughts to discern anything with clarity.

The conductor's booming voice broke through her musings as he announced their impending arrival at the next station.

From there, they would take a stagecoach. Then home.

"Thomas," Adsila said, licking her lips. A great urgency pressed into her chest.

He turned more of his body toward her. She had his full attention.

"My family—Father, Mother, Tsiyi… they have not accepted Jesus."

Thomas's mouth became a thin line. He nodded but waited. Did he wish her to continue?

"We must tell them about salvation. I cannot face what awaits us at home not knowing if they…"

He placed his other hand on top of hers already in his warm grasp. "We will. I promise we will tell them."

Something washed over her. Peace?

With Thomas's support, her chances of convincing them were better. Maybe.

Lord, be with us. Help us find the words. Help them see the truth. Help them see You.

She opened her eyes and looked at Thomas.

He, too, was in prayer. There was a tug in her core. Was his heart so turned by her parents' and brother's need for salvation? Warmth spread through her chest—a feeling that had become more familiar.

Was this love?

She couldn't be sure.

Her body pulled forward as the train started to slow, and a loud screech filled her ears as the great machine entered its station.

She turned her attention forward and gripped Thomas's hand even tighter. He pressed back.

They would have to release each other soon, but she would enjoy this simple contact for each second that she had.

Richard Clement wasn't an Army soldier but a carpenter by trade. That's what he knew. Not this. Not the army. Joining the state militia had been something he did because it was his duty. Or so he believed. Now he found himself in the middle of this business with the Indians. How had this not already been resolved? Wasn't this in the news years ago? And then it went away? Yet here he was, called up from his home and humble woodworking to bring final settlement to this Indian issue.

Oh, he had known there were still problems in Georgia with the Indians and their land. But who was to say who was right? He didn't know. His competence lay in saws and nails, not socioeconomic matters.

He wasn't even sure he knew what 'socioeconomic' meant.

No, it was best to leave that to the people who knew more about it.

Buttoning his uniform, he readied for morning troop inspection. He supposed he should be thankful it was springtime and the weather had been pleasant enough for camping. How dreadful it would be to have to do this in the dead of winter!

Just thinking of it made him shiver.

He pushed the last button through the hole and grabbed his firearm. As he stepped outside, another of his militia buddies, George, walked past his tent.

He nodded.

Richard took up step with him, and they walked to line up together.

"So, what do you think of New Echota so far?" George's accent was thick. Much more so than most.

Richard frowned, glancing around. "Nice scenery. Wish I was home, though."

George nodded. "Every time we get called up, it gets harder and harder to remember why I joined," George said almost under his breath.

Richard afforded him a short laugh.

They walked the rest of the distance in silence.

The captain was upon them all too soon, walking the line, looking for any soldier who might be out of place. Finding none, he seemed disappointed. "At ease, soldiers!"

A loud shuffle sounded as the soldiers adjusted their postures in unison.

"I would like to introduce you to your new commanding officer. You will join the U.S. Army troops recently arrived under the command of General Winfield Scott. He will take command of this unit."

If they had been free to speak, there would have been much to say about this. But they were not, so the captain's assertions were met with silence.

Richard searched the area and spotted a man standing off to the side. He looked older than Richard, or was it the years of battle experience weighing upon him that just made him seem so? Everything about the man appeared hard—his jaw, his stance, his chiseled features.

The captain stepped to the side and saluted the general as the man stepped into the center.

"Men, I will tell you what you are here to do. You are here to follow my orders. And follow them to the best of your ability. You are here to defend your country and your lives second only to my orders.

"Now, let me tell you what you are *not* here to do. You are not here to think. You are not here to question. You are not here to have discussions about what we should or should not be doing. You are here to do.

"But you are also not here to mistreat Indians. If that is why you are here, you can pack your bags and go home. I will not tolerate it. We are going to treat them with kindness and humanity. Those are my orders."

As the general finished his speech, the captain appeared out of nowhere. "Your commanding officer just gave you orders!" he yelled at them.

"Sir, yes, sir!" they said in unison.

"Attention!" the captain said.

Another shuffle rippled down the line as the soldiers shifted posture again, this time to salute.

What to make of the general's words? Richard wasn't sure. Of course he was to follow orders and not think. That was not news. But he got mixed messages about the Indians. Weren't they here to forcibly relocate them? How were they to do that and treat them with kindness? What if they refused to go? Was he to say, please?

He didn't understand.

But it wasn't his job to think after all.

Atohi watched as Yona laid their infant daughter down. There were far too few of these moments. Right now, everything in the world seemed right, at peace. And such moments would become fewer and fewer as the time of their relocation drew nearer. President Jackson had given them a deadline by which to voluntarily relocate.

The pro-treaty faction of the Cherokee people had taken the government up on their offer for assistance. And they had been the only ones. Precious few had gone.

Yes, most had decided to stay and fight.

For whatever that was worth.

He gazed at his wife and daughter. How would he protect them and their home? What was to become of them? Did they truly have a chance?

No.

That was the whole of it.

They would fight. And they would lose.

A knock at the door drew his attention.

Yona's eyes sought his.

He could guess what she thought—would it be another soldier?

He reached for his waistband and touched the handle of the knife resting there. Since the earlier unexpected visit, he had continued carrying his hunting blade.

Nodding to her, he moved toward the oak frame of the door, and she dropped the cloth partition to conceal herself and their infant.

Mohe had gone out with friends. Atohi was both relieved and concerned. While his son would be out of this potential danger, what trouble might he be in? If soldiers invaded the village, could he reach Mohe in time?

With a hand on the knife's hilt, Atohi opened the door and found himself face to face with Thomas Greyson.

He sighed, relaxing his posture and moving his hand to offer it to his friend. "Ah, pretty-pretty face, you have returned. I heard you had come back."

"I, um, yes." Thomas seemed unsure, hesitant in his movements. He glanced around Atohi and into the house. What for? Did he concern himself with an audience?

Atohi stepped back. "Would you come in?"

"Are you alone?" Thomas asked, still attempting to see into the recesses of the cabin.

"No," Atohi said, eyebrows coming together. "Yona is in the bedroom."

As if she had been summoned, she stepped from the partitioned off bedroom and nodded to Thomas.

"Good day, Thomas Greyson. I'm glad you are well." She lifted a hand.

Thomas nodded. "And you."

Atohi indicated the dining table. "Please, come in. We have coffee."

"I, uh, that is, I was hoping, er, wondering if I might speak with you alone." Thomas's gaze met Atohi's. He seemed out of sorts.

Atohi looked at his wife. "I think Mr. Greyson and I will take a walk."

She nodded, moving toward the kitchen.

Atohi stepped out of the small house, closing the door. Then he turned to his friend. "Now we are alone."

"Shall we walk?" Thomas jerked his head in the direction of the creek.

"All right," Atohi said; his curiosity grew by the second.

They strode down the path that led to the creek, walking several paces in silence.

Was Thomas waiting on him to make small talk? He would not. Whatever concerned Thomas, he must begin. Atohi would not make it easier. Though what disturbed the missionary was rather curious.

"Fine weather," Thomas said at last.

Atohi shot Thomas a stern look that he hoped told of his displeasure. Small talk did not suit him.

Thomas swallowed so hard Atohi heard it.

After several moments of silence, Atohi began to doubt his friend would ever speak to him again. Then, Thomas looked at him and said, "What will happen to the Cherokee that won't go?"

"The army will force us to go." He spoke so matter-of-factly that Atohi couldn't believe it came from his own mouth.

"And what of the ones who won't go? Those who choose to stay and fight?"

Atohi gave Thomas a long look. Thomas knew the answers to these questions. Perhaps more so than Atohi. He knew how his government worked.

A part of him wanted to walk away or to chastise Thomas. But something deeper softened his approach. "They will use whatever means they can to move us. Weapons, physical force, beatings... That is all I know."

Thomas hung his head.

"Let me ask you something." Atohi's voice was serious but he allowed the edge that came into it. "What will you do when that time comes?"

Thomas remained quiet for a moment. When he spoke, it was with conviction. "Anything I can to stop them."

When Thomas's eyes met Atohi's, they glistened. And Atohi knew.

"For her." It was not a question.

Thomas's gaze shifted, trained on something in the distance. Several heartbeats later, he responded. "Yes. For her."

"It is dangerous." Atohi's words came slowly. "For you and Adsila. You will not find more acceptance among the people in this village than you did your own. Some will understand, others will not."

"It doesn't matter what other people think," Thomas said, his voice sharp and short.

"But it will matter." Atohi attempted to keep his voice soft. "No man lives alone, unaffected by those around him. We need each other. And all the more for such times as these."

Thomas nodded but did not look at Atohi. "I hear you, my friend. And I don't have that answer right now. Perhaps that is something I must deal with when the time comes."

Atohi watched Thomas's eyes as they flicked back to him. And he understood then a couple of things about his missionary friend: first, he was in love and, second, he did not understand the true nature of it.

CHEROKEE REMOVAL

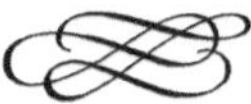

It seemed to Lillian Greyson that she would never stop crying. Until there were just no more tears. Her heart remained but a remnant of what it had once been, but no more tears would come. Had she cried herself out? Or merely become apathetic?

No, her heart still ached for her Tommy, no longer free to return to his home. She seethed under the surface toward her husband. How could he be so flippant? So brash? Was it nothing to him? What if Tommy never returned? If she never saw him again?

Her hands balled, scrunching her skirt at her knees. That future would not settle in her mind. Or her heart.

And prayer—the very thing that Thomas would have her do—was the last thing she wanted. No, she would not prostrate herself before God. Not after He had allowed these things to happen. What faith… what trust… could survive that?

She had trusted Him with her son, and He betrayed her. Now Thomas had gone away, chasing after a lost cause, placing himself in the middle of danger. Hadn't he already been arrested and imprisoned? Wasn't that enough to make him think twice? Of course not! Then he had taken up with an Indian girl.

It was too much.

No, she could not... would not trust God again with *anything* so near and dear to her heart.

A soft knock on the parlor door brought her solitude to an end.

"Come in." Her voice was almost caustic. She didn't care. Who would disturb her at a time like this?

A maidservant slipped into the room. All of her limbs were pulled in tightly as if fearful her mistress may bite at anything not well guarded.

Perhaps she would.

The young woman stopped several feet away. "Pardon, ma'am, a post came for you." She stretched the letter forth, but it would not reach.

Lillian's eyes narrowed. She had not the patience to suffer such nonsense.

The smooth hand trembled, but the girl's eyes remained on it. Perhaps, then, she was unaware of how her behavior had risen to a level of vexing her mistress.

Shuffling her feet forward, the maidservant brought the letter into comfortable reach.

Lillian still stared at the girl.

But her eyes were set upon the letter. Was there sweat upon her forehead?

Raising a hand, Lillian grasped the envelope.

An audible exhale drew her attention once more to the maid's face, but the girl turned too quickly for Lillian to discern anything more. And she tested propriety with the speed at which she quit the room.

Only after the door closed did Lillian peer at the missive.

The penmanship caught her eye.

Could it be...?

Yes—Thomas's hand!

Her heart skipped a beat as she turned the envelope over. But something gave her pause. Should she wait for Arthur? Perhaps that would be best.

But what if he refused to hear from Thomas and took the letter from her and she did not get to read it?

Then again, he may be angered that she did not give him the respect of delaying.

The thunder of her heartbeat grew louder.

Which was right? What was riskier? To face Arthur's wrath or the possibility of not knowing?

She ripped at the seal and revealed the letter within.

Dearest Mother and Father,

I am saddened by the circumstances of our last parting. And I cannot say enough how I wish it would have gone differently. Please know I love you both. So much. Yet I must be free to chart my life as God leads. I cannot let anyone stand in the way of God's will for me. You taught me that, Mother. Didn't you live that out, Father?

And I cannot deny my own heart. I understand your concerns. I do. But Adsila is part of my life, and I can no more disown her than I can renounce my own heart its right to beat. Please understand. I pray you can. Someday.

For now, know that no matter what happens, I will always be your son. And I will always love you. That will not change. Nor will my determination after God.

Sincerely,
Your Tommy

Lillian crushed the letter to her chest and heaved shallow breaths. More tears came. Fresh tears that stung her eyes. How was it that his words could both placate her heart and wound her? The more he strove to assure her of his love, the clearer the line between them became.

That was not what she wanted.

But was this about what she wanted? Or about what was right for Tommy?

How would she know if she wouldn't pray?

But that was the one thing she would not do.

It had long since been time for the Senate and Capitol, as a whole, to settle in to a new president. Van Buren had taken the White House. Without much chance of anyone catching him, too. Jackson hand-picked his successor, and the American people had agreed to it.

And just why did he choose Van Buren, who was first his secretary of state and then his vice president? Because the man would further Jackson's policies and continue his work.

There would be little hope of things changing where the Indians were concerned.

Frelinghuysen had read the poll results come in much the same as the previous election. His stomach sinking with each state counted.

But that was long past. He could not dwell on that now. No, he had to focus. What, if anything, could be done for the Indians? For the people who were being dehumanized, brutalized, cheated, and so much more?

Many days, it seemed as if his voice was only one. But he spoke for many. And he would not be silenced.

Knock, knock, knock.

He turned his chair toward the door, giving up the view beyond the window. "Come in."

"It's Walter," Mr. Buckner said as he cracked the door just enough to slide his head in.

"Do come in, Mr. Buckner," Frelinghuysen repeated. The young man had become a more frequent visitor to Frelinghuysen's private office. Not that he minded. He saw much of himself in the younger man—the idealism, the loyalty, the charm and charisma. How he hoped Mr. Buckner would use those things for the good of others and not only for his own gain.

Walter stepped into the office, his hand full of papers. "Pardon my intrusion. But I, um, have a few of these constituent letters that need your personal touch." He stepped closer to the desk, setting the papers down.

Frelinghuysen eyed the perhaps younger version of himself. Walter was probably his best supporter and perhaps the most reasonable man on his staff. But closer inspection revealed cracks in his exterior.

There were shadows under his eyes. Light as they were, they existed. The sides of his face as well had begun to hollow. Was the man not taking proper care of himself? Working long hours?

Reaching for the letters, Frelinghuysen cleared his throat. "Are we working you too hard, Mr. Buckner?"

"What? Of course not, sir." Walter moved a hand across his face.

"If I may," Frelinghuysen indicated the seat across his desk.

Walter sat, slowly. His strained features fixed in a somewhat confused expression.

"You don't quite seem your... energetic self. Are you sleeping well?" Frelinghuysen did not make it his business to inquire after the well being of his staff. If they weren't well, he expected they would stay home. But this was different.

"Yes, sir. I just... it's..." Walter's gaze bounced around the room as if the answer would be written, hidden in a corner somewhere. What was his struggle?

"Yes?" Frelinghuysen tried to catch Walter's eyes.

Walter dropped his head, gaze to the ground. "It's nothing, sir. Sorry to bother you."

Frelinghuysen leaned forward in his chair. "You are an important member of my staff, and I can see that something is weighing on you. If you do not wish to share it with me, that is your business, but I want you to know that you can."

Walter fidgeted with the arms of the chair. "There is something, sir."

Frelinghuysen arched a brow, but remained quiet.

Walter ran a hand through his hair. "It's the Indian issue."

Opening his mouth to speak, Frelinghuysen was cut off before he could form the first word.

"I know you're going to say that it's a settled matter, and I should let it go. There's nothing to be done. But still… I can't sleep. I almost can't eat. It just won't settle with me."

Was Walter finished? Frelinghuysen sensed it was important for him to. But Walter became silent. His eyes closed, and he pinched the bridge of his nose.

Frelinghuysen folded his hands on the desk. "I would not tell you any of those things, Mr. Buckner. In fact, I share your concerns."

Walter met his gaze. The sadness and grief was naked in his eyes.

"The burden is still heavy on me as well. I only wish there were some way I could prevent more removals from going forward."

The young man nodded and bit at his lip.

"I tell myself 'If only we could stand strong enough, if only our convictions were enough.'"

Walter's eyes did not shift. Did he think that Frelinghuysen had the key? Some grand unknown potion?

"The reality is that our ideals and strength are not enough. They're just not."

Jerking back as if stricken, Walter's brows furrowed.

Still, Frelinghuysen did not flinch. "All we can do is pray for the safety of the Indians that are yet to be removed. And I mean pray like we mean it."

Walter shook his head. "I'm not sure praying is for me, sir. I'm not that kind of person."

"What kind of person do you have to be to pray?" Frelinghuysen leaned back.

"Well… like you. Honest, good, noble."

"Prayer is for everyone, Mr. Buckner. Even for the sinner. Dare I say, *especially* for the sinner." Frelinghuysen brought his hands together, mimicking praying hands. "Start by praying for the Indians. At least you can do that. Who knows? It may bring you some peace. It will for certain do them some good."

Walter nodded, leaned forward, rested his arms on his knees, and folded his hands together.

Some moments of silence passed. Was Walter praying?

Frelinghuysen closed his eyes and focused his thoughts heavenward.

"I don't even know how to start." Walter's exasperated voice disrupted Frelinghuysen's concentration.

Opening his eyes, Frelinghuysen met Walter's gaze. "Then I'll help you."

Adsila listened as Mother sang Tsiyi a soft lullaby. He had become far too old for lullabies, but these last several days it had not mattered. Mother found reason to sing him to sleep anyway.

Closing her eyes, Adsila allowed the melody to take her back to her own childhood—a time when everything had been peaceful and good. There was no white man encroaching on their land. No Indian Removal Act looming, a dark cloud over them. And there wasn't the complication of love.

All that had existed was her and her people living in glorious freedom.

Caught up in this daydream, she imagined the thin blanket she had slept on as a child, the only thing between her and the warm earth. A teepee, the only protection from the wind and rain, surrounded and enclosed her. The men didn't farm. They hunted. And they were strong warriors, not the worn men she now saw.

Her people were a great nation. Proud. Noble. They did not deserve what was happening.

As she opened her eyes, she touched the place on her cheek where she sensed movement. Moisture? Was she crying? Wiping at the tears, she wanted to hide them from her parents. But when she looked up, she met their stares.

"Adsila?" Mother started.

"It's nothing." Adsila sniffled. "Just caught up in a memory."

Mother nodded. She understood. She always did.

Adsila's gaze fell to Father's face. The lines there seemed all the more drawn tonight. Their family's fate rested in his hands. What a weight to bear!

"Father," Adsila began, her voice slow and quiet.

His eyes caught hers.

"Please, listen to me tell you again of Jesus."

He shook his head, sighing and grunting.

"Father, He could lift this burden you carry." Her words poured out like water tripping over stones in the stream. "He could make you whole."

"You say I am half a man?" His face was stern.

"No, that is not what I mean. Each of us is missing something. There is a part inside of everyone that needs to be filled by our Creator."

"I have heard all of this from you." He stood abruptly. "And I will hear it no more."

She bowed her head, gritting her teeth. "Yes, Father."

He stormed off to his and Mother's partitioned off bedroom.

Tears fell anew. Adsila wept for her parents' unsaved souls and what may become of them. It terrified her more than anything else.

Gentle hands pressed her shoulders.

She jerked her head around and saw Mother's understanding smile.

"Do not lose heart," Mother said. "He hears more than you think."

Then Mother released Adsila and joined Father.

Adsila stared after Mother. What was she to make of that?

But she could not speak further of these things with Father. He had forbidden it.

Lord, give me guidance. Show me Your path. I believe it is Your will that my parents come to know You. Help me.

Chief John Ross prepared himself. Did he believe in the words he would deliver? He believed in his people, of that he was certain. And he did not think that more loss of life would further their cause. But was this the right course of action?

The letter from Senator Frelinghuysen had reached a welcome ear in Ross. How could he not be moved by the man's concern for the Cherokee? And so, the senator's words penetrated the hard exterior around Ross's heart and found a soft place to land.

Ross did care about the welfare of his people. Of course, he wanted them to survive. But at what cost? If they relented, were they merely sacrificing their land? Or would they lay down who they were as well?

From his seat on the stage, he searched the faces of his National Council gathered to hear his speech. Their conversations seemed rather lively. Were they, even now, discussing matters of the Cherokee and their well being?

Yet they looked to him for leadership. These men trusted him. To the end. Hadn't they committed to follow him for the betterment of their people?

The weight of their loyalty was an anchor, grounding him to reality. Did he choose the right path? More so than ever, he looked to the interest of his people above himself. If it were for him alone to consider, he would have them stand and fight.

Until the last one of them fell.

But his desire to do so did not make it the best decision for his people. Nothing would be gained. And all would be lost.

Taking a deep breath, he gathered his papers and his wits. Rising, he then stepped forward and took his place before the men he held in such high regard. The men who had sacrificed countless hours for their people. And they would do what it took to follow their chief.

"Council members," he began then paused, raising a hand to his mouth.

That wasn't quite right. These men weren't just councilmen. Not to him. They were so much more.

Friends? That didn't capture it either.

Men of noble cause? Hmm… that didn't fit this situation.

Dropping his hand once more, he took a breath before holding up his right hand and continuing.

"Cherokee warriors."

The eyes upon him gleamed.

Even at such a distance, he saw a fire lit anew in their spirits. A fire he had not seen in some time.

"I come to you with humility. In truth, I must admit that I have been thinking more of myself than the tribe. My stance on the decision to fight removal is selfish. As you know, brothers, if it were for only me, " —he looked down at his papers, unable to meet their eyes— "I would have us fight until the last Cherokee death. But I see that this would not further our cause.

"And so, I have a new message to the tribes: we will not risk our lives without reason. We shall not fight the removals. Stand your ground, yes. But only until your lives are threatened. Then we are to comply.

"How can we fight with knives and rifles against thousands of soldiers? We would only watch our wives and children suffer and perish. This is a war we cannot win."

Some of the men nodded along, but some were glaring at Ross. Perhaps part of the council still favored fighting. He could only hope that, in time, they would see reason as he had.

"My friends," he softened his voice, now certain this word was fitting. "This may be the last time we convene."

All was silent. No one moved. Every eye remained on Ross.

"Go home. Be with your families. Spread the words I have spoken. And let us ever look to the survival of our people and our culture. That is more important than some foolish idea of teaching the U.S. Government a lesson. Let it not be about them — it is only about us. I implore you—let that guide your actions."

With that, he stepped down and moved from the room, seeking privacy.

Murmurs filled the space behind him.

What did they say?

The papers fell from his hands. He dropped to a knee to collect them, but his fingers shook too much for him to grip the slender parchment. He stood. The papers would wait. For now, he had to find room to breathe.

There would be many questions that needed answers. He would have to return. But for now, for this moment, he needed a few minutes to himself.

Thomas walked up the familiar path. How long ago had he journeyed this way for the first time? It seemed only weeks ago, not months. That first meeting, dinner with Adsila's family, still brought a smile to his face. The two of them had made quite the turn around.

But one thing had not changed: even after all this time, his heart thumped quicker just thinking about her. Though they knew not what the next days or weeks would bring, with the removal deadline fast approaching, he was a man in love. Everything seemed new to him, and he felt more alive. The birds' songs were sweeter, the grass was greener, even the sky boasted a fresh shade of blue.

And the whirlwind of emotions that stirred within him in her presence—excitement, nervousness, joy... it overwhelmed him! But... did she feel the same?

He neared the house, unable to keep his smile from spreading across his face.

The door on the small cabin opened and a figure stepped out.

He paused. Who was that? A man... too tall to be Tsiyi, too short to be Gawonii.

Squinting in the dimness, he tried to make out anything that would mark the man's identity.

The door closed and the figure walked in his direction. It didn't take long before the man's angular features gave him away—Atohi.

Thomas raised a hand. "Atohi!"

Atohi offered nothing more than a head bob.

Thomas picked up his pace and closed the distance. "I didn't expect to see you." He smiled and stuck out a hand for his friend.

Atohi did not smile back or acknowledge the proffered shake.

Was Atohi bothered that Thomas had not spent much time with him? That didn't seem likely. "What's wrong?"

"I have been through the village, trying to speak sense to my Cherokee brothers. But they will not listen." His voice was gruff and his focus was on something in the distance.

"What is your message to them?"

Atohi caught Thomas's gaze. The Cherokee man's dark eyes were hard. "It is craziness to stay and fight. We cannot fight like braves *and* protect our families. Not in our own homes.

"If we could ride out and meet them..." His eyes drifted to the horizon again. "That would be different. But we cannot. All will lead to death. For everyone.

"We must go to the mountains in the east. Perhaps we can avoid the worst there. If the Great Spirit is with us, we might escape it all."

Thomas's eyebrows shot up. "Run to the east? You mean sneak off in the middle of the night?"

Atohi nodded. How could he not care that Thomas alluded to the cowardice of such an action?

"I... I don't know what to say." Thomas's eyes shot toward the house. Adsila's house. Would her father decide to take flight as well?

As if Atohi could read his mind, he said, "They will not go." He grunted. "They wish to stay and face their fate like the brave Cherokee they are." Atohi spoke as if he were mimicking Adsila's father.

Thomas could not deny the relief that rushed through him. But why? Which would be worse — facing the soldiers? Or being on the run in the mountains? He was unsure, but something deep within him did not want to sneak off in the night.

Turning toward his friend, he caught Atohi's gaze. "I have no words for you, friend. Except to wish you good journey and safe passage."

"Will you not come? Help convince others? Surely *you* must see I am right."

Thomas bowed his head. The words were difficult to find. When he raised his eyes to meet Atohi's gaze, he hoped he exuded more confidence than he felt. "I cannot. My path is intertwined with hers."

Atohi nodded. Had he guessed as much? He reached out his arm and took Thomas's forearm. "May the spirits be with you."

"And may God watch over you." Thomas shook Atohi's arm.

Atohi jerked his head once and slid free of Thomas's grasp. Then he turned and walked in the direction of the next house.

Thomas had a feeling he would never see his friend again.

Captain Samuel Jones stood outside General Winfield Scott's tent. He took a deep breath. His men were ready; he was sure of it. They would serve the general well. Some of them did have trepidations about what lay before them. And, he could not lie, what they had to do would not be easy. But he was certain they would perform their duty.

Clearing his throat, he attempted to alert the general to his presence.

Nothing.

"General Scott?" he called. Would his prodding be welcome?

"Come in." The general's rather gruff voice came from inside the tent.

Lifting the flap of the tent, Jones stepped inside.

The general hovered over his makeshift desk.

Jones moved closer, glancing at the map pressed out upon the surface. Some areas had been marked. Were these the places they would cover in the days to come?

A lump filled his throat, rising unbidden. And he did what he could to swallow it. To be sure—he was no Indian lover. Yet... he had no quarrel with them, either. Deep down, in those places he tried to keep separate from his actions on the field, he couldn't help but think that perhaps what they were doing wasn't right.

He straightened his posture and shot a glance at the general. Could the man read his thoughts? It would be best if he remembered that, like his men, he was not here to think, but to follow orders. Besides, General Scott had said they would treat the Indians with respect.

Jones waited while the general finished talking with his second in command. He tried not to listen, busying his mind with other things —like home. His wife was due in a month. Would he be home to see his baby enter the world? Not likely. This mission would keep him away for several weeks, perhaps months. The worst part was the uncertainty.

"Captain Jones." The general's voice broke into his thoughts.

"Yes, sir." He stood at attention.

"At ease." The general waved.

Jones adjusted his posture, keeping his chin up and back straight while awaiting his commanding officer's next words.

"I received word from President Van Buren."

Jones held his questions. It was not for him to ask anything. His job was to await orders.

"Tomorrow marks the deadline for the Cherokee to voluntarily remove themselves. The president made it clear that he does not intend to give them *any* additional days. We march tomorrow."

Jones clenched his jaw to keep his mouth shut and kept his eyes forward. "Yes, sir. I shall have my men ready to march out before dawn."

"Good man." The general nodded. "We'll show those savages that they cannot challenge the authority of the United States and get away with it."

Though he held a stoic posture and kept his face a mask, Jones's confusion risked breaking the surface of his features. Had the general not, just a few days ago, spoken words of respect and kindness toward the Indians? Pushing his own opinions on the general's slur to the side, Jones minded his duty. What the man thought and what his policies were could be two different things.

"Yes, sir."

"We will march east and take this village first." General Scott pointed it out on the map.

The village closest to their position would be their target.

"The Indians will be rounded up at gunpoint, if necessary. And, believe me when I say, it will be necessary. We will set up an internment camp here." The general made an X on the map in the middle of an open field.

"Yes, sir," Jones replied. He didn't trust himself to say anything else.

"Good. You are dismissed."

Jones shifted to stand at attention again and saluted. Then, turning on his heels, he marched out. Once the tent flap fell into place behind him, he took another deep breath.

He wiped a hand across his forehead, pulling it back at the moisture there. Sweating? He had been sweating? Did the general see? Whatever was bothering him needed to be put to rest. A unit of militia looked to him, and a general relied on him to carry out orders without question.

Weakness would not be tolerated.

The day had come. Dreadful day that it was. Black clouds hung over the capitol and rain poured upon the earth.

Suitable, Frelinghuysen thought. For this day was indeed a dark day.

May 26, 1838.

Would it be written into history books, as it would forever be etched in his memory? He hoped so. He hoped that history would remember this day as the dark day it was.

What would become of his friend, Chief John Ross? Would he be removed with the rest of the Indians or would they find some reason to kill him?

He was unsure. But he did not trust the military when given free reign.

Why had he even come to the office today? It would have been better for him to have stayed home with Charlotte. She would bring him comfort on this sad day.

Yet here he stood, by the great window in his small office,

watching the rain come down. Were these the tears not to be shed by the Indians?

Yes, these were a proud people. Even when removed from their homes, or with the atrocities committed against them, it was doubtful they would let the soldiers see them cry.

What kind of difference could he make in this mindset? Gloomy as he was?

Yes, he needed to go home.

Still, he couldn't force himself to move from the spot where his feet had planted.

And there he remained, gazing out into the black sky, allowing the sadness of the moment to pervade his spirit.

Thomas woke to an eerie silence.

No sound was discernable. Not even the chirping of birds nearby. Nothing. It was strange.

Opening his eyes, he scanned the cabin.

Everything looked the same. His things were all in their places. But something was terribly wrong.

The feeling overwhelmed him, threatened to suffocate him.

He rushed through getting dressed, glancing out the window when he was decent.

Again, nothing appeared the least bit out of order. Blue skies and a bright day greeted him.

Why, then, was everything in his spirit screaming out to him? Warning him? But about what? Perhaps it was the remnant of a bad dream?

Shrugging it off, he went to the creek for water. His walk was uneventful. And, as he dipped water from the stream, the fish swam by as if nothing were extraordinary.

Yes, it had been nothing more than a disturbing sleep.

Still, no matter how much he told himself that, something lurked on the edge of his consciousness. He pushed it as far to the back of his mind as he could. He must think on better things. What better than Adsila?

As he walked back toward his cabin, allowing his thoughts to settle on Adsila, an image of her appeared in his mind. It had been quite some time since they had been alone. They'd not had time to talk. Did she feel for him as strongly? It plagued him, but he was left without an answer until he could steal time alone with her. Perhaps, later today they could take a walk by the stream.

So much energy had been put into what would happen with the impending removals. Something had to give. She needed a break. And he could surprise her perhaps… take her away from all of this, if even for a few moments. If she would let him.

Maybe he could whittle her something new…

He neared his cabin, but something was amiss. There were men lurking outside. Five of them. With rifles. One preparing to break down his door.

What should he do? He alone couldn't stop so many armed men, neither did he want to stand by and let them tear into his home.

And what were they doing?

"Wait!" he called out. "Wait!" He rushed toward them.

The men turned around. It was easy to read the surprise on their faces.

"I will let you in." Thomas quickened his pace to close the distance. "What authority do you have to go into my home?"

The man closest to Thomas turned his rifle toward him, and Thomas took a step back. "This is my cabin. If you'd like, I can let you in. Please, just don't bust down the door."

The soldiers looked to the bearded blond-haired man at the door. He grunted and nodded.

Thomas moved to the door and opened it. They hadn't even tried. Without him being in the cabin, it wasn't locked. So, he simply opened the door for them to enter the one room structure.

The men exchanged looks.

"What does the army want with my cabin anyway?"

"We'll ask the questions." The blond man by the door said as one of

the others, a brown-haired man with a curious mustache stepped inside, rifle leveled, prepared to attack.

"What is a white man doing on Indian land?" The brown-haired man snarled as he walked past.

"I am a missionary to the Cherokee people," Thomas said, offering nothing more.

"Missionary?" the blond man said, cocking his head to one side. He turned his attention to the soldier within. "Anyone in there, Smithers?"

"No one," the man Smithers called back.

"Leave the cabin untouched," the blond man yelled to Smithers.

"I'll give you fair warning, missionary," the blond man said. "Though I'm not certain whether or not I should."

The other men eyed him.

"We are here for the Indian removal. Starting with this village. But they didn't say anything about what to do with the missionaries. So, lay low. Get out while you can."

"Removals?" The warmth drained from Thomas's face.

Adsila... he had to get to Adsila. He nodded to the soldier, but he couldn't follow the well-meaning advice. No, Adsila needed him.

Dropping his bucket, he ran toward her house.

And prayed he wasn't too late.

Adsila picked at her food. She glanced around the table. None of her family members seemed any hungrier than she this morning. No surprise there.

Yesterday had been the day—their final chance to get out without repercussions. Now what? There had been some speculation as to what the government would do. But no one truly knew. One thing was certain: today began the waiting.

Would they have days? Weeks perhaps to change their minds? Or would the removals begin immediately? And if so, where would they start?

A hardness had formed in the pit of her stomach. Would it begin here? In their village?

She forced those thoughts to the side.

There were many places for them to go. The odds were against their tribe being first.

Pushing her plate forward, Adsila then scooted her chair back. "I'm going to work in my garden."

Mother nodded but didn't speak.

No one did as Adsila rose and walked to the door. Too much emotion had already been spent. Too many words already said. Was there nothing more to say then?

The air had become thick with anticipation. It was the fifth person in the house, always sitting, watching, bearing dreadful expectations.

A shiver slid down her spine as she opened the door. She could not step out fast enough. But as she shut the door on the reminders of what was, she turned toward the sun. Leaning against the hard wood surface, she basked in the early morning rays. The day was bright, full of life, and held every promise in the world.

Perhaps she might even find time to ask Thomas for a walk by the stream.

The thought warmed her core even more.

Then she frowned. She had avoided time alone with him of late. Why? He had become a source of joy and comfort. Their... friendship was a place of security and peace.

Why then?

But she needn't bother asking herself. For she knew.

She didn't understand her feelings about him. And she feared he would seek to know them.

How could she put into words something that was still... so... indescribable?

Her heart fluttered when he drew near. Or even at the mention of his name. But her head and knees became weak when he held her. Was this normal?

She shrugged. There was no sense in it. Try as she might, she would no more be able to piece the myriad of emotions together now than the many times she had attempted before.

Pressing against the door, she pushed herself off and walked around the simple structure to the side of the house. Ah, her garden. If only life could be as simple as plants.

She opened the gate and stepped in. Breathing in, she imagined she could smell the vegetables and herbs. Some did have a subtle fragrance. And if she bent closer, she would certainly pick up their perfume. But she longed to take in a bit of the vibrancy, the strength and promise of new life coming forth.

Springtime always held such eagerness. She had planned and worked out a most bountiful harvest. Now, she could see it take form. Her efforts had not been in vain.

Dropping to her knees, she stuck her hands into the dirt. Was anything better than the feeling of earth between her fingers? No, nothing felt this good. She closed her eyes and gripped it. The land. It belonged to her and she to it.

But for how long?

Her eyes stung.

No.

Not today.

There had been enough of that.

She pulled her hands free and focused on the tender sprouts and what they required.

Working the rows of plants helped the time slip away. And, while she remained here, she could be encased in this world unaffected by the chaos. No government, no removals, no Indian Removal Act. Here she was just Adsila… and the life she'd brought forth.

Crunch!

The sound came from behind the house. It almost escaped her notice.

Still, something gave her pause. She jerked her head in that direction.

Nothing as far as she could see. "Tsiyi?"

No response.

"Tsiyi, I'm not in the mood to be scared today." He'd best not jump out and frighten her. Not unless he wanted to end up in the creek.

He did not answer.

Perhaps a rabbit or something.

Shrugging, she turned her attention back to the tomatoes, humming a tune as old as her people. There, the tomatoes seemed much more content. She put a foot under her to rise.

Rough hands gripped her and jerked her up.

Who? What?

She fought the unseen attacker. Scratching and kicking.

His thick arm wrapped around her waist and another held her face still, hand clamped on her jaw.

Twisting and trying to turn her head from side to side, she continued to thrash about.

The bayonet of a rifle appeared in front of her, the blade inches from her nose.

Drawing in a breath, she bit her lip to hold back a scream.

Her eyes sought the owner of the rifle. A man in a soldier's uniform stood behind the weapon, sneering. Likely it was another soldier who held her.

"There now," came a gritty voice, hot in her ear. "Be still. Don't cause trouble."

Dread rushed through her, and her limbs tingled with the desire to go, to run, to fight, to do something… but what? What would happen to her?

Her eyes shot from side to side. Other soldiers come forth from the shadows. She counted six in all.

"What do ya say, men? Shall we have some fun with this one?" the man holding her continued. His voice rasped as he spoke.

One of the soldiers off to the side gave the man a disgusted look. "Remember, Johnson, our orders are to treat them with kindness."

"Oh, I'll be nice," he snickered. "If she will."

Adsila fought to draw in a breath. It wouldn't come. She pulled against the man's hand.

His body shook with laughter, and he clamped his hold tighter.

Her eyes widened. She couldn't breathe!

She looked toward the sky. *God, help me!*

"That means no, Johnson. We have our orders." The other soldier gave the man a stern look.

Johnson grunted.

Her breaths were ragged, but they were coming in and out again.

The soldier with the rifle in her face moved toward the one who seemed to be leading the group.

"If you scream," Johnson said into her ear, his breath seeming to sear her skin, "So help me, I'll break your neck." He then dragged her to where the soldiers gathered, behind the house.

What could she do? Her parents and Tsiyi were inside. What would the soldiers do to them? Could she warn them? Would Johnson make good on his threat?

She cut a glance toward the man.

He seemed sincere. But her family was more important than her life.

Bracing herself, she sent up a silent prayer. And screamed.

Johnson's hand clamped over on her mouth. Hard. And he jerked her body against his, knocking the very breath out of her.

She tried to gasp for air, but his hand covered her mouth.

Was she to suffocate?

Her vision blurred. Some of the soldiers ran around the corner. How many?

Had she just made things worse? Father would run outside to aid her, unaware of anything but her scream, and be captured.

A dark haze came around what she could see. Her breaths shallow, not able to fill her lungs.

Another voice spoke. Had one of the other soldiers remained? "Johnson, put her down and help the others."

"But, I..."

"Do it!"

Adsila dropped to the ground. She landed hard. Had he thrown her?

She dragged air in. The breath of life had never been so glorious.

Rolling onto her back, she closed her eyes and concentrated on bringing air in and pushing it out.

A few moments later, she remembered her family and jerked up.

She nearly struck the soldier squatting, crouched over her. Leaning back, he gave her room to sit fully.

"Are you well?"

She nodded. "Thank you—"

"Shut up!" the man snarled, rising. "*You* are not to speak to me!"

She nodded, looking down.

Sounds came from the front of the cabin.

What was happening? Adsila's heart ached. Father had been a capable warrior. But he didn't have a rifle. And he had Mother and Tsiyi to worry after.

She peered at the soldier.

His features were drawn. Was he, too, eager to know? Did he worry after his men? Or was it possible he was unsure what they might be doing to her family? As uncomfortable as he had been with what Johnson want to do to her?

A shot rang out.

Her heart stopped. "No!" she screamed. One of the soldiers must have shot at her family!

The man grabbed her arm, jerking her to her feet. He rushed around the house.

Vision blurred by tears, Adsila stumbled after, nearly falling as he pulled her along.

When they turned the corner, Adsila's legs gave way at the sight and she fell.

Father was on his knees, hands tied behind his back. Two soldiers circled him. Johnson was one of them.

Mother and Tsiyi huddled together off to the side. Three more soldiers had rifles trained on them.

"Who fired?" the soldier dragging her demanded.

As she wailed, he released her, but remained at her side.

"I did." The dark-haired soldier by Mother and Tsiyi lifted a hand. "The boy became… restless."

Adsila narrowed her eyes, clawing at the ground. How could such anger and sorrow live together in her heart?

The soldier with her frowned, but he said nothing.

Nothing.

The only man here with any semblance of decency said nothing.

Adsila's gaze was drawn to her proud father, forced into the stance of a prisoner.

His eyes met hers. There was such depth in that moment. A depth she could not read. Sorrow, regret, pride… even in the midst of everything, relief at the sight of her, and so much more.

"Go there." The man pushed her toward Mother and Tsiyi.

She rose and did her best to put one foot in front of the other, tripping over her feet, her dress, random rocks as she went. It became impossible to see through the blurriness of her emotion.

"And what were you planning to do with *him*?" the man asked the two soldiers circling Father.

"Just teach the others about obedience," Johnson said as he lifted his rifle and smashed the butt against the side of Father's head.

Father landed hard on the ground, unable to break his own fall.

The man that had previously insisted Adsila be treated with kindness did not protest such treatment of Father. Why? Why was this different?

"Pick him up," Johnson commanded.

The other soldier did so, lifting Father back to a kneeling position.

Johnson backhanded him across the face, but Father remained upright.

Johnson's face reddened. He raised the rifle again. Over and over, he hit Father either with his fists or the rifle.

Mother whimpered and pulled Tsiyi's face to her stomach. She hid her own face in Adsila's shoulder. But Adsila could not look away. No, she held Father's eyes.

"Stop!" a voice called.

Who? Who would dare?

Adsila scanned the area. The voice had come from a distance.

Indeed a man ran up the path.

Her heart leapt. Thomas!

No… not Thomas. He shouldn't be here. They would kill him for intervening.

Everything slowed as Thomas ran in between Johnson and Father. He panted and heaved. Had he run all the way from his house?

The soldiers seemed stunned into inaction. Were they so surprised that a white man would stand up for an Indian?

"If… you… want… to… beat… someone… give… me… a… try," Thomas said as he caught his breath.

"What are you?" Johnson asked, now recovered from his momentary shock. "Some kind of Indian lover?"

Thomas held his chin up and met the man's gaze. But he remained silent.

Johnson walked to Thomas, not stopping until he was nose to nose with the missionary. "If that's the way you want it, that's the way it will be."

He pulled his hand back, curling it into a fist.

Thomas did not flinch.

"Stop!" the lead soldier shouted.

All froze, but Johnson continued to hold his hand up, ready to strike.

"We are not here to lay a hand on a white man," the lead soldier said.

"But he said—" Johnson started.

"Let's get on with our job," the man in charge said. "We must finish and move on." Turning his head toward the house, he stepped in that direction.

Johnson gripped his rifle and smashed the butt into Thomas's midsection.

Thomas crumpled.

"No!" Adsila wailed.

The lead soldier spun around. He took in the situation and narrowed his eyes at Johnson.

Johnson shrugged and moved toward him.

The four remaining soldiers gathered the family and Thomas

together, all but dragging Thomas and Father to where the women and Tsiyi stood.

Adsila fell by Thomas's side.

"Are you well?" she asked in hushed tones.

He nodded, an arm still on his midsection.

"Can you stand?" She brushed hair from his forehead. Letting her caress speak what she dare not.

He nodded.

She gripped his arms and did what she could to help him rise.

The lead soldier gathered all but one soldier, left guarding them. He motioned at the house and they moved toward it.

As Adsila watched with her family, helpless, the soldiers plundered her home. They smashed things that had been priceless, some of which had been passed for generations. Barbarians. Satchels appeared on the soldiers' hips that she hadn't noticed before. And they put anything that could be considered valuable in them.

When she could watch no more, she huddled against Thomas's chest. His arm came around her shoulders. And his embrace anchored her. She closed her eyes and rested in the feel of him. It was perhaps the only sure thing in her life.

A great commotion shattered her daydream. She looked up, careful to not let her expression betray what she was thinking to these white dogs.

They had left the house. Now, they huddled and spoke rapidly to each other, motioning now and then to her family.

Johnson held up his hands, made a loud exclamation and walked back toward the house, reaching into his pockets.

He stepped into the small cabin and one of the other soldiers followed. Not long after, they came back out. They weren't smiling. Or anything. It seemed as if they had become bored.

But there was a smell. What was it?

Smoke.

Then the dark gray cloud began seeping from the windows and door.

They were burning the house down?

Adsila's knees went weak. But Thomas's strong arm her held her upright.

She couldn't turn away as her family's home burned.

Did the soldiers watch them? Did they gain some kind of sick pleasure from it?

Before long, the soldiers forced them to move. Almost as if they allowed them to watch long enough to draw out a sense of hopelessness, but not long enough to give them closure. Could these evil men taste these emotions? Did they derive some enjoyment from them?

Adsila forced her mouth to become a thin line and dried her tears. These men would get no more from her.

The short trip to the next place, what she heard one of the men call 'internment camp,' was difficult for Father. His injuries and wounds were severe.

Once they arrived at the place set up to detain the Indians, the men there were reluctant to imprison Thomas.

But then Johnson told his version of what happened. And Thomas refused to be removed from Adsila and her family.

They walked, spent, into the fenced in camp prepared for them. Already there were others. In all states of injury. And as they met Adsila's eyes, she noted that some family members were not among them. These were the lucky ones who survived. Or were they?

Such a sad ending. Then again, even that wasn't true.

This, after all, was only the beginning.

INTERNMENT CAMPS

Richard Clement ate his rations in silence. The first round of Indian gatherings was complete. One village had been culled. The soldiers were now coming together for dinner, but it was quiet, too quiet for a camp of thousands of soldiers. But Richard didn't have anything to say to anyone.

Movement nearby drew his attention, and he looked up in time to see his friend George sit beside him. He nodded at George and got a nod back, but neither spoke.

As Richard watched the fire, he couldn't help but reflect on his actions of the last twenty-four hours. Why did his stomach turn as the images crossed through his mind? It had not started well. That first family he encountered had not eased him into the process. And Johnson had been so flippant about the whole thing. It didn't make things any better.

Still, he couldn't deny the part he played in their suffering. How could he? Though he had not laid a hand on any member of that family, he had not made a stand for them either. No, he stood by and let it happen. The memory of it caused his stomach to now twist painfully. He looked at the hard tack bread in his hand and set it to the side. There wasn't room for anything else.

This place was too constricting. He needed space. Room to breathe. Distance from all these uniforms. His own collar was choking him.

Pulling at the edge of the material around his neck and nodding at George again, he stood and walked into the night.

Where should he go? Looking to the right and left, he saw many choices and few at the same time. One direction would bring him closer to the internment camp, the other a thick forest. Though he did not wish to be swallowed up by trunks and low hanging branches, the trees it was.

He focused on the moon as he walked. The perfect round orb shone its light, illuminating the soldiers' camp and the tree line.

But if he were to look far left, he could make out the outline of Indians huddled together. How many were crammed into that enclosed area? He shivered despite the fact he was rather warm in his uniform jacket. Why must he think of them? Out in the open air with naught but the clothes that had been on their backs. Some soldiers had been kind enough to grant them a few of their possessions, but some were detained without even their shoes.

None of it seemed right. But he was not here to think. And he wouldn't. Not about them. Not anymore.

As he approached the tree line, he heard a rustling in the bushes. He was immediately on alert.

Had they missed one? Was someone about to jump out and attack him? Or was it some wild animal? He wished he had thought to grab his rifle.

Stopping, he planted his feet and hunched over. The rustling became louder and the movement of the short branches drew closer to the surface. Whatever was in there, came closer. A moment later, a figure emerged.

He let out a breath. It was one of the army men.

The moonlight gave Richard a clear view of the man. He stood up and came out of the tree line, his hand against his mouth. Had the man been sick?

The soldier noticed Richard and nodded as he stepped that way.

Though he truly didn't want to, Richard felt compelled to ask after him. "You okay there…" He looked at the stripes on the man's uniform. "Private?"

The man's head made slow bobs. "Just a little… overwhelmed… after today."

"Yeah." Richard crossed his arms. "That was…" He hunted for the right word and came up short. "…something."

The man's eyes gazed into the distance. From the direction of his stare, Richard guessed he looked at the Indians' camp. This private was young. He could almost have been Richard's son. Almost.

Richard put a hand on the younger man's shoulder. "Don't let it get you down. We were just following orders. That's what we're here for, remember?"

The man nodded, eyes still on the people imprisoned beyond the army's camp. "Do you think when our children look back on this, they'll remember that?"

Richard's head fell, examining his shoes. That was a good question. He thought of his own children sleeping at home. Would they understand? How he prayed they'd never know of his involvement in such as this! Couldn't they go on in their innocent admiration of their father?

"I don't know," was his quiet reply to the private.

"I saw things today… I did things today… that I… I…" He put the back of his hand against his mouth and his eyes watered.

Richard put both hands on the slender shoulders and gave him a slight shake. "Calm yourself, private! Hang in there."

"I… I have to tell someone," he finally managed.

Richard was quite certain he didn't want to hear it. But he swallowed the lump in his throat and nodded anyway.

"I saw… General Scott forced four Cherokees to shoot their village's chief and his children." The private's eyes filled with moisture.

Richard's stomach lurched. He knew the man spoke the truth but it was unimaginable. Hadn't General Scott told them… no, commanded them to treat the Indians with respect and kindness? One of his hands went to his chin, rubbing his beard.

"Private—" Richard started.

"Burnett," the man offered. "My name is John Burnett."

"John," Richard started again. "I regret that you saw things today that disturbed you. But I daresay, it will not be the last. There will be more removals. We must gird ourselves for what is to come. Above all, do not forget, we are just following the orders of our superiors."

Burnett nodded, taking in a deep breath.

Richard clapped the man on the back. "Now, let's get some sleep. There's not much a good night's sleep can't improve."

But Richard knew… this would not be one of them.

Walter moved through the halls of the Capitol, making his way to Senator Frelinghuysen's office. He passed other aides along the way, including Harry. But his friend barely acknowledged him as they moved along in the corridor.

That was what their friendship had become. And Walter couldn't blame him. There was much tension between them. It would be short-lived though, once Walter's decision was made public.

Walter had wrestled with this decision. He'd even tried praying about it. There was no peace to be found, but still, he was certain he made the right choice.

This whole business with the Indian Removal Act and the atrocities committed against them… it was all too much. Still, he'd been helpless to stop it. Frelinghuysen with all his status had been equally helpless. And the senator had done everything in his power—filibustering, being vocal in the senate chambers, bringing forth legislation. What good was a career in politics if you couldn't change anything?

As he drew near to the senator's offices, Walter sucked in a long breath through his teeth. What did he owe the senator? Could he realistically just write his resignation out or did the man deserve a face-to-face?

There was no question about it.

The man had been good to him. He deserved more than a handwritten notice.

Walter owed him an explanation.

Only moments later, he entered the main office.

He was not the first person in the office. Mason sat at his desk sorting through papers, and a couple aides worked quietly in the corner.

Walter strode to his own desk and sat. Shuffling papers, he attempted to lose himself in his work, but it was not to be. His mind was on his resignation and the conversation he was due to have with Frelinghuysen. Glancing at the door to Frelinghuysen's inner office, he swallowed. How was he even to begin such an exchange?

No matter what it would look like, it might be best he get it over with. He had rehearsed an opening statement in his head. Perhaps now was the time. Now... or later. It had to happen.

Standing, he moved toward the senator's inner office.

As he neared the door, he glanced at Mason. "Is the senator busy?"

He cleared his throat. "There's nothing on his schedule until 9:30."

Twenty minutes. He had twenty minutes. That would give him plenty of time, but push him to stay concise. Yes, this would be best.

Stepping up to the door, he knocked.

"Come in," the senator called.

Walter closed his eyes and turned the latch. Moments later, he was looking at the senator behind his massive desk.

"Can I do something for you, Mr. Buckner?" Frelinghuysen said, brow arched.

"I felt... rather, I *thought* that I should... that is," Walter flustered. *Oh, I'm going about this all wrong!*

He worked to gather his words. Why would he become tongue-tied now of all times?

"I need to turn in my letter of resignation." He produced a folded paper and laid it in front of Frelinghuysen.

"Resignation?" Frelinghuysen said, the shock evident in his voice. "But why?"

Sweat beaded on Walter's forehead. He fought the urge to wipe at it. "I've given this a lot of thought. I don't believe politics are for me."

"If I might be so bold." Frelinghuysen leaned forward. "I disagree."

Walter stared. He respected the man's opinion, and it was true that he expected no less out of this confrontation, but his decision was firm.

Or was it?

"You see, sir, I got into politics to make a difference, to be a voice for those who needed one. And I've watched the *voice* of the Indians become silenced. Even here in Washington, D.C. Despite the fact that there are those, like yourself, who have tried to speak for them. And if you can't make a difference, I don't see how I can."

"Please, sit." Frelinghuysen indicated a seat in front of his desk. "While it is true that my actions and *voice* may not have changed the outcome, I refuse to believe that I did not give them a voice or that their voice, my voice, has been silenced.

"How can I say who has been affected by the things I've said? Or who has become more aware of the plight of the Indians by the things I have done? Maybe other politicians will think twice before supporting legislation like this in the future. Perhaps constituents will change their votes after they are made more aware of what the Indians are being forced to endure.

"But I cannot and will not, while I have breath, be silenced."

Walter nodded, looking at the floor. He had insulted the man. "I apologize for my words, senator. You are right."

"And that's why it is so important that the Mr. Buckners... the Walters of the world stay in the race! Do you think your friend Harry Corbell will be a voice for the disenfranchised? Too many politicians are in the game for themselves, for the fame, for the money. We need *you* to stand up and be a voice for the people! Even if you stand alone."

The senator's words were a salve to Walter's wounded heart. Frelinghuysen made sense. Maybe he needed to rethink his decision.

While the senator's belief in him was a high compliment and his speech inspiring, the future he painted was not exactly pleasant, but fraught with difficulty.

Was Walter ready to take it on?

Lillian took careful steps through the hallway of her house. The very halls that haunted her. Mocked her. With memories of life before. With how life should be.

If only.

If only Arthur wasn't so hard headed. If only her Tommy wasn't so stubborn. It would have been better if he were dead and she could mourn him properly, instead of all this worrying.

She stepped into the parlor and held a hand up against the light. The maids had opened the curtains. Whatever for? Hadn't she given instructions to the contrary?

There was no sense in it.

Turning, she opened her mouth to call for one of the maids. Then she remembered. Today was different. That's why they had gotten her dressed and done her hair.

For Emma.

Emma would come for tea.

Bless it all. Why had she agreed to this?

Oh yes...so that Emma could be assured that her mother was just fine.

If she hadn't decided to drop in unannounced last week, there would be no need for this charade. When Emma had come, Lillian was having one of her days. Doesn't everyone? So, she was still abed. And Arthur, how he does exaggerate... claiming she kept to her room and her bed most days of the week! Had she ever wanted to raise her voice to that man so much?

Yes. The day he banned Tommy from his home. But she had been weak. Trusting. Next time...

Oh, what was the use?

She dragged herself to a chair and awaited her daughter's arrival.

How much of this joyful, merriment would she have to play? Would a plastered-on smile do it? Well-contrived chitchat? A practice well kept by the lady of this house.

Looking around the room, she mused at the colors. It may be time to redecorate. When had she thought such bright colors a good idea?

The bell rang, and voices down the hall confirmed that Emma had arrived.

Straightening her shoulders, Lillian pressed her lips into the best, most realistic smile she could manage. There. That would do it.

But it hurt. Her muscles ached. Were they so strained?

It would not hold.

She lifted a hand to her face as the simple expression fell.

This would not do. Should she try again? Perhaps not. She certainly didn't care. Why should Emma?

Lillian's gaze caught on the chair Thomas sat in the last time she saw him. She closed her eyes and took a deep breath, shutting out the memory. Emma would have to understand.

What was there to smile about anyway?

"Good afternoon, Mother." Emma bustled into the room, making straight for her. Her face was lit, a larger-than-life smile filling her features. "You are looking well."

Lillian glanced toward her hands. It became difficult to look at Emma. Was she truly so happy? "It is all an appearance, I assure you." Lillian neither cared about nor peered up to see Emma's reaction.

Silence fell in the room. Did Emma expect her to elaborate?

After a moment, Emma sat on the settee next to Lillian's chair. "The children send their love." Emma leaned closer to Lillian. Was she attempting to engage her mother more deeply?

"That's nice."

Two maids came in with trays—one bearing tea, one biscuits.

"Thank you," Emma said. Even her voice held a smile. How had Lillian never noticed this side of her daughter before? It seemed exhausting.

When Lillian did lift her gaze, Emma opened her mouth to speak further. She frequently inquired after the servants' wellness, habits, and whatnot.

"That will be all," Lillian interrupted.

Not even that disrupted Emma's smile.

After the maids left, Emma turned to Lillian, folding her hands in her lap. Lillian picked up her teacup.

Emma's brows furrowed. "Shall we pray?"

Lillian lowered her cup. "Oh, I'd rather not."

"Rather not?" Emma spoke with slow, careful words as if she hadn't actually heard her mother. "Perhaps it would be best if we… see, I just…"

Was Emma flustered? She wasn't smiling anymore.

Emma met Lillian's eyes. "I think we should."

Lillian shrugged, setting her cup on the tray. "Go ahead."

Emma bowed. "Heavenly Father, we thank you for this lovely summer day and for your many blessings upon us."

Lillian could not help the snort that came from her. Blessings. What blessings?

Emma paused. Her features contorted slightly. But she continued. "We thank you for this time. We also pray for Tommy."

Lillian lifted her head. She would not bow. Would not close her eyes. She could not participate in this prayer. She just couldn't.

The prayer flowed from Emma's lips. "Keep Your mighty hand on him and bring him safely home when his job is done. May that be soon. In Jesus name I pray, Amen."

Emma lifted her head and caught Lillian's eyes. Her expression became one of confusion.

Lillian cared not. She did not seek Emma's permission or approval. Shifting her focus out the window, she said, "The garden is lovely this season."

Emma turned then nodded.

The garden… That's where the Indian girl spent most of her time. She had some kind of fascination with it. A sharp burn in her chest threatened to color Lillian's features.

"Shall we have our tea before it gets cold?" Emma reached for her cup.

Lillian nodded, picking up her own.

Silence fell between them, lingering for several moments.

Did Emma have something to say? What kept her from doing so? Was she fearful?

Lillian sighed. *Bless it all.*

"Mother," Emma began, hesitation in her voice. "Why do you not wish to pray?"

"I am no longer convinced there is anyone to hear." There was little emotion in her response. Why should there be? It was a fact, was it not?

Emma had to catch her toppling teacup. When she righted it, she set it down. "Of course, God hears you. Why would He not?"

Lillian sighed. Innocent, naïve child. "I prayed over Tommy. And this is God's answer, if it be God's work at all: your brother is in love with an Indian girl, he insists on walking this terrible path with those people, and he refuses to see reason. And now he's been banished from my home."

Emma leaned a little closer and peered at Lillian, almost as if she searched for something. Tears, perhaps?

She would find none. They had been cried out.

Clearing her throat, Emma placed her hands in her lap. "But, Mother, how can you know that these things are not God's will?"

Lillian's eyes widened. What was Emma saying? "How can they be the will of a loving God? A God who claims to love me? To love Tommy?"

"Tommy wrote me." Emma spoke slowly, as if measuring her words. "He knows Father did not mean whatever he said."

Lillian sighed. However, the relief she expected to come did not.

"But more than that is what I know of God. Did you not teach us that there are things about God we may not necessarily like? Yet, that doesn't make them any less true or Him any less God?"

Lillian met Emma's gaze. She saw how pained her daughter had become. Over her resistance?

"Mother, could it be that *your* faith is being tested? That you are being refined by fire?" Emma spoke with gentleness. Her words so tender and loving that they snuck through the hardened exterior of Lillian's heart.

Lillian's gaze fell to the teacup in her lap. Were these not her own words? Her own truths learned over her years of walking with the Lord? How could she abandon them so quickly? And so completely? When faced with a test of faith. Was her trust not stronger than this?

Emma held something out to her.

Lillian looked in her direction.

A handkerchief.

Was she?

Yes, there was moisture in her eyes.

"I have missed Him, Emma. So much."

"Call on Him." Emma scooted closer. "You know He cares as much about Tommy as you do. More even. And He cares just as much about you and your struggle. Let Him be your Rock. Your strength."

Lillian nodded. *Bless me... this moment, this encounter.* "Thank you for speaking truth into my life."

"I learned it from a great woman of faith." Emma's smile seemed to light up the room. "Can I pray for you?"

"No," Lillian said, pulling the handkerchief down.

Emma's brows came together. "But—"

"We should pray... together."

Two weeks. They had been here two weeks! And that had not been the entirety of their imprisonment. That did not include the time spent in the internment camp near their village. Days after lingering there, they and thousands of other Cherokee had been marched here, to the Indian Agency near Cleveland, Tennessee. Here they were to remain in this internment camp for who knew how long.

Thomas sighed and gazed out the barrier fence.

The soldiers on the other side sneered at him. They seemed to have a special hatred for him and the handful of other white men imprisoned with the Cherokee.

He could only imagine why.

Crossing his arms, he was thankful he could do so without pain shooting through his torso. It had taken almost the entire two weeks for that pain in his midsection to subside. There was no way to know if internal damage had occurred. For certain, he'd had bruised ribs.

Gawonii's injuries had been worse. He continued to heal. And these soldiers did not provide any assistance though the Cherokee had nothing with which to nurse their wounded.

Many of the men that survived the culling were injured in some way.

Perhaps this was the one blessing of the internment camp — time for rest and whatever limited wound care could be provided.

A hand pressed onto his back.

He jerked his head around.

A bump here and there was nothing in such crowded quarters, but a hand on his body was intentional.

It was Adsila.

He offered her a weak smile.

She slid her hand from his back, down his arm, and into his hand.

He pulled it to his chest.

"How are you today?" Her voice sounded small. Too small.

He hated the way this place was crushing her spirit.

"Better," he patted his ribs. "And you?"

She shrugged. "Father is over the worst of it. He is luckier than most, I suppose. I just…"

Turning her face away, she scanned the outskirts of the camp. Why? Or was she avoiding his eyes?

He angled his body toward her and reached his free hand to her chin, nudging her face back until their eyes met. Tears welled in hers.

"Adsila," he said, his voice soft and gentle. He longed to kiss away her tears, to hold her and tell her everything would be all right.

But he could do neither.

Not only would that level of contact be unacceptable, he would not lie to her. Not even to placate her for a moment. He would not insult her with hollow platitudes.

All he could do was pull her closer. "Talk to me."

She shook her head against his chest.

"Know that I'm here."

She nodded, reaching her free hand up to cling to his shirt with a ferocity that surprised him.

His gaze drifted back toward the soldiers; they started moving. Rations time.

"Hey," he shook her ever so gently. "We'd best get back to your family."

Her eyes sought his. She seemed sad. Did she think he didn't want to hold her? He would do so forever if she would let him!

Raising an arm, he pointed at the soldiers.

She nodded. Pulling back, but keeping a firm grasp on his hand, she led him to the corner of the enclosure occupied by her family.

Gawonii leaned against the fence with his makeshift bandages. Adsila and Inola had sacrificed the hems of their skirts to make them.

Inola sat to one side of him, retying a bandage. Had she just checked his wounds?

But Tsiyi reclined to the other side of Inola, half leaning against his mother. That was unusual. He was almost always off with a friend making up some kind of fun.

"What's wrong with Tsiyi?" Thomas asked Adsila under his breath as they neared.

"I'm not sure." She didn't look confident in her answer. "He said he didn't feel well this morning."

"Perhaps he's just tired," Thomas offered. Though he didn't believe it.

Adsila nodded slowly.

He would bet she didn't believe him either. They were each trying to assuage the other.

Disease had become rampant in the camp. This was not a good sign.

Thomas crouched next to Tsiyi. "What's going on, young brave?"

Tsiyi moaned. "I'm tired. And my head hurts."

Thomas put a hand to his forehead.

Tsiyi burned with fever.

Lifting his eyes to meet Adsila's, he could not hide his concern. His gaze followed Adsila's over to Inola and Gawonii.

Were they as oblivious as they seemed to the potential seriousness of Tsiyi's condition? Perhaps they were unaware. Too focused on Gawonii's improvement?

Tsiyi coughed. Did his chest rattle as his body shook?

Thomas stood and stepped closer to Adsila. "It could be something small." He attempted to convince her. And himself. "Tsiyi is young. His body is strong. All we can do is watch and hope his body can fight it."

Despite standing in front of her parents, Thomas risked grasping Adsila's hand and squeezing it once more before releasing her.

A great commotion erupted nearby.

Turning, Thomas spotted soldiers coming through the camp.

Rations.

He'd best sit and prepare himself for his day's meal.

Chief John Ross was led by two soldiers. What did they fear from him? That he might run? Leave his wife and his people behind? Or did they think it would take two with rifles to subdue him? They need not concern themselves. He had no fight left in him.

His people had depended on him, and he failed them. They were suffering. Some had died. And they were all looking to him for answers. He had none. But he was still chief. And he would do every-thing in his power to ease the remainder of their confinement and eventual move to their new home.

The thought of it made him sick. *This* was their home.

No, not any more. Their homes were gone... destroyed, burned to the ground. Their possessions strewn about the fields, pilfered, plun-dered, destroyed.

The door to the general's office opened, drawing his attention forward.

One of the soldiers all but shoved him into the room.

The man he had never met, but had heard plenty about, sat behind the lone desk occupying the space—General Winfield Scott. This supposedly great military leader stared him down.

The general glared at him smugly. As if he were the victor and Ross the loser.

Did he regard Ross as his counterpart? The leader of the enemy army?

Nothing could be further from the truth.

This had not been a battle. Innocent people ambushed in their homes... dragged out... women and children...

And the treatment of his people... Ross doubted that the government treated even prisoners of war this way.

But this had not been a war. The Cherokee were not the enemy. And he was not the military commander of some organized army.

The two soldiers with Ross pulled him to the desk but did not untie the binds on his hands nor sit him in one of the chairs. They left him standing in front of the desk, facing the general.

"My captain has said you wish to speak with me," the general said, his crooked smile dropping. He turned his attention to other things on his desk. Was he so bored with the plight of the Cherokee? Had he better things to do than speak with the Cherokee Principal Chief?

It was too much. Ross tasted bile and felt heat rising into his face. Many things about this situation angered him. The least of which was not the way his people were treated. But nothing would be gained by a display of such emotion.

"Yes," was his only response.

"What can I do for you, *chief.*" General Scott fairly spit the word out and glanced up from his papers, but briefly.

"I wish to negotiate the voluntary movement of my people to our new home." It was difficult for Ross to speak it without his voice breaking, but he kept his tone strong and firm.

"You wish to what?" Now he had the man's attention. General

Scott's voice seemed caught somewhere between shock and laughter. "After all of this, *now* you want to just go? Voluntarily?"

Ross nodded. "Yes."

The general shook his head and slapped his knee. "Well, I never!" He laughed.

"I think," Ross continued. "It would be to your benefit for me to supervise the continuing removal process with, of course, military presence."

"And just why do I need you?" All hint of laughter was now erased from Scott's face. Replaced by a dark expression. "We seem to be doing quite well on our own."

"My people are in fences right now. Do you think when you try to march them that they won't try to revolt?" Ross countered.

"We gathered them from their homes rather... easily," the general argued, leaning forward.

"Do not take for granted what a band of Cherokee might do. Once together, we are stronger. And without that fence to protect your soldiers, I cannot guarantee what might happen."

The general became quiet. He watched Ross, studied him.

Ross held his chin high. Now was not the time to show weakness or indecision.

"What are you proposing? Not that I'm saying I believe you."

"Let me oversee the removal process, the movement of the Cherokee to the new land west of the Mississippi. Nothing will change except in the eyes of my people. They will see me leading them and not a military general. They will follow me and not make trouble."

"Everything will be the same?" the general asked, eyebrow quirked.

"I'd like it if your men were treating my people with a bit more respect." Ross's voice was level.

"Those are my orders. Any man not following my orders will have to answer to me," General Scott said, dismissing Ross's concerns. "We are agreed then?"

Ross had heard stories about atrocities that had occurred under the general's direct orders. He did not truly believe the man. But this may be the best he would get. So, he nodded.

"Good. We shall move out in a week's time.

Had he heard the general right? One week? They had been in this internment camp for almost a month, and he declares they shall leave in one week as if it means nothing to him!

Ross opened his mouth to speak, but was cut off as the general motioned for the two soldiers to take the chief back to the enclosure.

That was the last the chief was to hear on this matter.

TRAIL OF TEARS

Adsila stared up at the barren branches reaching down as if to snatch her out of the crowd moving along the trail. The earth had become cold and dead. Snow crunched under her feet. How long had it been since she felt warm? She couldn't remember. All she knew was this chill that pervaded her body. But she kept moving. There was no other option. So, she focused on putting one foot in front of the other, and then again.

They moved in silence. No one wished to expend the energy for conversation. Even if they did, what was there to say?

How are you today?

I'm cold.

Me, too.

Any of your family members die this week? Friends?

Survival was all that was relevant. And the prospect of continuing this journey for days, weeks, perhaps months on end made death look like a sweet release.

Still, she was comforted that her loved ones were still by her side. Tsiyi's illness had taken him far into the depths, but he was now well on his way to recovery.

She suspected Mother gave him her rations, but said nothing. Who would it hurt? Perhaps it was the extra nourishment that strengthened his body.

And Thomas was with them. She couldn't quite understand that. Why would he continue on this hard road with them?

Every day, she prepared herself that at any moment he would admit he'd had enough, that she wasn't worth the sacrifice.

But still he endured.

The depth of his consideration for her must be great. Indeed, he must love her.

She stole a glance at him.

He walked alongside her, arms crossed over his chest just as everyone else's, a feeble attempt to conserve heat.

His gaze turned to her. Did he feel her eyes on him? The weak smile she had become accustomed to broke across his features. And those eyes, which would have lit up under normal circumstances, remained serious.

Why shouldn't they? What they faced was serious.

The small smile he afforded her was all anyone could give under a weight such as they bore.

Her foot caught a tree branch, and she stumbled.

But Thomas's hands were on her—one around her waist and one gripping her arm. Of course, he would not let her fall.

Looking up at him, she nodded her thanks. But in this bitter cold, she could not even force a half smile.

He nodded and, as she regained her balance, he withdrew his hands.

She regretted the loss of contact immediately. It seemed his hands, his eyes were all that could bring warmth into her body.

At night, when they bedded down on the cold earth, the family units would huddle together for shared warmth. Thomas's spot was next to Tsiyi on the opposite side of her parents from where she lay.

How she longed for the private moments with him that had once been so easy! If only they could steal away for even a few minutes.

But that was not to be. Not in this crowd.

How long it would remain a crowd was uncertain. There were

deaths every day. Her people suffered from disease and cold. It was the worst nightmare she could imagine.

Worse yet, they had lost all hope.

All around her, she saw a people, once strong. Now all that remained was a crushed spirit. This once proud, great nation had been summarily defeated, pushed down, and broken.

There had been no news from Thomas for weeks and Lillian feared the worst. More than that, she knew. Deep down, she knew what had happened to her Tommy.

He joined the Cherokee people... joined *her* in their forced relocation.

Tears came anew, and Lillian did little to fight them.

What would become of her Tommy? Who could survive such a trek in this weather? Would the soldiers treat him with kindness because he was a white man? Or would they single him out with cruelty because he had chosen to side with the Indians? While she could not be certain, she feared the latter.

The front door opened. Was it Arthur? No one else was expected. He had come home rather late.

She wiped her eyes; there would be little tolerance for tears in Arthur's presence. He had a hard approach to Thomas's choices. Something about 'reap what you sow.'

The dinner hour would be here soon. No use having tears at the table.

Arthur's footsteps fell heavy on the floor as he came down the hall toward the parlor.

Lillian lifted her eyes to meet his gaze as he appeared in the doorway.

He looked into the room, his eyes searching. For her?

"For goodness sake's, Lillian, have the maid light a lamp! I can barely see anything in there."

Lillian stood. "I am well enough, dear." Clearing her throat. "But I will call for one of the maids as soon as we finish with dinner. I'll have her light as many lamps as we need to chase away the darkness."

He smiled. Or she thought it was a smile.

She did see him extend his arm. Rising, she went to him.

"I can't tell you how hungry I am. Shall we then?"

She nodded, wrapping her arm around his.

They walked the short distance to the dining room in silence.

What was there to say? All Lillian thought of was Thomas and his well-being. And that was the one subject Arthur refused to entertain.

And so, Lillian was made to suffer in silence.

Captain Samuel Jones found himself, yet again, face to face with Chief John Ross. The man was becoming a bit of nuisance. But Jones tried not to think of him that way. He was only concerned after his people and their welfare.

And things were not going well for them. Not at all. They lost more Indians each day. As much as he wished he could do something about it, he had his orders.

The chief approached him, and even from a distance, he saw that the man steamed. And why shouldn't he? There was everything in the world to be angry about and not too many things about which to be pleased.

"Why do we take such round about routes?" he demanded. "Don't think I haven't noticed! We are going out of our way to bypass villages and towns, making our trip that much longer!"

"Those are my orders, sir. Directly from the general." Jones met Ross's glare. If he could, he would duck his head in shame, but he dared not show such a display. No, he needed to stand his ground.

"Why? It doesn't make sense! Unless you're afraid the display of some poor Indians being mistreated will entreat the people to pity us."

Jones did not reply. How could he? What response would not be a lie and yet not affirm Ross's words?

"Can we at least pass closer?" Ross pleaded. "Anything to cut time off our journey. Can you not see my people are dying out here?"

Jones swallowed past a lump in his throat. But he dared not show what he felt to this man. "I am not blind to what happens under my purview, sir, but I have my orders. The routes have been laid out. I may not change them at will."

"Stubborn man!" Ross threw up his arms. "I can't imagine why you are so afraid of the populace coming in contact with us. Do you think we will contaminate them with our Indian ways?"

This man deserved an explanation, but it was not Jones's job to think. Dare he risk it? Just this once? After all, he was in command. Didn't he have *some* leeway to make decisions? "There is the concern of spreading disease."

"Spreading disease?" Ross's words echoed his expression—incredulous. "You prolong my people's suffering to keep the townsfolk from catching a cold? While *my* people are dying from these infections for lack of treatment?"

"We're doing all we can," Jones insisted, but he knew the military only provided fine words. That he was just spewing the same rhetoric. "We simply do not have the resources to provide care for this many people under these conditions."

Ross looked at him through narrowing slits. "I wonder, sir, if that would be the case if this was a group of white settlers instead of a group of Indians."

Jones had no response. Ross had spoken the truth, and there was nothing he could say to contradict it.

"If you have nothing further," Jones broke the silence, finding refuge from Ross's gaze by looking at his papers.

"Oh, I have more to say," Ross interjected. "But I fear it would fall on deaf ears." With that, he turned and marched out of the tent.

Jones, now alone, laid his head in his hands.

What have I done?

Thomas cleared snow by the base of a tree, making a suitable place for him to sit. He plopped down, taking the weight of his body off his aching legs. They tired of carrying him day after day on this horrid trail. Rubbing life back into his cold feet, his mind went to where it did of late: where was God in all this?

His time for prayer and reflection had seemed scarce. Yet all they had was time as they walked. Perhaps the real truth of it was that he hadn't wanted to pray. Did he not want to talk to God? He didn't like that thought, but he couldn't deny that it resonated. Why? Why would he not want to turn his heart, full of questions, full of hurt, over to the One who could do something about it?

An emotion rose in him. But it couldn't be. Not him.

Yet he didn't wish to lie to himself. That would not serve him.

He tested the emotion, examined it… Yes, he was angry with God.

But to run from Him because of anger would not fix anything. He had to face it.

Was God truly, as they say, big enough to handle human anger?

Where are You? Have You abandoned us?

Silence.

Didn't You call me to witness to these people? How then could You allow such suffering? How can you expect them to believe in a God that allows this?

Silence.

He gazed up at the sky, as if that would bring an answer. Drawing his knees to his chest, he laid his arms across them and dropped his head. He'd best not expect an answer. Not after so much silence on his end.

There was a gentle whisper. Faint. Not audible really. But he heard it.

Remember the Israelites.

It came on the edge of his mind. Like a caress.

Thomas looked up and glanced around. Was someone nearby? Had someone spoken to him?

Those closest were still several feet away and were engaged in their own conversations, almost all in Iroquois.

Remember the Israelites in the desert.

No, the voice came from within. His eyes fixed heavenward, *Yes, Lord, I remember.*

I led them through the wilderness, through the desert. Cloud by day, fire by night.

Thomas nodded. *Yes, Lord, I know. But I see no cloud, no fire to tell me You are here.*

But, You can know I am with you... always. Even now. I am guiding you. I am moving in your midst. I am hemming you in behind and before.

Thomas remembered Psalm 139 — how it spoke of God's enclosing His followers, laying his hand upon them. And Thomas's favorite part—that there is nowhere God's child can go where His presence is not.

You are great, Oh God, but I wonder... what of all this suffering?

Are not two sparrows sold for a cent? And yet not one of them will fall to the ground apart from My knowing. Know that I am with them in their suffering.

Thomas began to understand, as much as he could. This might very well be one of those things not intended for the finite mind of man. As he sat and continued to listen, he remembered in Romans 12 that the Lord spoke of His wrath. That vengeance was His, not Thomas's, not the Cherokee's.

Thank You, Lord, that You are with us, that you are enclosing us on this terrible journey. We need You, God, in a real way to be with us.

As he continued his prayer, a strange warmth filled him despite the cold temperatures. All remnants of the coolness left his body. It wasn't that he was not cold. Rather, he did not perceive it. Was this what it was like to feel the spirit move?

After some time, a touch on his shoulder shook him from his prayerful thoughts.

Looking up, he saw Adsila's concerned face.

"I was worried." Her brows furrowed, mouth turned downward. "You have sat here so still for a long time."

His features broke into a smile. "I was talking with the Lord."

She balked, but recovered quickly. "Come, night is drawing closer. They are delivering rations."

What was that reaction about? He wanted to ask her, but now was not the time. There would be another moment.

Rising, he took her hand and followed to where her family sat.

The warmth that had entered his body continued to surround his heart for the remainder of the evening and on into the night.

Even after it dissipated, he continued to hold God's words close.

Walter pulled his coat more tightly around himself as the wind shot a chill through his body. Thankful for his coat and the short distance he would travel outside, he picked up his step. An image of the Indians traveling in this same cold, almost all without the aid of an overcoat or even warm clothing came into his mind unbidden.

He paused.

They would walk for miles… for weeks in the frigid air. And here he was, worried about the few feet between the Capitol and his apartment. He felt so small, belittled by his realization.

As much as he wanted to continue the few yards that would find him safe and comfy in his apartment, he didn't want to be alone with these thoughts.

When he did put one foot in front of the other, it was to carry him to a nearby bar that served a decent sandwich. It would be warm there, but not too warm.

Perhaps he could sit by the door.

Why did he feel the need to punish himself?

Walter neared the establishment. It didn't look too crowded through the window. He caught the door as a man stumbled out, a little more inebriated than he would have expected for this early in the evening. Ignoring the man, he shuffled inside the sparsely decorated business and found a table in a corner where he could be left to himself.

A waitress came by soon after.

He ordered a sandwich and a beer. No sense being in a bar and not partaking. Perhaps a beer was just what he needed to dull this ache.

There wasn't anything else he could do about it anyway. Senator Frelinghuysen had proved as much. That man had done everything humanly possible to stop the Cherokee's removal. And all to no avail.

The waitress returned with his beer and sandwich in due time.

He took a long swig of the brew, hoping the alcohol would dull his senses. His gaze rested on the foam trail formed when he tipped the glass.

The foam was not unlike snow.

Snow-covered sidewalks and snow-covered paths...

He was so lost in thought, he hadn't noticed Harry until the man stood over him, his voice booming and slurring.

"Well, if it isn't my pal, Walter! Hey, guys, look! It's Walter!"

Walter raised his glass to Harry. "In the flesh." He took another long drink.

"It sure is nice to see you out in polite society, my friend." Harry slapped a hand on Walter's table. "I figured you'd be off somewhere crying about those Indians."

Walter gave Harry a harsh look. "You've had too much to drink, Harry." He turned his attention back to his sandwich and the amber liquid before him.

"No, I mean it." Harry nodded. "You've been moaning and groaning about those Indians like one of 'em was your own mother!" Harry leaned over Walter. A little too close. Walter smelled alcohol on Harry. Strongly. "Is that it, Walter? You really a red-skinned savage underneath all that?"

Rising, Walter threw some bills on the table to cover his order. "You've had too much to drink," he repeated. "I'm going home." He moved past Harry and toward the door.

"Aw," Harry called after him. The word was drawn out, exaggerated. "Now, don't go away mad, Sassagawatcha." He laughed at his own joke.

Walter stopped. "You don't know what you're saying." Walter spoke more for his own benefit.

Harry put his hand over his mouth, moving it so as to make a sound like a put on Indian war call.

Walter turned.

Harry clumsily pulled an imaginary bow and arrow back to shoot Walter.

Walter marched up to Harry, stopping only when he was in Harry's face. His voice was even, though his anger threatened to boil over. "You're drunk. You don't know what you're saying. Go home and sleep it off."

Harry stood to his full height. "Or what? You can't do anything! You... you spout off about the Indians, and look where it got them. You're just as impotent in your politics as Senator Frelinghuysen."

"You take that back," Walter seethed.

If possible, Harry rose a half-inch higher. "Impotent," he spat.

Walter threw a punch to his stomach; it found its home.

Harry's breath rushed out of him as he swung wildly at Walter.

But Walter evaded Harry's weak jabs at the air and landed another hit to the right side of Harry's jaw, knocking him to the floor.

There he crumpled and moaned.

Walter straightened, shaking his hand. "Now, go sleep it off."

Looking for the barkeep, he spotted the man several feet away, watching them. "Sorry, sir. I'll pay for any inconvenience."

The barkeep waved him away.

Walter understood—the man just wanted one of them out of the establishment.

He had no problem obliging.

Chief Ross walked along the trail with his head down, hands in his coat pockets. He had struggled over and over many times about his coat. Why should he have it? So many of his people barely escaped their houses—no, were driven from their homes—with naught but the clothes on their backs. There were many without shoes. It wasn't right.

He had offered his coat to many only to be turned down. Each person insisted that he needed to remain in good health, strong to fight for them.

Why must they be moved in this bitter cold? He blamed it for the loss of so many lives. His people were not so weak. In better weather, their bodies would be more resilient.

He watched the movements of those around him. Family units, staying close together, almost huddling as they walked… anything to fight this bitter cold.

Where was Quatie? He preferred his wife to stay close. But she frequently wandered among the people, ensuring what comforts she could provide.

There, she had gotten several paces ahead.

"Quatie," he called.

She looked over her shoulder. Smiling at him, she paused and let him catch up to her. "Yes, John?"

He took her hand. "You know I like to walk beside you."

She squeezed his hand. Her fingers were like ice.

"Put your hands in your pockets for a while. You will…" He glanced at her.

She frowned. "Do not be angry."

"What happened to your coat?"

She coughed. It didn't sound good. "There was a child a mile back. She cried because she was so cold. I just… I had to give it to her."

Ross drew his mouth into a thin line. Yes, Quatie would do whatever she could for their people, but at what cost? Her own comfort? Her own life even?

"Come here." He waved her closer.

She moved toward him.

He wrapped an arm around her. Could he shield her from the worst of it?

But as they walked along, they bumped into each other. Their steps became more laborious.

This is nonsense! He stopped.

She caught his eyes as she paused, too.

"You need this." He stretched his arms back and wrestled with the coat, sliding out of the arms.

"No!" She placed a hand on his arm, pulling at the opening of the jacket to keep him from making any more progress. "You can't!"

"Why not? You're my wife. I must see to your well-being."

"No." She shook her head. "Above all, you are my chief. And your life is valuable. Much more so than you think. You need to be a voice for our people."

Yes, he'd heard all this before. And he refused to hear it again. Opening his mouth, he caught her eyes and saw something there in those depths. Something he had only seen but few times in their many years of marriage. And he knew. It would be pointless to argue.

He groaned and shrugged the coat back on. Still, he drew her to his side again, encircling her as best he could.

"I may be your chief," he said for her ears only, "but you are my strength."

She snuggled as close as she could. "I'm sorry," she said after a moment.

"For what?" He was surprised at her apology.

"I know you are not happy with me for giving up my coat."

"You misunderstand." He looked ahead at those in front of them. "I am not happy with our circumstances."

She nodded.

"How could I fault your sacrifice? Your kind heart? Some of the things I love most about you."

Quatie was quiet.

Would things ever be normal for them? What would life be like once they reached their new land? They would be a different people, for certain, having endured this trek. But would they be stronger for it?

If more of them were like his Quatie, he was certain they would be just fine.

Adsila continued to trudge through the snow. The days melted together. How long had they been on this trail? Weeks? Months? She couldn't remember what summer felt like. Gazing up at the sun, she silently cursed it for its lack of warmth. Even nature had failed her people in these hard days.

Mother heaved beside her.

It drew Adsila's attention.

"Mother, are you well?" Adsila moved closer.

Mother shivered uncontrollably.

She had noticed the older woman had become thinner of late. Was it because she had given so much of her rations to Tsiyi while he was sick and recovering? While it was true they had all thinned from less food and excess of exercise, Adsila worried after the severe lack of anything on Mother's body. What was there to keep her warm? As she came closer, she heard Mother's teeth chattering.

"I… am… just… like… everyone… else. Cold." Mother's sentence may have been broken, but her voice was firm.

Adsila wanted to argue, but there was little point in it.

"Adsila…" Mother started, her voice low and quiet.

Drawing closer again, Adsila inclined her ear.

"I… want… you… to… know… that… I… listen… when… you… talk… of… Jesus," she said between chatters.

Adsila drew an eyebrow upward. Talk of Jesus did not help her heart. Rather it twisted an already pained place. Jesus was not a subject she wished to visit right now. She was not happy with Him. How could he let His creations suffer like this? How dare He claim to love them and then allow this!

"I… think… about… it… about… Ye… oh… waa… come… down… to… earth," Mother continued.

"Don't try to talk," Adsila mumbled. "Conserve your strength."

"You… need… to… know… that… I… believe. I… believe… in… Jesus."

Adsila nodded but she didn't know what to say. Too much pain filled her heart for her to be excited about her mother's faith. She wasn't even sure where her own was.

Just then, the soldiers called for a break in the trip.

Good. Rations would come. Maybe that would give Mother some warmth. Maybe.

Adsila walked Mother to a nearby tree and helped her settle at the base.

"Here," she said, smoothing a hand over the hair she had admired as a child. "Rest. I'll let you know when the soldier is here with your rations. And you must eat mine, too."

"No—"

"Yes," Adsila said, her voice firm. "You are too thin." She met Mother's eyes. How had Mother become so distant? Looking in her eyes disturbed Adsila greatly. Still, she could do nothing about that right now. Only day by day, she would help Mother regain her strength. Somehow.

Where were Father and Tsiyi? They must have been walking farther ahead.

It wasn't long before she spotted her father and brother a little ahead of where she and Mother had been as they walked. Thomas had already joined them.

Adsila waved.

They nodded at her and moved in her direction as people around them found places to sit for the short time they'd be allowed to stop.

"Where is Mother?" Tsiyi bounded up to Adsila.

"Over there." Adsila nodded behind her. "But don't bother her. She needs her rest."

"Shall we join her?" Thomas sounded tired, as tired as Adsila felt. They were the younger adults, the stronger and more capable of the small group. It was up to them to carry the weight of the family.

Adsila nodded and led them to where Mother slept, leaning against the oak's sturdy trunk.

As they approached, Adsila signaled for everyone to be quiet.

Poor Mother! How she suffered from the horrid weather and the never-ending journey.

They stopped several feet short of Mother. No one wished to end her peaceful rest one minute sooner than necessary.

"I wonder," Father said as they sat. "Greyson, what your God says about this."

Adsila sighed. She couldn't even muster the energy to be shocked by Father anymore. But she did wish to be anywhere else. How had she found herself in a conversation about God yet again?

Thomas nodded, slowly. "God's word tells us about His people, the Israelites. They went through great trials. They were enslaved for hundreds of years in Egypt. Many suffered, many died. They thought God did not hear them.

"And one day, He delivered them from their oppressors. Not the way they wanted to be rescued. But the way they needed to be rescued."

Father grunted. "So happy ending?"

Thomas frowned. "Unfortunately, not right away. They wandered in the wilderness for forty years. God led them, though they lacked faith many times along the journey.

"There is a song in the Bible that talks of how God leads His people, how He encloses them in before and behind. Though it is difficult to believe, He is with us. We may never understand His ways, His plan, or why we must endure such hardship. But that is what faith is about. Trusting when it is difficult."

Father grunted again.

Adsila looked down. This was a lot to think about. For each of them. What could Thomas expect them to think of a God that allowed this to befall their people?

The soldiers neared, handing out rations.

As much as Adsila hated to, it would be best to wake Mother so she could eat. She rose and walked to where Mother reclined.

Crouching in front of her, Adsila shook her shoulder gently but there was no response. Adsila gripped her more firmly and shook harder. Something wasn't right.

The shoulder under her hand... there was no semblance of warmth coming from Mother's body. She shook Mother harder, and shouted, "Mother!"

Nothing.

"Mother! Wake up! You have to wake up!"

A hand fell on her back. She didn't have to turn to know it was Thomas. He reached around Adsila to Mother's neck. His hand remained there for several moments, adjusting position a few times, before falling.

"No!" Adsila cried, shaking her head. "No! Mother!" She continued to shake her mother.

Thomas grabbed for Adsila's arms. "Please, Adsila. Leave her be!"

"No!" She fought against him. "No! Mother!"

Thomas pulled her against his chest. "Adsila, she's gone."

She continued to fight him, but weakened and drained, she relented and fell against him. And when he wrapped his arms around her, his embrace was tighter than she could remember.

Snow crunched.

She looked up.

Father stood over her mother's body.

Before she could speak, he released a loud mourning cry that pierced the silence, echoing in the forest, bouncing off the trees, as he sank to his knees. His cry became a song of sadness that her father sang right there in the middle of the wilderness.

Lillian stared at the back of Arthur's paper. It had become the norm between them. She on her chair, he on his. Apart. There might as well have been a gulf separating them. Where was their sense of camaraderie? It seemed to have followed Thomas out the door. Or had it been lost before then? Either way, the back of the paper had been her only companion these last weeks.

Turning back to her cross-stitch, she attempted to work the thread, but the stitches blurred. The rustling of paper drew her gaze upward. Arthur turned another page.

For a moment, she had hoped he might have noticed her tears and come to comfort her. Such a silly notion.

He grunted at some tidbit of news.

How much longer would they remain in this stalemate? Her heart was broken, and his heart had become hardened to the very thing that wounded hers.

Yes, they were quite the pair.

He chuckled. A throaty sound. Something in the article now amused him?

Her palms stung. She looked down to find that her hands had balled into fists. How much more could she take? How much was she willing to take?

No more.

Without another thought, she rose. Her cross-stitch fell to the ground, but she made no move to catch it.

Arthur glanced up from his paper. His brows rose. Did she, too, amuse him?

She met his gaze with an intensity all her own. "You can sit there and pretend, but I won't have it! I'm done!" The sharpness of her voice surprised even her.

"Lillian!" Arthur jerked back as if she had slapped him. She had never spoken to him like this. "Whatever could you mean?"

"What do I mean, Arthur?" Her hands opened and clenched at her sides. "I will no longer pretend that everything is well and good when our son" —her voice broke on the word, but she regained her strength and remembered her anger— "Our son is out there... somewhere... suffering, maybe dying. And you sit here with your *paper*, refusing to acknowledge his plight."

Arthur's eyes widened. His mouth moved ever so slightly. Was he trying to form words? Searching for the right ones?

But nothing came forth.

"If you so care, you will find me at Emma's house." She turned and stomped out of the parlor.

Nothing diverted her attention as she walked straight for the door, not the sense of what she had said, or the reality of what she was doing.

She had her wrap on before the maid could reach her and was out the door before the butler could grab for the latch.

Frelinghuysen entered the place he called home and closed the door behind himself, trying to keep as much of the winter weather out as possible. The dreariness need not invade his sanctuary. Today had been a tough one at the office. So many sad faces.

"Home at last," Charlotte said, coming down the stairs. A beautiful sight, lovely to his weary eyes.

He welcomed her into his embrace before he shrugged out of his coat.

"Let's get you in front of the fire with a hot cup of tea before you freeze." She rubbed his arms.

"I'm all right." He placed hands on her shoulders. "Just a little chilled."

"I insist all the same." She grabbed his hand and led him farther into the house.

Soon after, she had him seated as close to the hearth as possible with a steaming cup of his favorite tea. She took a seat nearby and watched as he sipped his body back to warmer temperatures.

He couldn't help but admire how the firelight danced in her eyes and highlighted her features. Truly, he was a lucky man.

"How did the staff receive the news?" She broke into his musings.

Taking a long swig of tea, he delayed his answer for a moment. The faces of those who had worked with him, many for quite some time, were easy to recall. Their resigned expressions, their saddened faces... but was it more for him or themselves? For some, the fact that he would not run again for his senate seat, would be a setback in their political careers. "It was as expected."

"Hmmm," she muttered, but said nothing further.

"I think it came as no surprise for several. But still it was hard news." He wrapped both of his large hands around the cup; they overlapped the delicate china.

"Will you invite any to come along in your bid for mayor?" Her eyes shone even brighter.

He had considered this very thing and thought on it anew as his gaze shifted to the fire. "There are those that would come along for the ride but only a few I would care to bring with me."

"Did any ask after your decision not to run?" Her voice had become soft, almost small.

He sighed and set his now empty teacup aside. "I didn't give them a chance to ask questions."

Charlotte wrinkled her nose, and her mouth made a thin line.

"I thought it best to tell the staff what I wanted them to know and leave it at that. It didn't seem wise to open myself to topics I wasn't prepared to discuss."

Her features softened somewhat, and she nodded.

He reached a long arm across the space between them.

Her hand met his in the gap.

"As long as we're a team we can weather any political storm."

She nodded. "But it's nice to have a supporter base."

Smiling, he nodded. He, too, remembered the early days when they first got into politics, when they had no one but themselves and their family and friends. It wouldn't be like that again. No, he had a constituent base now. A strong group of supporters back in New Jersey. They wouldn't be starting over again.

"And, we have God on our side. With Him, all things are possible," he said as he turned back toward the fire.

Charlotte squeezed his hand. "He has never led us astray."

CROSSING THE RIVER

Thomas huddled with Adsila's now smaller family by the river. Steamers would carry them across to continue their journey on foot. The Cherokee standing at the banks gathered close for warmth, but it was no use. Everywhere he looked, the people shivered. Nothing, it seemed, could chase the chill from their bodies. Still, they crouched together in futility for what shared body heat existed and perhaps for sake of camaraderie.

At last, the steamers finished their work for the day, carrying white passengers, and could avail themselves to the Cherokee.

Thomas motioned to Adsila as he stepped toward Father and Tsiyi, offering a hand to each. Their grief had taken more energy from them than they perhaps could afford. But he tried to encourage them forward. The sooner they were on the steamer and then to the other side of the river, the sooner this nightmare would be over.

But would it truly ever be over? Or would the journey echo in their minds? That was if they were to reach their destination. Or would they, too, die on this terrible trail of tears?

Shaking his head, he attempted to loose the thoughts from his mind. He had to plant his trust firmly in God's hand and believe that

God was with them, sustaining them. If he didn't, his faith would be lost. Yet another victim of this trial.

Now on their feet, Thomas pressed Father and Tsiyi to move forward, shuffling them through the crowd.

Adsila's presence was ever behind him, moving with him, albeit ever so slowly.

The loss of her mother had done serious damage. Her spirit was completely broken. Indeed, a part of her had given up.

And, for the first time on this journey, he sensed that she doubted they would reach their new land. Death had cut her deeply. More so than ever before. She became vulnerable, fearful perhaps.

It was too soon, the wound too fresh, her faith too young, for him to wager a guess as to how things would fall for her. Would she cling to God? Or turn from Him?

Drawing closer to the steamer, Adsila paused.

He turned. What could be so important that she would risk herself?

Then he heard it.

The distant cries of a small child.

Scanning in the direction of the cries, he found the source of the wails. But the scene surrounding the sorrowful mourning sounds caused his heart to sink.

A young girl pressed against her father. The man was motionless.

And Thomas knew.

He saw in the man's body what he had seen in Adsila's mother two days prior. The father was dead.

Adsila took a step in that direction.

Thomas reached out and grabbed her arm. He ached for the child, but he needed to get them on the boat. This family had endured too much. They couldn't take another loss.

"We must go!"

Adsila met his eyes. A deep sorrow flashed back at him.

The grief for her mother shone through, but he knew her. Regardless of what had happened, she would not leave this child to die in the cold.

With little effort, she pulled her arm from his grip and rushed in the opposite direction.

What was he to do? Should he follow her? Or ensure the safety of her father and Tsiyi?

Gawonii laid a hand a hand on his shoulder. The man took Tsiyi's hand in his and nodded. Something unspoken passed between him and Thomas. Gawonii would be well. And would ensure Tsiyi's safety.

Without a word, Thomas turned and pushed through the crowd, following the path Adsila had taken. When he reached her, she already knelt in front of the small child, encouraging her to release her father's arms.

The child refused, clinging to the lapels of the man's shirt, crying and pleading in Iroquois.

Thomas checked the man's pulse, shaking his head, but Adsila showed no surprise at his confirmation. Working together, they carefully disentangled the small child's limbs from her father's body.

Adsila gathered the flailing girl into her arms and spoke gently in Iroquois. Thomas did not need to know their language to guess that she asked after the child's mother.

The girl cried harder, now turning and holding onto Adsila, and spoke only a few words.

Adsila frowned.

And Thomas knew—the mother no longer lived either.

His heart softened toward the girl. Only just old enough to go to school and already an orphan. But there would be time to commiserate on that later. Their prospects here were not good.

He looked at Adsila. "We must get to the steamer!" It was their only hope of escaping this man's fate.

Adsila rose, trying to lift the squirming child, but she couldn't seem to raise the child more than a few inches off the ground. Had her body become so weakened from days of malnutrition and the intense cold?

Without a word, Thomas reached for the small girl, taking her from Adsila and gathering her close. He then grabbed Adsila's hand, tugging her to her feet, and moved toward the steamer.

He pulled at Adsila, but they could not seem to move fast enough.

They had to make it! Their odds of survival would decline drastically if they were forced to remain here any longer.

But as they neared the boat, he heard the unmistakable sounds of the steamer revving up. His heart sank. All they could do was stand at the bank and watch as the steamer pulled away.

What were they going to do? Remain huddled here? Face the same fate as this child's father? He couldn't let that happen.

He just…

Looking toward the sky, he thought, *Aren't you done testing me yet?*

Chief John Ross looked across the Arkansas River. His people's suffering weighed heavily on him. How many had they lost in the last week? As the days passed, the number grew, and he had a difficult time keeping count. They were into the thousands.

At some point, the reality of that growing number lost its bite. Had the dead become a faceless mass? Perhaps for a moment… for these next hours he would allow himself to be numb to the grief of those around him and he would be naught but 'John Ross,' the man who loved his wife.

For his Quatie had become ill.

A doctor had been found and was examining her even now.

Ross fought to keep his eyes open, exhausted from too many nights sitting up with her. He should sleep, but nothing could keep him from his constant vigil. Not then, not now.

A coughing fit racked her body. Everything in her seemed to vibrate.

The doctor glanced at Ross, slowly lowered his gaze, and shook his head.

Ross nodded, but his attempt to grasp the truth of it was akin to gripping water in hand—it continued to slip through.

How? Why? Had he not done all he could? Why then should his

wife be taken? Stripped from him? The one thing... the *one* thing he held to himself in this life.

The ship rocked them gently as they continued down the river, but nothing could soothe the gaping wound in his chest.

He wished the doctor would leave so he might let loose some of this emotion.

"John..." The tender word was soft, raspy.

Looking at the one who was dearest to him in the world, now in his arms, he clenched his jaw. Would that stave off the tears?

Weak hands pulled at his jacket.

Did she fear he would not listen? She was his world. Had he given her reason to doubt that?

He gazed into the kind face of his wife.

"John," she repeated, the effort of talking brought on another coughing fit.

When it subsided, she opened her mouth.

He found his voice, "Quatie, save your strength."

She shook her head. "I need you to know..."

He cupped her face with a shaking hand. "I do know." A tear escaped his well-guarded exterior.

"You must be strong. For our people." Her voice was not much more than a whisper, her breaths ragged and raspy.

He nodded. But how? It wouldn't be possible. Not without her.

"And I... I..." She gasped for breath.

It would not come.

He pulled her more tightly to himself, hugging her body against his.

But he could not hold back the loud mourning cries as he held his wife. In a matter of moments, her journey came to its end.

Walter kicked off his shoes and flung them across the room.

That was that.

Frelinghuysen was done with Washington, D.C.

Just as well! So was he. He'd had his fill of Washington politics. A lot of difference he'd made when it really mattered.

He scanned his small apartment—an eclectic collection of random things he had picked up along the way. Things from his childhood and on through the years.

Home.

Should he go back home? Not that anyone there cared much for his opinion on anything. He couldn't make a difference there.

That was the root of it—he wanted to make a difference. But where? How? He still cared about what happened to the Indians, but their fate was sealed. Or was it?

He pinched the bridge of his nose and fell back across his bed. Great. A headache was the last thing he needed.

He pulled his hand away from his face and stared at the ceiling. What was it Frelinghuysen had said? About God? About prayer? Could it be true? Could the same God that created everything truly care about what happened to him? It seemed like a nice idea, but not something he was ready to put stock in.

"Are you there, God?"

Nothing.

Just as I thought.

Sighing, he got up and walked across the room to pick up his shoes. One of the shoes had knocked into a side table and caused a book to fall. He picked it up. Rubbing a hand across the cover, he saw it was the Bible Senator Frelinghuysen had given him. One of the pages had become crumpled when it fell.

He opened it to smooth out the page. His eyes caught the words at the top: *"For I know the plans that I have for you," declares the Lord, "Plans for welfare and not for calamity to give you a future and a hope."*

Plans. *God has plans for me? What plans does He have? Plans I can get excited about? Or plans to be a missionary in Africa?*

He walked the Bible to his chair and sat, looking over the page. Dare he read further?

"You will seek Me and find Me when you search for Me with all your heart."

There it was again—prayer.

Frelinghuysen had talked about how important it was. They had even prayed together. But it hadn't changed anything. Walter still felt lost. Useless. All his efforts had been wasted. Still, he turned the Bible over in his hands, loving the leather of the binding.

Could this book be more than it seemed?

Adsila placed her feet on firm ground. The steamer trip had not been pleasant. Her body might have ached from walking, but it had wrenched and churned from the movement of the boat.

No, the trip, though short, had seemed an eternity to her stomach.

Thomas had been helpless to do anything to comfort her, as he held onto the orphaned child.

It had been fortunate a second steamer came along soon after the first departed. Their chances were much improved.

Now on the other side of the river, she searched the crowd for Father and Tsiyi. But the moving bodies blurred together, and she could not make them out. Perhaps they had moved on.

A hand pressed her shoulder and she turned.

Thomas. An unspoken question in his eyes. Had he, too, been searching for Father and Tsiyi?

She shook her head and he frowned.

"We will have to keep moving," he said, adjusting the child on his hip. "We will come across them along the way." He seemed confident, but she knew he was just as worried as she.

They all needed to be together, to look after one another, to keep each other safe. But there was nothing more they could do here. So, she conceded, falling in step with the rest of her people as they moved ever forward toward their promised destination.

Thomas had the little girl walk at times, but mostly he carried her. At first, she was closed to them, but as the day wore on, she exchanged smiles. Particularly with Thomas. And she shared her name—Salali.

When they stopped for evening rations, it was not a moment too soon. Adsila became more and more certain that her feet would fall off, and the temperature had already started to drop. The day had been cold, but the night promised to be every bit as frozen as any other night on this dreadful trail—downright frigid. Without the others for added warmth, what would she and Thomas do?

Would she and Thomas lie side by side? There didn't seem to be any other option.

As she and Salali finished their rations, Thomas began clearing the snow near a tree. She did notice that he cleared only one space. Perhaps he did intend for them all to lie together.

She watched him, a tingling sensation running through her limbs. From the cold?

He met her gaze and offered a small smile before resuming his work.

She turned away but could not turn her thoughts. What would it be like in a position so intimate with Thomas? There, of course, would be nothing inappropriate. Not in the cold, surrounded by so many, and he such a gentleman.

Still, it did make her wonder.

She yawned. As did Salali.

Thomas's hand appeared in front of her face. "The place is as ready as it will be."

Following the outstretched hand all the way to his eyes, a slight warmth crept into her face.

Would he notice? Hopefully not!

She slid a hand into his and let him pull her to her feet. He then leaned over and gathered the child into his arms.

How had Adsila not noticed that Salali had started to drift into sleep?

Thomas strode toward the place he prepared. Once there, he laid Salali on the cleared spot, but Adsila remained rooted where she was.

Thomas seemed surprised that she had not followed him. Lifting an arm toward her, he beckoned her.

She encouraged her feet to move, but they wouldn't.

He looked down at Salali and then to Adsila. Was he attempting to make a choice?

It had not been her intention to put him in such a position. She forced her feet to move once more.

His brows furrowed; his features spoke of his concern as she approached. He held out his hands for hers.

Should she place herself in his care? He had never given her reason not to trust him. So she did, putting her hands in his.

"Is something wrong?" Thomas's eyes softened.

"I find myself... uneasy... about this." She shivered. Because of the breeze or because of this conversation?

His eyes moved over her face like a caress. "If there was any other way..."

"I know."

"It is not my intention to take advantage of the situation—"

She put a hand on his chest to stop him. "I do know that. It's just... a lot."

He nodded.

They stood watching each other for a moment.

"How about you sleep with Salali, and I'll be nearby against the tree. I don't want to be far—"

"No... It's all right. I think you are right. Neither Salali nor I will be able to keep the other warm enough. Not as much as if we all three..." Her sentence trailed off as she stared into his eyes.

He wrapped his arms around her. "You can trust me," he said into her ear.

"I never doubted that."

And so, they lay on either side of Salali, keeping the small girl between them to provide her the greatest warmth.

As the minutes stretched into hours, Adsila continued to lie awake, staring at the sky. She comforted herself with the deep, rhythmic breathing of the two sleeping beside her.

Still, she kept her face toward the stars. Was Mother up there somewhere? What had Mother's faith brought her? Contentment in some afterlife? Peace in death?

A death that should have been prevented?

How long Adsila lay there, considering these things, she did not know, but after some time, Thomas's breathing shifted. Had he awakened?

His hand covered her shoulder. "Adsila?"

"Um hm?" She did not turn toward him, but fixed her gaze on the sky.

"What are you thinking about?" His voice was deep, but soft.

"Many things." A tear escaped her eye.

"Thinking about your mother?"

She closed her eyes to keep more tears at bay. "I think of many things," she repeated.

"Please, tell me." His fingertips grazed her cheek. His touch was so gentle on her face, as if he sought to soothe her features as much as his voice sought to soothe her aching soul.

"I do think of Mother. But I also think about Father and Tsiyi— where they are, how they are doing. Are they safe? Are they well? I think about how we're going to survive.

"I think about Salali. She's an orphan now. She has no one. What will become of her?

"I think of my people. What will become of us? We are all much like Salali—orphaned, homeless."

She sniffled.

"The government says we have a new home. But will we be safe there? Or will they take this home away from us, too? Nothing can be for certain."

She turned toward Thomas.

His features displayed his concern.

"There is great turmoil in me, Thomas." She sighed. "And I wonder... where is God?" More tears fell. "Where is your God in all this?"

He didn't speak for several moments. Was he searching for the right words?

Her sadness was a deep ache in her chest now, and her body shook as tears came.

Thomas's breathing became ragged. Was he so moved?

She pierced him with her gaze, letting her anger cover her grief. It was safer. "Where is He? I trusted Him. I believed in Him. And He took my mother."

Thomas took a deep breath. "There are no good words for times like this. But God does not promise us tomorrow. Or a safe life. Or even a pleasant one. The one thing He does promise is that He will be with us. And I believe He is."

Adsila frowned. "Where? Where is He?" The anger grew, taking on a new form. "In this child's tears? Is that where He is? In all this death? Is that where you see Him? Where do you see Him, Thomas? Because I cannot."

Thomas became quiet, and she turned away. It wasn't fair to make him bear the brunt of her anger. Hadn't he been through the same nightmare she had? How could he not share her doubts? Whether or not he realized it, he didn't have the answers.

This winter would never end. What was the date? The days drudged by on this horrid trail, and there didn't seem to be much use in keeping track of them.

Richard Clement grumbled and took a swig of his now chilled coffee. It was impossible to keep anything warm for any length of time. But at least he was slightly better off than the Indians. They dropped like flies! Sickness and the elements took their toll on the Cherokee.

At first it had bothered him, all the deaths. But now, it had become almost common. He'd been numbed to it all.

Private Burnett stepped out of his tent, stretched, and shivered in one fluid movement.

"Harsh morning?" Richard almost smiled.

Burnett nodded, shaking.

Richard handed him a cup of cold coffee.

The private felt the mug and frowned.

Richard shrugged and turned his attention to cleaning his rifle.

"Wonder how many deaths we had last night," Burnett mused.

Richard grunted. It was a wonder that Burnett still cared. But he was young. This took its toll on him in a very different way.

Burnett sat and crossed his arms. An attempt to conserve heat? Laughable. He pulled his jacket tighter around himself. Marginal.

"Guess this is a Christmas Eve we'll never forget." Burnett took a sip.

"Christmas Eve?" Could it be?

Perhaps the Cherokee deaths weren't the only thing Burnett kept track of. Everyone else had stopped counting the calendar days, too.

"Yep." Burnett looked off into the distance.

Richard thought on it for a moment. What would his family's day be like?

This holiday was all about family at his home. He should be with them, not out here in this wretched wasteland escorting Indians. Who knew if there would be any of them left to inhabit the land they were promised? Whenever that was.

What would his family think of what he had done? He prayed they would never know.

"I wonder if they'll give the Indians a reprieve from walking tomorrow," Burnett said.

"Doubt it." When did he become so apathetic?

Burnett's gaze rested on him, but he didn't speak.

Just as well. I'm not in the mood for any handholding.

Knock, knock, knock.

What was that sound?

Walter pulled himself out of bed. Hadn't he heard something?

Knock, knock, knock.

The door. Someone was at the door.

He glanced down at his rumpled clothing. He hadn't even bothered to change before falling into bed last night. Quite a sight. The last couple of days had been full. Long nights and late mornings did not help. For certain he could benefit from a shower.

Would they go away?

The knocking continued.

He sauntered toward the door, praying it was nothing more than the neighbor or the some other such nuisance.

But as he pulled the door back, he found himself face-to-face with Senator Frelinghuysen. Immaculately dressed, as always, with top hat and coat in place.

They would stand in stark contrast to one another if any were unfortunate enough to see them, with Walter appearing a mess of untucked clothes, haggard hair, and unshaven face.

Frelinghuysen's eyebrows shot up.

Not that Walter needed the reaction to feel shamed.

"C-Come in, sir," Walter said. If it wasn't bad enough, his words were slurred. How deeply had he been sleeping?

He waved his boss in as he stumbled backward into his apartment.

"Good gracious, Mr. Buckner," Frelinghuysen said, taking off his hat and stepping through the doorway. "Have you been drinking?"

Walter's face heated. "No, sir. I... was up late. Praying. I only now awoke. Forgive me," he said, pressing a hand to his forehead. "I think I'm still half-asleep."

"Praying?" The senator seemed truly shocked. Perhaps more so than if Walter had said he intended to join the circus.

Walter nodded. "Yes, sir. And reading."

"Reading?" The man's eyes were still wide. Was he so disbelieving?

Thoughts began to cut though the fog of his sleep-soaked brain. He smiled and shook his head as he moved farther into the apartment. "Are you just repeating me?"

"No... that is, not intentionally," the senator stumbled over his words. Did he still not believe Walter?

Now in the small space Walter called his great room, he motioned for the senator to sit on an old armchair, while Walter pulled a dining chair over.

The senator eased into the seat, still watching Walter as if he waited for something. An explanation perhaps?

Silence fell in the space.

"Can I get you anything, sir? Coffee? Tea?" Walter started to rise.

"No, I thank you." Frelinghuysen held out a hand. "I am intrigued to hear more about this... Bible reading."

So that was it. He was cautiously reserving judgment.

"Yes." Walter settled back down. "I sort of found myself picking up the Bible the other night, truly for the first time, and was quite unable to stop."

Frelinghuysen nodded and cleared his throat. "And..." His words came slowly. "What have you discovered?"

Was this yet another question to determine the truthfulness of his claim? Walter pushed that thought to the side. This wasn't about the senator. How could he put it into words? Everything that came to mind seemed inadequate.

He needed to say what was on his heart.

Taking a deep breath and letting it out, he hoped his gaze spoke to his confidence. "I found a God I never knew—a God who cares about me, Who is intentional, and Who has a plan."

Frelinghuysen leaned back. He seemed thoughtful.

"Even a plan in all this mess."

One of the senator's brows arched.

"It's been hard to see that. Still is, I think. But that's where faith comes in—*real* faith. Those times when belief becomes... challenging."

Frelinghuysen nodded. And... could it be? Smiled?

"Seems as if you have something."

"I tell you, sir, I've experienced so much... freedom in the last couple of days, as I've come to know God."

"I know quite well what you mean." Frelinghuysen's smile broadened.

Then there was that silence between them.

"Did you... I mean, was there something you needed, sir?" Walter gripped the arms of the chair. Otherwise he might slump. And that may find him soon off to sleep. He had only stopped reading for rest perhaps three hours ago.

"Yes." Frelinghuysen straightened, shifting his hat to his other knee. "I have come to admire a lot of things about you, Mr. Buckner. You have good work ethic. But it's more than that. You have principles. And passion. You care about the people who rely on you, who count on you to speak for them."

"Thank you, sir."

"And I hoped you would consider coming with me to New Jersey. I need men like you on my team—running my campaign and, eventually, my staff."

Walter feared he wouldn't be able to speak. Such high compliments from a man whose opinion he valued. But, as he needed them, the words came.

"I… I'm honored by your words. And that you would think of me."

The senator's eyes brightened. "So, that's a yes?"

Walter paused. If he had learned anything from his reading, it had been that moves like this required prayer. He shot Frelinghuysen one of his half grins, hopefully a charming look. "I'll have to give it some prayerful consideration."

The smile that marked the senator's face was the first truly happy expression Walter thought he had ever seen on the man.

"You wouldn't be the man I want for the job if you didn't."

There was no fanfare the day the Cherokee arrived in their promised land. A solemn silence ushered them into their new home. The large group that had wandered for so many months joined the small contingency that had already laid claim on the land as part of the voluntary relocation. Together at long last.

Those who had already established themselves welcomed the Cherokee that had trudged through the winter months with open arms, taking the more serious cases — those sick and ailing — into their established homes. The season had started to turn and the weather became milder each day. Shelter was no longer the dire necessity it had been. Still, the Cherokee worked together to build tents and teepee homes.

Thomas, though exhausted and spent physically, emotionally, and spiritually by the journey, took much joy in this experience. He would not be parted from Adsila as she searched for Father and Tsiyi.

Their reunion was brief and sweet before their attentions turned toward creating shelter. Nothing more was spoken of Mother's absence.

This did not surprise Thomas. These people were survivors. They had proven that quite well. And they would continue to strive for their livelihood. Come what may.

Once things calmed somewhat, Thomas became eager to find solitude. After having been surrounded by crowds constantly for nearly a year, he needed time to think on all that had happened. Time to reflect on the impact to his faith. And whatever was between him and Adsila.

What would he do now that he had seen this thing through? Would he go east? Would he seek another mission field? Or was his future here?

The bright spring afternoon drew Thomas up a nearby hillside that overlooked the valley opposite the large settlement. This was his place. His refuge where he found solitude and peace.

Sitting cross-legged on the ground, he breathed in the scent of the coming spring. The fragrance of sweet grasses filled his senses.

Life from the earth, hope anew.

His eyes slid closed, and he raised his face toward the heavens.

But prayer would not come. Was he too distracted by his lack of faith? His doubts? Or that he hadn't had the answers Adsila sought in her grief? Nothing for her pained heart in need of reassurance about God?

Didn't God call him to minister to these people? To be a light?

And in a moment of great weakness and need, Thomas had failed them, had failed *her*.

His head dropped.

It was not that God faltered. But that he, Thomas, doubted.

And so, after all this, where did he stand with God?

Or with Adsila?

The time they had needed to strengthen their bond and be sure of what they were to one another never came. It, too, had been taken, stolen when they were collected by the soldiers.

He never was assured of how she felt about him. And he feared his heart might soon be beyond repair, that he could find himself at her mercy. And that was a place he didn't want to be… completely lost to himself.

Lillian sat in Emma's parlor, chatting about the changes she had made to the room. The curtains were a nice touch—sewn by Emma herself. And the furniture had been rearranged to take better advantage of the fireplace this winter. It also made more use of conversation spaces. All in all, Lillian overflowed with compliments for her daughter's good taste and homemaking skills.

The butler stepped into the room.

"Yes, William?" Emma set her teacup on its saucer.

"Mr. Greyson has arrived. He wishes to see Mrs. Greyson."

Emma shot her mother a look.

So, he comes at last. Lillian nodded.

"Please, do show him in." Emma set her teacup and saucer on a nearby side table. She stood then, running her hands along her skirt, smoothing down any creases.

Lillian mimicked her actions.

It wasn't long before they heard the twin set of footfalls coming toward them.

Lillian held her breath. How would Arthur be? Apologetic and pleading? Or perhaps angry, demanding that she return home at once?

Two heartbeats later, Arthur stood in the doorway. When his eyes met Lillian's, his eyes betrayed a sadness, his features an apology.

"Father," Emma stepped to Arthur and embraced him.

He welcomed her affection.

As Emma pulled back, she glanced between them. "I'll leave you to speak in private." She stepped into the hallway, closing the door behind herself.

Lillian and Arthur's eyes met again.

Then he looked away.

There was silence in that space between them. Arthur clasped his hands and twirled his thumbs.

Lillian sat down. Placing her hands firmly on her knees, her gaze was glued on Arthur, watching, waiting.

He glanced in her direction from time to time, but did not speak.

Was he waiting for her to say something? To make this easier?

She was not about to. Not after the way he had behaved.

At long last, he cleared his throat and shifted his gaze to meet and hold hers. "Lillian," he started in a somewhat uncertain tone. "It seems I owe you an apology."

Then came that silence again.

What was he waiting for? She refused to help him in this.

One of his eyebrows lifted. Then both furrowed. "That is, I have come to say… to admit rather… that I may have been a bit… harsh with Thomas."

She nodded, blinking. The mention of Thomas's name caused her to well with emotion.

Arthur took slow, tentative steps toward her. He sat beside her, taking one of her hands in his. "You must know, Lillian, I am every bit as worried as you. I only hide my concern behind a perhaps too calloused exterior. And I apologize if that has hurt you."

She felt moisture on her face. Yes, she was hurt. Hurt by him and pained by the fears of what may have befallen her Tommy.

Arthur lifted a hand to wipe away a tear. "It *will* be all right."

"How can you know that?" Lillian's voice broke.

"Because I know who holds the future." He offered her a half smile. "And He is capable."

Adsila helped Salali stretch out inside their family tent. The small child was beyond tired, and Adsila was ready to have her rest for a couple of hours. Taking on the added responsibility of a young child had not been an easy fit, but it suited her. Taking care of Salali gave Adsila something to do, something to keep her mind off Mother, and more importantly, an excuse to keep Thomas at arm's length.

Since their arrival, she had successfully avoided being alone with him. It wasn't that she no longer cared for him. Quite the contrary. Her emotions overwhelmed her. He had become so much more to her in these last months. It almost seemed he was a part of her now. Was that possible? She didn't like the way it felt to be so dependent on someone. Or what it might be like to lose him.

Between her thoughts of Thomas, her intense grief over the loss of Mother, and dealing with the hard work of re-establishing a community, she hadn't the time to sit down and sort it out.

How could she talk to him about her feelings when she could hardly think about it without bursting?

"Adsila?" Salali's sweet, but tired voice called.

"Yes?"

"Will you sing to me?" The girl's innocent brown eyes pled. How could Adsila say no?

Shifting her legs, she settled herself more comfortably and began a lullaby. Salali loved these lullabies, but they cut through Adsila's heart. They were Mother's songs. Not even a year ago Mother sang these words to Tsiyi.

The song came to a close. Adsila wiped at a tear and looked down at Salali.

Her eyes were closed and her breathing was even and deep.

Adsila slowly slipped free of the child's body and crept out of the tent.

Once outside, she raised her arms and let the muscles have their release. She closed her eyes and enjoyed the feel of the sun on her skin. Warm. Finally.

Where had everyone gone? Oh, yes. Father went to a council meeting, and Tsiyi was off causing some manner of trouble. She spotted

Thomas several feet away, speaking with a young man she didn't recognize.

His eyes caught hers, and he motioned for her to wait a moment.

Adsila moved off in the opposite direction, stepping as quickly as she could. She went between tents and small groups of chatting people until she broke free of the village.

Now alone, and only now, she could breathe. Taking in a deep breath, she closed her eyes. As she held the breath, she imagined it cleansed her body and renewed her strength. Then she pushed it out through her mouth fast and hard.

Eyes open again, she continued the few steps it took to reach the stream. The water was every bit as refreshing as the stream back home.

Home.

She shook her head. *I have to stop thinking like that.* When she had more time, she would explore this stream farther away from the village. This place was far too close for her to feel alone, but she dared not venture too far with Salali sleeping. Still, it would do.

She settled herself on the bank and listened to the sound of the water, allowing the simple glub-glub of the tripping water to calm her spirit.

Adsila had not thought much about the state of her spirit. But hadn't she given up on faith? On God? After watching her people suffer and die... anyone would. No good God would allow that. What was out there in the spirit realm? Did she believe in anything beyond herself? Did someone or something control the earth and the great forces of nature? Even the ways of man? Of powerful men?

A loud cry rang out from the village.

Adsila startled, putting a hand in front of her, prepared to jump to her feet.

The cry rang out again.

A call for help.

She was on her feet in a moment and running toward the voice.

A small crowd had gathered by the time she arrived. People pressed in and spoke rapidly to try to assist the poor man.

Someone spotted her.

"Here is hope!"

Her? Hope?

The woman who had shouted about her grabbed her wrist and pulled her through the thick of people to the man.

He looked desperate, harried, scared. His hands went to her shoulders. "My wife… she's in labor. So much pain!"

Adsila shook her head. "No." She looked around at all the eager faces. "You don't understand. My mother was a midwife. She died. I cannot help."

"But you were with her when my youngest was born. I know you were," the woman who first spotted her argued.

"Please," the man begged. "I don't want to lose my wife."

"Where is the doctor?" As soon as she said it, she knew. He would be at the council meeting. Far, far away.

Someone pushed through the crowd. "What's going on here?"

Thomas appeared, concern shone plain on his features. "Adsila, are you all right?"

She nodded.

The young man looked to Thomas and swallowed. "My wife is dying."

Adsila put a hand to his upper arm. "You don't know that."

"Will you help then?" The man's voice lifted.

"I will try. But, I don't want you to have false hope…"

Thomas stepped to her side. "You are capable of more than you think."

She met his gaze.

He loved her. He truly did.

"And I will be praying."

In that moment, she wanted that. So very much.

Turning her attention toward the young man, she nodded. "Let's go."

He spun toward the collection of tents.

Just before she stepped after him, Thomas reached for her hand and squeezed it.

The simple contact ignited something in her. A fire. It traveled through her body, giving her strength and comfort.

She prayed that if God were there, He would help her recall what she had learned.

Chief Ross cleared his throat. He had gathered the men of all the village councils together. They were greater in number than he had dared hope. Although, still fewer than they should have been. It would be their job to establish a new governing council for the new land and give the people some sense of continuity.

"Gentlemen," he said, standing. "I cannot tell you how honored I am to see every face present. We have endured much these last months, and there is not one among us who cannot speak of great loss. But I charge you now to put that to the side. Let it fuel your passion to continue on. For we must forge ahead and lead our people. We cannot remain in the past. Certainly not in a past as trying as the one we have walked through."

There was a space of silence. He would allow anyone to speak that wished to.

No one spoke. No one said anything about their losses. No one spoke of the recent murders of the Cherokee men who had signed the much-opposed treaty. It came as no surprise though. Any Cherokee would have known when they signed it that they signed their own death warrants. This was just how things were done. And that's why no one questioned it now.

"It is up to us, men. We will once again be the strong people we have been for centuries. We will let the U.S. Government know that though they may take away our land, they cannot take away who we are. We are Cherokee. And we are united."

Adsila had never been so tired. The intensity of the birth and the relief as the baby cried was beyond compare.

When she handed the small wriggling bundle to the woman who withstood more pain than Adsila could have imagined, she wanted to collapse against the wall.

Instead, she took a step back and watched.

A baby had been born. A new life had entered the world. And she had been a part of it. More than that, this was the first baby to arrive since they arrived in their new home.

Despite herself, it brought a smile to Adsila's face.

A blessed child, even, to have been born in the spring, when the earth brings forth fresh life.

The father was allowed into the room and he rushed to his wife's side. It was as if he didn't know where to look first—the face of his beloved, or that of his child. He kissed both with equal ferocity.

And all of a sudden, she became the intruder. She slipped from the room and, though her body ached, she walked toward the stream.

Spring had always been her favorite season... new life after a season of death.

She halted.

That was so. The earth moved in seasons, cycles. Perhaps that was true of life as well. None could stop it, none could tame it.

Maybe...

Maybe in a sense, the trail they had walked... was their winter. Now came spring, and new life. New life for Salali, for this baby, for her people, even for her.

Could it be that life was a rhythm? A time for winter, for death, for mourning. And a time for newness, for spring?

But why was there winter? Need there be such death? Such suffering?

Was there an answer? Or perhaps it just is. Is there is no answer for death? Maybe it, too, just is.

And that would make faith all the more important—faith in the winter knows that the spring will come. Trust that there is life after death. For what is faith without trust?

Thomas…

Perhaps, spring meant a new life, a new hope for her and Thomas, too. Her heart stirred at the thought of what that might mean. Yes, she could no longer imagine a life without him. And she had let that scare her. Scare her into pushing him away.

But fear was not the way. No, in this she needed to trust also. Trust in him. Trust in the love she felt for him.

Realization poured over her.

She *loved* him. She truly loved him. Where was he? She had to tell him!

Dusk had fallen. The sounds of the village were but a noisy din, somewhat muted, from where Thomas sat. He loved this spot, perched on the hill overlooking the valley where the village rested. But he couldn't bring himself to join in.

Did he belong?

It was no longer a certainty.

As much as the people became more welcoming since he walked the trail with them, Adsila had become all the more distant.

Wasn't it clear? She didn't love him.

And so he sat, deep in thought. So much had gone wrong. He was not the missionary he was sent to be. He'd had doubts. Adsila didn't love him. Perhaps because he'd failed her, too. Maybe it was time for him to pack it up and head home.

But where was home? Charlotte? That didn't seem like home anymore.

Gazing at the heavens, he longed for a word, for direction.

Nothing.

Sensing he was being watched, his eyes fell forward again. And there she was.

Adsila.

He was on his feet faster than he thought possible.

"Thomas, I—"

"Adsila, you don't have to explain. I understand." He found it diffi-cult to look her in the eye. "I've failed you. I wasn't there when you needed me. In the way you needed me. How can I ask for anything from you? I want you to know that I'm leaving tomorrow. I—"

"Leaving?"

"Yes, I just... I don't know where I belong." Unable to show his pain any longer, he looked away.

She took a step toward him. "Don't know where you belong? A failure?"

"Please..." He wanted to beg her not to taunt him.

"Thomas, you have been my strength when I had none. My hope when all was lost. How can you even think—?" She choked on the word. "You belong," she said, leaning forward, a breath away from his lips. "With me." She pressed her mouth to his.

He responded but held something back.

Her hands found his and intertwined their fingers.

When they broke apart, he had great difficulty finding his voice. "But I have lost my way." His voice was quiet, uncertain.

"Then we'll find it... together."

Their lips met again. His heart swelled anew.

Yes, he was lost to himself. And she had become everything to him. She was home.

He wouldn't have any more answers for her tomorrow than he did yesterday, but maybe, just maybe, that would be all right.

EPILOGUE

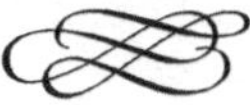

Dearest Mother and Father,

I hope this letter finds you well. I apologize that I haven't written in some time. Your letter arrived well enough. I cannot imagine what Emma will do with another baby in the house, but I am certain, Mother, that you are excited. Please, tell Emma that I, too, hate she missed our wedding. If only it had been possible for us to have all been together.

The village continues to grow strong. Truly, the Cherokee are an independent and hard-working people. We started classes again. There isn't a schoolhouse yet, so we meet near the stream, but the children are happy to learn, and I am happy to teach them.

Tsuji decided he would like to take up teaching, so I am training him as well. Hopefully, he will be able to take a class of younger students soon. There is a great need for teachers.

And Emma is not the only one with good news. Adsila and I are expecting a little brave next spring. We are so excited, but I must confess I am also nervous. Adsila is radiant. She has a special glow about her. Salali could not be more excited about a baby brother or sister.

I cannot say enough how much your support has come to mean to me. I know it is not easy, and there are many, if not all of your friends and connections, that do not understand or accept my new life. On that count, your approval means everything. I look forward to hearing from you soon.

Your loving son,
Thomas

Keep reading for a preview of the first book in the Cripple Creek Series!

Thank you, dear reader, for for reading along with me! If you enjoyed this story, I would sincerely appreciate if you would submit a review. It would mean so much to me!

The stagecoach moved along, bumping and rocking as it went. Trees and other green scenery whisked by the window. Views of mountains and open plains were visible from the seat of the coach, vistas familiar to its occupant. Katherine Matthews was coming home. She returned to Cripple Creek, no longer the scared, unsure teenager who had left to further her education so many years ago with hopes and dreams of a new life in a new place. No, she had matured into a confident young woman who had grown in stature and in beauty. Her hair was no longer the mousy color she always hated, for it had deepened into the same beautiful chestnut brown she had always admired in her mother's appearance. She'd grown out of her awkward teenage features, and was now well regarded among her peers as a rather handsome woman.

Returning to Cripple Creek brought many rather-mixed emotions to the surface. Imagine, one of her first postings would be at the same schoolhouse where she received her educational start. When her mother wrote to her of the interim need, she was glad to help out. What an odd coincidence that the letter would find her, too, in transition. Would this turn into a permanent placement? Did she want it to?

The mountain scenery became more recognizable, and she thought back on her childhood. There were so many happy times here. Unbidden, her mind wandered to the day of the great tragedy that had marred her spirit—the day Ellie Mae died.

Even all these years later, she carried the scar in her heart. The events of that day had left her broken. Why must thoughts of Ellie Mae plague her so? And all the more as her return became imminent? She shivered as the images from her nightmares the previous evening flitted across her mind. They would not stop. These same visions visited her in sleep night after night. All the more frequently these last weeks.

Closing her eyes, the hazy images took form and became memory. It was as if no time had passed. She and Ellie, walking through the schoolyard just as they did every other day . . .

Hooking arms with Ellie Mae, Katherine stepped out of the schoolhouse and into the yard. A rather large group of students gathered off to the right near the old tree. It didn't bother Katherine. She turned her attention toward the path that would lead home.

"What do you think they're up to?" Ellie Mae whispered.

Katherine glanced in that direction and noticed Betsy Callaway at the center, flapping her jaws. Why would anyone listen to anything she said? But they did. The class at large seemed to adore Betsy. It didn't make sense. Clenching her teeth, Katherine grabbed for Ellie Mae's hand. "Whatever it is, we don't want to be involved." She pulled Ellie Mae along as she walked on, trying to pass the gathering.

"I know Miss Matthews couldn't do it," Betsy said loudly.

Katherine froze in her tracks. What had she just said?

The crowd of students parted and glared at Katherine and Ellie Mae.

"Let's keep going," Ellie Mae pleaded, tugging on Katherine's hand.

She should listen to Ellie Mae and not become a part of whatever game Betsy played. But she could not let Betsy get the best of her. What would everyone think of her?

So, she turned to face her accuser. There stood Betsy with Wyatt Sullivan, the most popular boy in school, right beside her. Betsy's blonde pigtails, tied back with perfect pink ribbons, shone in the sun. Her dress was no less perfect, pink with just the right amount of lace and even a slight puff to the sleeves.

"Do what, pray tell?" Katherine shot back. Her heart beat furiously in her chest.

"Go down through the mine shaft." Betsy folded her arms in front of her chest and raised an eyebrow.

Katherine's heart skipped a beat then, but she tried not to show her fear.

Ellie Mae's grip tightened on her hand.

"I assure you, Miss Callaway, it's not that I can't do it. It's simply that I have better things to do than to be traipsing about a mine shaft." She turned to leave and hoped that would be enough to silence Betsy.

"Prove it." Betsy's voice rang out after her.

Katherine's eyes slid closed. Was there any way around this? "I have nothing to prove to you," she called back over her shoulder.

"Fraidycat!" Betsy laughed.

The other students joined in.

Katherine's face burned. A fire had been lit within her. She was not afraid of anything! Releasing Ellie Mae's hand, she then whirled around. "I am not afraid!"

"There's only one way we'll believe that." Betsy's hands moved from her chest to her hips.

There was no way this would be a one-way challenge. "Are you going?" Katherine poked her chin out, putting her own hands on her hips, attempting to puff up her chest as much as she could.

"Of course," Betsy said, though her voice caught.

"Then, let's go." Katherine grabbed after Ellie Mae's hand and headed out in the direction of the old mine shaft. She hoped Ellie Mae didn't feel how her palms had started to sweat. Perspiration covered her whole body. How was she to keep up this façade?

The group of students followed, a din of voices behind. As they neared the cavernous opening, they became quiet as they halted several feet short of the forbidden place.

Wyatt pushed through the crowd once they had stopped. "Now, girls, this is foolishness. Talking about it is one thing, but you're not actually going down there, are you?"

Katherine glanced at the mine opening. It looked dark and ominous. Not what she wanted to see. Then she eyed Betsy. She had everything—the popularity, the most handsome boy in school ... But she would not have Katherine's pride, too. "I am."

"Then I am, too." Betsy stared at Katherine, matching her glare through slitted eyes.

"Kath-rine," Ellie whispered, tugging on her hand.

Katherine looked over at her friend. Ellie's eyes begged her not to go. Katherine wondered again at the danger. Her friend had every right to be concerned, she supposed. But it would not last. Betsy would go but a few steps in and give up. Katherine was sure of it. So, she would not be dissuaded.

Wyatt's eyes moved from one girl to the other. A couple of years older than the girls at their thirteen years, he stood a good head taller than Katherine. At last, he threw his hands up in the air. "Then I'm going too."

"And so am I," came Ellie Mae's quiet response.

Katherine leaned toward her friend. "Ellie, you don't have to go." Her eyes held Ellie's. What was she going to do? She couldn't take Ellie into that place. But something had eased in her when Ellie Mae volunteered to go. Was it selfish of her to want her friend to accompany her?

"Yes, I do." Her voice was firm, though her chin quivered. "I'm sticking with you."

A bump in the trail jolted Katherine from her reverie. The scenery outside became blurred. Or was it her? Touching her face, she felt moisture. She wiped at the tears. This would not do! Whatever happened when she returned, Katherine was determined she would face it with as much bravery as she could muster.

To read more, find *Hope in Cripple Creek* here:

https://saraturnquist.com/hope-in-cripple-creek/

ACKNOWLEDGMENTS

This has, by far, been the most difficult novel I have ever written. The research was tough, and walking through the suffering in some small way was really difficult. Knowing that the Cherokee and these other Native American groups suffered these things and much more…was hard. And this question: where is God when things don't make sense? It's still a challenging question. One not easily answered.

But, at the end of today, as I am putting this book together to go out into the world, there are many people who made this work possible. And I cannot begin to name everyone who has encouraged my career and prayed over me! You are all truly appreciated. I am so blessed.

First, my editor, Julie Sherwood. Thank you for making my work stronger and keeping me on my game. You make everything that much more polished. And still keep the heart of my books intact.

Cora Graphics, you continue to put out such amazing work. Consistently. There is no end to your talent.

The photographer who makes me look good, VerBull Photography, I know I'm taking full advantage of your skills.

The Clarksville Christian Writers, my critique group, you support me and spur me on more than you know!

My Beta Readers and Turnquist's Troupe…you all encourage me and provide such valuable feedback.

My husband and children, you help me push through when the going gets tough.

For Rachel, you keep me honest. For my dad, knowing you are proud of me fills me with joy.

For my mom, I will love you forever.

For my Lord, You are everything.

Last, but certainly not least, my readers, you give me every reason to keep writing.

ABOUT THE AUTHOR

Sara is a coffee lovin', word slinging, Historical Romance author whose super power is converting caffeine into novels. She loves those odd little tidbits of history that are stranger than fiction. That's what inspires her. Well, that and a good love story.

But of all the love stories she knows, hers is her favorite. She lives happily with her own Prince Charming and their gaggle of minions. Three to be exact. They sure know how to distract a writer! But, alas, the stories must be written, even if it must happen in the wee hours of the morning.

Sara is an avid reader and enjoys reading and writing clean Historical Romance when she's not traveling.

Please follow along with her journey through her newsletter at: http://saraturnquist.com/list

Happy Reading!

SARA R. TURNQUIST
Author
Editor
Speaker

facebook.com/AuthorSaraRTurnquist

instagram.com/sararturnquist

x.com/sararturnquist

youtube.com/@SaraRTurnquist

pinterest.com/sararturnquist

ALSO BY SARA R. TURNQUIST

CONVENIENT RISK SERIES

A Convenient Risk

An Inconvenient Christmas

A Less Convenient Path

A Convenient Escape

An Inconvenient Acquaintance

These Golden Years

A Less Convenient Arrangement

Ranch Hands Collection (ebook only)

CRIPPLE CREEK SERIES

Hope in Cripple Creek

Christmas in Cripple Creek

Faith in Cripple Creek

Love in Cripple Creek

~Prequels~

Leaving Waverly

Leaving Stoneybrook

LADY OF BOHEMIA SERIES

The Lady Bornekova

The Lady and the Hussites

The Lady and Her Champion

The Lady and Her Secret

RAILWAY ROMANCE SERIES

Laura, The Tycoon's Daughter